LONG GONE

DCI PAUL CULLEN MYSTERIES BOOK 1

PAUL PILKINGTON

For AP

ALSO BY PAUL PILKINGTON

Emma Holden Trilogy:

The One You Love

The One You Fear

The One You Trust

Standalone Mysteries:

Someone to Save You

I Heard You

For Your Own Protection

DCI Paul Cullen Mysteries:

Long Gone

Fallen Angel

PART I

1

Monday morning

DETECTIVE CHIEF INSPECTOR Paul Cullen gripped tight hold of the overhead hand support as the packed tube train jerked to a stop. Caught off balance, he swayed against the back of the woman who was pressed close to him and mouthed an embarrassed sorry as she turned. Even just a nudge couldn't be pleasant from a six foot three, fourteen stone police officer. Apology accepted, his attention turned back to the young man he'd been watching for the past few minutes on this journey below London towards Euston.

'Apologies for the slight delay as we're held at this red signal,' the driver announced to the weary commuters over the inadequate speaker system. 'Hopefully we'll be on our way in the next minute or so.'

The young guy under Cullen's informal surveillance was standing against one of the glass panels, next to the sliding external doors, side-on to Cullen. From his vantage point across the carriage, the guy wearing a bright yellow construction worker style jacket looked to be really tight in to a young woman, his crotch sometimes brushing against her rear.

There weren't any signs that they were a couple – no communication between them, no acknowledgement of the other's presence.

Was the physical contact deliberate?

There was a time when the thought wouldn't have occurred to him. But not any longer. Such crime was a real problem on the tube network. London was no different to any other city on the planet, where heaving rush-hour transportation systems offered the chance for offenders to take advantage of the sardine-like conditions on trains, trams and buses and 'have a feel'.

And there were plenty of people, a depressing number, ready to use the conditions on the London Underground for their own pleasure. Almost always men. Young, old, suited City types, t-shirted tourists, teachers.

Operation Archangel had caught all these, and more.

Involving hundreds of uniformed and plain clothes officers from the British Transport Police stationed across the capital's rail network, Operation Archangel had been remarkably successful at identifying and catching offenders who had previously got away with crimes that had often left women and girls terribly traumatised.

For Cullen, as lead officer for the operation, the sheer number of offenders who had been caught in just a few months was satisfying and depressing in equal measure.

Was this another one?

The Northern Line train jerked again as it rocked forwards, not far now from Euston. This was Cullen's daily commute. An early-morning, packed overground train from just outside the M25 into Waterloo, then onto the tube. Alighting a couple of stations early, the fifteen-minute walk from Euston to the British Transport Police Headquarters in Camden Town gave him precious time to think – about ongoing cases and, in recent months, about how to rescue his marriage.

But at least there was now a solution in sight.

The train emerged into the bright light of the station as Cullen kept his gaze on the man. People around him began shifting into position for disembarkation as the train's brakes screeched. The guy bent down and picked up the rucksack that had been wedged between his feet. He was about to disembark.

If he were going to do anything more obvious, it would be now.

Cullen allowed people to slide past on either side of him as he watched on. The adrenalin was really pumping now. He craned his neck to keep eye contact with the two people. The train juddered to a stop and, just before the doors swished open, it happened.

The guy's hand snaked around the girl's waist and slithered up her right side. The girl, still with her back to him, reacted instantly, shrugging him off in disgust and shrinking back into the carriage, her face full of shock.

The guy darted out through the doors, not looking back.

Cullen had just a few seconds.

He moved quickly towards her as the rest of the passengers exited. 'That man, did he assault you?'

She was tearful. 'Yeah, he did.'

'Don't worry, he won't get away with it.' Cullen looked across at the doors. He didn't have much time. People were already boarding. He shoved a hand into his pocket and placed the card in her palm.

'Paul Cullen. British Transport Police. Call me.'

And then, against the tide of incoming commuters, he headed for the doors.

A MASS of people flowed onto the train, clutching bags, carrying cases or hand in hand with children. For such a large guy, Paul Cullen weaved impressively around the incomers, apologising as he went, his chances of disembarking and giving chase to the offender slipping away. Just as he reached the exit, the warning beep to indicate the doors were about to close sounded. He threw out a powerful hand, jamming the door open. Straining against him, the door resisted. Cullen thrust his right foot to its base, bumped the doors open with a shoulder charge and, as expected, initiated the tube train's safety mechanism. All the doors slid open.

He slipped out onto the now quieter platform. The eyes of an old couple directly ahead were on him, their anxiety obvious, before they looked away.

'Oi!'

Cullen looked up as a visibly annoyed underground worker strode towards him, wagging a finger.

'You can't do that.'

There was no time to show ID. 'Paul Cullen. British Transport Police. Operation Archangel.'

'Oh,' the man said, standing down and flushing crimson. He would be well aware of the high-profile police operation. 'Well, sorry, officer.'

'Sorry to delay the train.'

'That's fine... can I...'

But Cullen was already off down the platform, flashing past the still-waiting train. The man he was pursuing had long gone. But there was still a chance of intercepting him, even if he had left the station – especially with his distinctive jacket.

But the opportunity faded with each passing second.

Soon the guy would disappear into London's maze of people-filled streets.

Fortunately the platform was quiet, and Cullen hit a strong stride around the corner and up the well-worn stairs: quicker and quieter than the escalator. All the time, he scanned for the neon jacket.

Out on the concourse he reached the back markers from the train he had just left. A young family of American tourists talking excitedly about the day ahead, an old man, head down, with a walking stick, an elderly lady with a wheeled shopping trolley, bumping it over the uneven floor.

No sign of the man in the neon jacket.

Still he remained hopeful that he was closing the gap, given that the guy didn't know he was after him and presumably wouldn't be hurrying.

But if he were getting on a bus directly outside the station...

He picked up the pace.

This was one reason why he loved his job.

You never knew what was coming.

He scanned through the ticket barriers and out into the main concourse of Euston's mainline overground station, trying to spot the guy. To the right the electronic boards displayed the 9:35am train to Edinburgh, via his home town of Wigan: the town made famous by George Orwell, with its tiny pier by the canal.

He thought momentarily of Sarah. She would be packing at home, finalising things for her journey up North.

Would she ever come back?

Snapping his attention back to the task at hand, he spotted two uniformed officers over to his left.

Both recognised him as he approached.

'Sir.'

Cullen didn't have time for pleasantries. 'A young black guy in a bright yellow neon jacket. Like a construction worker's. Have you seen him?'

'No, sir.'

'He would have come up the escalator from the tube. Just a minute or so ago.' He looked around again, but still no sign.

Unless he'd connected with another service underground...

Damn.

Both officers shook their heads.

'Sorry, we've just been helping a member of the public who'd lost their bag. Really sorry, sir.'

Cullen suppressed his frustration. It wasn't their fault. 'Can you put a call out, black male, short dark hair, yellow neon jacket, in the vicinity of Euston station or travelling from there on the network. Suspected sexual assault. He might be long gone, but worth a shot.'

'Of course.'

Cullen moved towards the exit, still not giving up, as he heard one of the officers radio through his instructions.

And there he was, exiting the pastry shop just outside the station, paper bag up towards his mouth.

Cullen jogged towards him, adrenalin pumping, his prey in his sights. He waited until the man was just a few metres away and came at him from the side.

'Hey!'

The man's head snapped sideways in surprise.

'Police. Can I...'

The man shot off at speed, as if the words had been the firing of a starting gun in an Olympic sprint final. Cullen gave chase, nearly slipping on the bag that the man had dropped to the ground. He thought he heard a girl shout from behind as he pursued the man down the path from the station, but he couldn't really take anything in apart from his goal.

'Stop!' he shouted, as the man increased the distance between them.

But he didn't stop. Didn't slow. Bemused passers-by turned their heads as the two men continued their race.

The man, now quite a few metres ahead of him, approached the always-busy main road that traversed the front of the station, connecting North London's great main-line stations of Paddington, Euston, St. Pancras and King's Cross. The crossing was on red, with several people waiting as four lanes of London traffic rushed by.

Maybe he would turn sharp left and continue along Euston Road, try to outrun him and then dart into one of the many side roads.

But Cullen thought not.

He would more than likely take the much riskier but potentially more effective option.

And he did.

The man hardly slowed as he reached the crossing, darting through the first lane of traffic, a black taxi blasting its horn as it was forced to push on the brakes.

Cullen, too, reached the crossing, heart pounding as he stood shoulder to shoulder with the other pedestrians, willing the lights to go green. But they remained steadfastly red.

Another horn blared as the man stepped out in front of a delivery van coming from the opposite direction of the taxi, this time causing the vehicle to come to a complete stop. Several horns blared as the ripple from the sudden braking stopped three more vehicles behind.

Cullen dismissed the idea of traversing the dangerous road himself. He didn't fancy his chances. And a dead detective would never catch the guy. Surely the lights would turn any second.

But not in time.

Maybe the man's attention had been taken up by the near-miss with the van, or maybe he was so close to the other side that his concentration had faltered.

He stepped right in front of the oncoming red double-decker bus.

With a shocking thud the man was propelled along the road from the force of the impact, skimming along the tarmac and into the oncoming traffic. An articulated lorry coming from the opposite direction crunched over his body, dragging it under its large wheels as it slammed to a halt with a hiss just in front of them.

Surely the guy had no chance.

Screams rang out from both sides of the road as Cullen hurried up to the vehicle. The man's body – he was just a boy, really, maybe nineteen or twenty – was crushed and broken, his face twisted in shock.

There was blood everywhere.

Cullen cradled his head, supporting the limp and lifeless neck, looking him in his dead, questioning eyes. Just seconds ago this person had been in flight, full of life, but now the lights were out.

'Oh my God, oh my God! He's... oh no, please no, please...'

Cullen turned to see the girl skid to a stop, feet from him. It was the victim from the tube carriage.

Her face was twisted in despair and shock, tears gushing. A woman who had been waiting at the crossing instinctively placed an arm around her back.

'He's dead. Oh my God, he's dead!'

Cullen didn't understand.

'My boyfriend!' the girl screamed at him, her eyes flaring with sudden anger. 'You've *murdered* my boyfriend!'

2

Previous Friday evening

NATALIE LONG GAZED at the Edwardian building in London's Mayfair and took a deep breath before moving to the door and pressing the security intercom.

'Brand New. How can I help?'

'Hi, I'm here for the selection weekend. It's Natalie Long.'

In the moment's pause Natalie convinced herself that there had been some embarrassing mistake. The selection letter had been posted out to her accidentally. Maybe there had been some mix-up with the mail merge, and she was supposed to get the brush-off version, the one that said thanks but no thanks. She'd have to return to Bristol with her tail between her legs...

'Natalie, do come in.'

She brushed down her shirt and pushed open the grand door, emerging into a brightly lit reception room, with a chandelier sparkling above like some UFO about to land.

This place was other-worldly. She could already see that.

To the smell of vanilla and something exotic she couldn't put her finger on, Natalie signed in at the reception desk, beaming.

'Here's your keycard,' the glamorous young receptionist said. 'The welcome reception is at six.' She looked across at the grandfather clock in the corner. 'You're nice and early, so there's plenty of time to settle in and explore.'

'Thank you,' Natalie smiled, taking the card. 'I'm really looking forward to it all.'

'Your welcome pack is in the room. It outlines what you should expect during the weekend, and spells out the ground rules.'

'Ground rules?'

'Oh, don't worry. It's all pretty standard for this kind of thing.'

Natalie nodded, never having had any experience of anything remotely like 'this kind of thing'.

Would the rest of the applicants be just as naive as her?

She doubted it.

What is it that Amy had said? 'Fake it till you make it.'

'Your room is on the top floor, second on the left,' directed the receptionist. 'Sorry, there's no lift. Just the staircase.'

Natalie was about to quip that she could manage the walk, even with her suitcase, but before she could speak a porter appeared at her shoulder and grabbed the case. 'I'll take that for you, madam. Please, do follow me.'

She followed the porter up the wide, winding staircase, glancing back as she went – self-conscious that if she'd carried any dirt on her shoes it would really make a mess of the cream carpet. Fortunately the carpet remained pristine in her wake.

'Here you are,' the porter said, as they reached Room Fourteen.

'Thank you.' She reached into her bag.

'That won't be necessary,' he said, smiling. 'All part of the service. Would you like me to carry the bag into the room?'

'No, it's fine, thank you.'

'Very well.' He half-bowed. 'Have a pleasant stay, Miss Long.'

She watched as he set off back towards where they had come from. She could get used to this.

'Wow.'

Natalie stood open-mouthed as the door closed behind her. She stepped slowly into the luxurious room, savouring every moment.

'This is... just... wow!'

She turned in a small circle, not quite believing just how amazing this room was. There'd been a programme on television a few months ago, featuring the world's most glamorous hotels – spa resorts in Switzerland, gold-laden towers in Dubai. And this property was right up there.

The room was about twice the size of any hotel room she'd ever been in. There was an inviting-looking Super King-sized bed, a flat screen so large it covered half the wall, and a sofa area complete with a bean-to-cup coffee machine.

The bathroom had a superb-looking shower, and a sensational roll-top bath at its centre. There were two marble sinks and a huge wall-to-wall mirror, with angel-white lighting around.

Kicking off her shoes, she flopped onto the bed and stared up at the ceiling, still not quite believing that this was real.

Things were really looking up.

After a few minutes of just taking in the ambience, she found the welcome pack and, legs tucked underneath her on the sofa, began to leaf through it.

The inside page had a short welcome message from Sir Kenneth New, complete with a close-up professional photo of him smiling to camera. The photo looked like a recent one. He was sixty-five, but had youthful, enthusiastic, bright-blue eyes. His close-cut red beard matched his still full head of hair.

Welcome to New House, in the heart of the great city of London! And congratulations for doing brilliantly enough to get this far. You stand on the edge of a great future. For one of you, this weekend will mark the beginning of an amazing journey with me and my company. So, best of luck to you all and may the best person be triumphant!

Natalie's nerves returned. This was for real. Somehow her speculative application had won her a place here. How on earth had she stood out of the crowd? Surely there must have been hundreds, if not thousands of people desperate for such an opportunity?

Why her?

She leafed through the rest of the welcome pack, which contained details of mealtimes, and the locations of the dining area, gym, and even a small swimming pool in the basement. Applicants were free to use any of the facilities outside of assessment hours. But she didn't have a swimming costume or clothes suitable for working out – who would have brought those things with them?

She was just checking out the coffee machine when there was a knock on the door.

'Natalie, so *lovely* to meet you.' The woman proffered a hand, smiling with teeth so white, it looked as if they'd been painted with emulsion. She was dressed in a black suit, and her hair was pulled tightly back into a ponytail.

'Hi,' Natalie replied. The woman's grip was stronger than she had expected. 'Lovely to meet you too.'

'I just thought I'd see how you were settling in.' The woman seemed to steal a glance past Natalie into the room. 'I'm Tabitha Blair. I work with Sir Kenneth. I'll be your relationship manager for the weekend.'

'Oh, hi. It's great to be here. A real honour.' She immediately regretted sounding so sad, but it gained another smile from Tabitha.

'It will be such an experience for you,' she said. 'I was wondering, have you watched the video yet?'

'Video? No, what...'

'The induction video. There's a note on the table? Maybe it wasn't...'

Natalie twisted and saw it there. She turned back, more embarrassed than she should have been. 'Really sorry, I didn't see it.'

'That's fine, no problem, no problem at all. It's just that it would be really great if you could watch it before the get-together this evening. As soon as possible.'

'Sure, I'll watch it now.'

Another beaming smile. 'That's great, then. I hope you have a lovely stay with us, Natalie.'

'I'm sure I will.'

'And if there's anything you need, anything at all, just call down on the room phone and we'll get onto it straight away.'

Natalie returned to the coffee machine, managing to produce a good-tasting latte before powering up the TV to watch the video that seemed so important. Her phone buzzed. It was a message from Amy, wishing her luck. She would answer it after the video. But she noticed the battery was down to thirty percent, so she fished out the charger from her case.

Where were the wall sockets?

She looked on each side of the bed, but there was nothing. And nothing above the table, or underneath. All the lights were set into the walls and ceiling, so it wasn't even possible to use sockets from there.

'There must be a socket somewhere...'

But there wasn't.

She gave up looking and switched on the television to watch the induction video. The screen sprang to life: another close-up headshot image of Kenneth New, smiling right at her. It kind of gave her the creeps, like one of those paintings where the eyes seem to *really* look at you, and follow you around the room.

A few seconds later, the video began. It must have been set to autoplay upon switching on the system. Natalie hoped that she wouldn't have to watch it every time she switched on the TV.

'Hello and welcome to New House,' a female voice said. Then the video played through a high-spec production of the company's history, accompanied by vox pops from several beaming company staff, unanimous in their love of both Brand New and Sir Kenneth. One of the workers was Tabitha.

'I've been with the company just under twelve months now, and it's been the most fantastic experience imaginable,' she said to camera. 'I really couldn't imagine a better place to live out my career!'

Five minutes in, and Natalie was tiring of the bombardment of positivity. She glanced down at the remote control and wondered whether they had *Netflix* piped through. Maybe this evening, after the activities, she could catch up with a box set.

'So,' the narrator said to a black screen, 'we hope you enjoy your weekend stay at New House, whether or not you are ultimately successful. To maximise your experience, we ask all participants to comply with the house ways of working and living.'

'Ways of working and living,' Natalie repeated.

'Firstly, New House does not permit the use of electronic communication devices. Please deposit your mobile phones, personal computers, smart watches, fitness trackers and other electrical equipment with a member of staff. Your devices will be held securely and returned to you at the end of your stay.

'Secondly. New House does not permit guests. Guests must not enter the property at any time. This includes family, friends and partners. Any family member, friend or partner who arrives at New House requesting to meet with you during your stay will be politely asked to return after the recruitment experience.

'Thirdly, New House does not permit intimate relations between participants.

'And finally, participants are asked not to leave the premises during the duration of the experience, unless express permission has been given by your Brand New relations manager. In the event of a fire or other emergency, then please follow the evacuation procedures as outlined in your welcome pack.

'Your continued presence at New House represents your express agreement of the aforementioned ways of working and living. Should you decide that the ways of working and living are unacceptable to you, then we politely request that you leave the property immediately. You will then be withdrawn from the recruitment experience. This decision is final and return will not be possible. You will be unable to apply for any similar opportunities with Brand New going forward. Do think extremely carefully before making your decision and its implications for your future career prospects.'

'Heavy stuff,' Natalie noted.

'If you contravene any of the aforementioned ways of working and living, you will forfeit participation in the recruitment experience and will be immediately asked to leave the property. You will have no longer than ten minutes to gather your belongings and leave. Any participant who, upon request, refuses to leave the property will be questioned initially by our experience manager and house security. Any escalating situation will involve law enforcement officers.'

'Very heavy stuff.'

'Thank you for your co-operation. Enjoy your experience!'

Natalie just stared at the screen. These 'ways of working and living' sounded over the top. But then again, Brand New was a company known for its eccentricity. Now that she thought about it, there had been something in the news a few months ago about how the company offices had introduced an 'email-free day' each Friday, where no one was allowed to send or look at emails. This was about focus and productivity, or so the company had claimed. Supposedly quite a few companies had done likewise. But a total ban on electronic equipment? It seemed extreme.

Still, rules were rules. Even if they were called the rather strangely worded 'ways of working and living'. She pulled out her phone and began to text Amy. Her friend and housemate had asked to be kept up to date with events over the weekend; she might get worried if she didn't hear anything. If Natalie just texted to explain the situation, then it would stop her from...

Knock! Knock!

Phone in hand, the message half-written, she moved towards the door.

'Miss Long.' It was the guy who had carried up her case. 'I'm here to collect your personal electronic devices.'

'Oh,' Natalie replied, the phone in her hand hanging down by her side. 'I was just in the middle of messaging my...'

'The ways of working and living are clear. Use of electronic communication devices on site are forbidden.'

'Yes, but I thought I'd better...'

'You did watch the induction video.'

'Yes. But...'

'Then you know that you do have free choice to leave the property and forfeit your participation in the recruitment experience.'

Natalie nodded. She turned the phone off and handed it to the man.

'Thank you. Do you have any other devices?'

'No, that's it.'

Then she had a thought. 'The room phone. We can use that for outside calls?'

He smiled sadly. 'I'm afraid not. It's on the internal network only. If there are any emergencies, then we do have external phones down at reception. The staff would be happy to make calls, should the need arise.'

'Okay.'

'Have a pleasant stay, Miss Long.'

Natalie closed the door and surveyed the room again, wondering what on earth she had walked into.

3

'Paul. I hear you've had a busy start to the week.'

Paul Cullen grimaced as he took the seat that had just been offered by Detective Superintendent Maggie Ferguson, Cullen's senior officer at British Transport Police's Central Division, based at BTP's Camden Town Force Headquarters.

'You could say that.'

Despite being offered a lift in a squad car, Cullen had decided to walk the few minutes from the tragic incident to HQ, an unassuming high-rise block of offices on Camden Road. It was home to the Major and Serious Organised Crime department that Cullen headed up, working on cases nationally that involved the rail network, alongside his colleague DCI Harper and her team in the Leeds northern office.

'Talk me through what happened.'

Cullen exhaled, still trying to process the events himself. He'd already told them to one of the uniformed officers who had followed him out of the station. And without doubt he would be telling the story a number of times more yet, including during the Coroner's inquest and inevitably as part of the Independent Office for Police Conduct investigation.

'I've been briefed already, of course.'

Cullen couldn't help but smile at the honesty of his boss. She was a tough Glaswegian who didn't suffer fools. Upon her arrival from Police Scotland, she'd certainly stamped her authority on the division, taking on some of the more difficult characters with gusto. But she was also a fair-minded person and had backed him for his promotion to Detective Chief Inspector just a short six months ago.

'I was on the tube, a few minutes out of Euston, when I saw what I suspected was a case of ongoing sexual assault, involving a young male against a young female.'

'Suspected?'

'Yes, ma'am.'

'And you tried to confirm your suspicions?'

She pulled across her keyboard.

'I asked the... the victim for confirmation, and she gave it.'

'I see.'

She tapped away into the computer. 'I just want to get this clear, for any further investigations.'

'Of course.'

'So you asked her if she'd just been sexually assaulted and she said yes.'

'That's correct.'

'It all happened very quickly,' she commented. 'You were trying to get off the train and had limited time. It was a high-pressure situation. Are you sure you heard her correctly?'

'I'm sure.'

Warning bells were sounding. Something wasn't right here.

He asked the question. 'Has she denied it?'

Ferguson's brow creased, giving him his answer.

'I'm one hundred percent certain that she confirmed the assault,' Cullen stated, trying to remain calm. 'There might be witnesses from the train carriage who heard what she said.'

'We'll certainly pursue those lines if we need to,' she replied. 'So, you then gave chase.'

'Yes.'

'Do you think that was wise?'

Cullen shrugged. 'No less wise than not giving chase. He was wearing a distinctive yellow jacket. I was confident of apprehending him before he left the station.'

'But you didn't.'

'No.'

'Go on...'

'It took a bit of time getting out of the carriage, and then I was stopped briefly by an underground worker. I caught up with the guy outside the main concourse.'

'And he ran.'

'As soon as he heard the word "police".'

She was typing again. 'Seems an odd thing to do if you haven't done anything wrong.'

'Uniformed found a small amount of cannabis on his person. But only enough for personal use.'

'Maybe he just panicked in the moment,' she offered. 'He knew he had the drugs on him, and his first instinct was to run.'

'Maybe.'

Ferguson detected Cullen's mood. 'I'm with you on this, Paul, believe me. I'm just asking the questions to get it clear in my mind from the source I trust the most. I have total confidence in you.'

'Thank you.'

'But... we *do* have a problem. We have a dead man, who was killed whilst being pursued by one of our officers. We have a suspected victim who now denies being one and is very angry and upset. And we've got a potential media storm about to break across the capital. It's not good.'

'No, it's not.'

'The girl is key. We'll be questioning her again shortly, obviously mindful of the sensitivities. Hopefully she'll go back on what she said in the immediate aftermath and confirm your version of events.'

'What did she say?'

'You know I can't tell you that.'

'Of course. Sorry I asked.'

She pushed the keyboard away from her. 'Paul. How about having a break, just until this blows over?'

'You're not...'

'No, not suspension, of course not. Just a break. Call it a holiday, whatever you like, maybe for a week or so.'

Cullen was about to argue – there was so much to do in the office and he didn't like how this might look to those on the outside. 'Do I have a choice?'

'Yes, of course you do. But that would be my strong recommendation.'

He thought about his wife packing and travelling up to Wigan alone. A week off would enable him to accompany her, help her settle in, show her that he really cared and supported her in her decision to move back up North for the short term.

It could save his marriage.

'Okay,' he said, although part of him was still fighting the decision and wanting to instead get cracking with the

working day downstairs with his team of officers. 'Just a week,
until things blow over.'

CULLEN SPLASHED his face with ice-cold water and stared hard
at himself in the toilet mirror with his striking emerald green
eyes as the drips fell like tears into the basin. He'd been
replaying the events to his tired-looking reflection, from the
first moment he had spotted the guy on the train, right
through to the moment of impact and the way his girlfriend
had screamed and then crumpled in despair at the foot of her
dead boyfriend.

Great, heaving, guttural sobs.

It had only been a couple of minutes since he'd agreed to
the time out, and he was already regretting his decision.
There was so much work to do, for a start. And he didn't like
the way it looked, him disappearing at the first sign of trouble. It wasn't the way he worked.

But was Maggie Ferguson really giving him the choice?

He doubted it. Yes, suspension was probably too far, and
she certainly wouldn't want to go down that route, risking
alienating a senior officer and fanning the flames of blame
that the media might well be stoking at this very moment.

He could just imagine the way The Daily Post would play
it, despite his relatively good working relationship with a
couple of their more experienced journalists.

But if she was being pushed into a decision, and if he'd
resisted her 'offer', he didn't doubt that she would have acted
swiftly and decisively.

He eyed the toilet door as it swung open.

'Boss.' DS Tony Beswick let the door close behind him. 'I've been looking for you.'

Cullen smiled, flattening down his short, dark but greying hair with one last look in the mirror. 'Well, looks like you've found me.'

'I heard about what happened.'

'The jungle drums are working well today,' Cullen deadpanned. He leant against the sink with the back of his hands.

'You want to talk about it?'

Cullen nodded. 'Not in the toilets, though.'

'Why ever not...'

'Call me picky, but I'd prefer somewhere that didn't smell of urine.'

'YOU'VE CHANGED,' Beswick joked as Cullen ordered a skinny flat white. At Cullen's suggestion, they'd gone to the branch of Costa Coffee that was just a few metres down from Headquarters.

The girl behind the counter looked across at Beswick. 'Just a black coffee for me,' he said.

'Americano? Would you like to try our new Nicaraguan blend?'

Cullen smiled as he watched Beswick's mind whir, a slight panic behind his eyes as his salt and pepper moustache twitched.

'Err, just a black coffee.'

They retreated towards a quiet corner when the coffees arrived.

'I bloody hate all that choice,' Beswick said, pulling up his chair with an ear-splitting scrape. 'I preferred it when a coffee was just a coffee. What the heck is skinny anyway?'

'Skimmed milk.'

'Oh,' he said, non-plussed. 'And the flat white bit?'

'No idea. But it tastes great,' Cullen said, taking a sip.

Beswick was more than just a colleague. Now good friends, they'd worked together for the past eight years, ever since Cullen had transferred to the capital from the North West. The born and bred East Ender had always looked after him, and as Cullen had climbed the ranks rapidly from Sergeant to Inspector and then to Chief Inspector, there had never been a hint of jealousy from his older but now technically junior colleague.

'So, what happened?'

Cullen recounted the events as Beswick looked on without comment, his facial expression not giving anything away.

'And that's it,' Cullen finished. 'I came straight to the office.'

'And how are you feeling?'

'Okay. I think.'

In this job, you got to see some horrific sights, but this morning had been particularly shocking. The face of that boy, the way his wide eyes seemed to bore into him; he would never forget it.

'Maybe you should take some time off?' Beswick suggested. 'Just a few days,' he added quickly. 'To let it all sink in.'

'I am,' Cullen replied. 'The whole week, at least.'

'Oh.' Beswick sounded surprised. 'Well, that's a good decision, I think.'

'The Super made me an offer I couldn't refuse,' Cullen

said. 'Take a holiday or else.'

'She said that?'

'Not in as many words, but you know how it works.'

'Yes. I still think it's for the best though.' He looked closely at Cullen. 'You don't?'

'Maybe.'

'Look, Boss, I understand it goes against your instincts. But you've got a good team, the world won't stop turning if you take a few days off.'

'I know. I'll probably go up to Wigan with Sarah.'

'So she's not left yet?'

'This afternoon.'

'It's a good idea. It must be difficult for her with what's happening to her brother. I'm sure she'll appreciate it.'

Sarah had made the decision to be close to her brother, Philip, whose early-onset dementia had been getting worse in recent weeks.

'Hopefully.' Cullen looked off to his left. 'I keep thinking about what happened this morning... it doesn't really make sense.'

'Why his girlfriend changed her story?'

'Not just that. Why he ran. And he didn't just run, he ran for his life.'

'Bad choice of words.'

'Indeed.' Cullen struggled with his thoughts. 'I know they found the cannabis, but it was such a small amount. I just don't think that's the reason he ran.'

'Any theories?'

'Well, the girl changing her mind, that seems pretty obvious. They'd had an argument, she was spurning his advances on the tube, and when he copped a feel I presented her with an opportunity to get revenge. She probably thought it would just teach him a lesson, no real harm done.'

'I can see how getting the police to put the wind up him would have been tempting.'

'Particularly on the spur of the moment.'

'And then she followed you off the train and out of the station, maybe already regretting what she'd done.'

'Just in time to see him hit by the bus.'

'And then, scared and guilt-ridden by what she'd said to you, she changed her story.'

'Exactly,' Cullen said. 'Sounds plausible?'

'Eminently.'

'But why he ran, with such urgency, I don't really have any concrete ideas. You?'

'No. But I'll give it some thought.'

'It might all come out in the wash, once the background checks have been carried out. He might have a history.'

'Hopefully.'

'Do you think I overreacted?'

'Not from what you've told me. I would have done the same. Except with this body, I don't think I'd have caught up with the guy anywhere north of the Thames.' He offered a smile.

'You should try the skimmed milk.'

'No thank you. Anyway, *you* always do the running.'

4

Cullen was standing on the platform at Waterloo station, waiting for his train back home, when his phone rang. He thought it might be Sarah, calling back about something she'd forgotten to say when they'd spoken just before he'd left HQ.

But it was Amy, their nineteen-year-old daughter.

'Dad, thank goodness you picked up.'

'Amy, are you okay?' She didn't sound her usual self and Cullen felt sick as a terrible thought flashed in his mind.

'Not really.'

Cullen, phone pressed tightly to his ear, moved away from the others on the platform. 'What's up, love?'

Please let her be okay...

'It's Natalie. She's gone missing.'

'Natalie, as in your housemate?'

'She went to London at the weekend for a selection event at *Brand New*, you know, the big international marketing and branding company.'

Cullen was aware of the company. Their mercurial and charismatic founder, Kenneth New, was a well-known celebrity who had recently fronted a reality TV show called *Pitch Your Life*.

'She was due back on a train from Paddington last night. I went to bed early and this morning I realised she hadn't come back.'

'You've tried her phone, presumably.'

'Permanently off.'

'Battery ran out?' Cullen tried.

'Maybe. But it still doesn't explain why she didn't come home.'

'No,' he agreed. 'She got friends in London?'

'Plenty.'

'So maybe she decided at the last minute to stay over Sunday evening with one of them? And in the meantime her phone went dead? She could be on her way back as we speak.'

'I don't think so, Dad.'

'Why so sure?'

'Because the last text message I got from her was from Paddington, just as she was about to board the train back to Bristol.'

'What did it say?'

'It said *Can't wait to get home. Made a terrible mistake coming here.*'

'Right. And that's the last you heard from her?'

'I didn't spot the text for a few minutes. By the time I tried to call back, there was no answer. I texted but no reply. Can you see why I'm worried?'

'Yes, I can. How about her boyfriend? Has he heard anything?'

'Ex-boyfriend. They split up a couple of weeks ago.'

'Oh.'

'I did call Jack, first thing this morning, but he says he hasn't heard anything from her since the night they broke up.'

'Her family, have you checked with them?'

'She's just got her brother left...'

Of course, he knew that her mother and father were dead.

'...And he's trekking in Nepal. So Natalie isn't in regular contact with him at the moment.'

'How about contact with Natalie over the weekend? Any indications that something was wrong? Anything that might explain what the terrible mistake might be referring to?'

'Apart from the last text message, the only other time I heard from her was just before she entered the selection centre, on Friday evening.'

'Tell me about this selection centre.'

'Well, it was at a large property in Mayfair, a weekend-long residential event, staying on site for two nights. As far as I know, they had to do a series of tasks, as well as having interviews. Natalie told me that there were eight people who got through to this stage. It's a really competitive process, with thousands applying. She was desperate to get a job with them. Said it would be a dream come true.'

'So the terrible mistake, maybe it relates to applying to the company.'

'Maybe.'

'What would you like me to do?'

'Investigate. This is your remit, isn't it? She's gone missing on a train.'

'We don't know that.'

'Well, she was last heard from at a Network Rail station, at

London Paddington, and that's also British Transport Police jurisdiction.'

'True.' Cullen always admired Amy's determination. At least she wasn't one of those sons or daughters that knew nothing of what their parents did.

'Can't you launch a missing person's alert?'

'It wouldn't be me. That would be the London division. We only deal with major and serious crime. Anything else, the regional guys deal with. That includes missing people, unless it's escalated, in which case we would get involved.'

'So can you liaise with them?'

'I can do that. Of course.'

'Thanks, Dad. That's brilliant, I'm so worried... oh!'

'What is it?'

'Natalie's just texted.'

'That's great.'

There was silence from his daughter.

'Amy? That's good news. What does she say?'

'It says: *Sorry I didn't come home. Just need some space. Staying with friends until I get my head together Nat x.*'

Amy sounded very hesitant as she read it out.

'You okay, Amy?'

'I... I just have a bad feeling.'

'You're worried about her state of mind? That she might do something silly?'

'I... I'm not sure about this.'

'About what?'

'I don't really know.'

CULLEN WAS HALFWAY HOME, twenty-five minutes into the journey from Waterloo, when Amy called back.

'Amy.'

'Hey, Dad.'

She still sounded troubled.

'Not heard anything more from Natalie?'

'The phone's off again,' she replied despondently. 'I've tried and tried. Fired off a couple of texts, messaged her on WhatsApp, sent a direct tweet, but if the phone isn't ringing through, there's not much point.'

'Just give her time, Amy. She'll get in touch when she's ready. It won't be long, I'm sure.'

'I've just sent her an email, in case she's on a computer somewhere. But her laptop's back here, at the house. She travelled to London pretty light.'

'Try not to worry, love.' Cullen checked his watch. 'Haven't you got classes this morning?'

'Yeah. I've skipped the first one,' she admitted. 'I just couldn't go in as normal, while Natalie was missing.'

'But now you know she's not missing...'

'Yeah, I guess so.'

'What's bothering you so much about this?' There definitely seemed more to her skittish behaviour. The way her voice faltered between words, her mind processing things not quite as fluently as usual. He worried whether her anxiety issues might be surfacing again, the dark, destructive monster emerging from the swamp to wreak havoc on his beautiful daughter and on those who loved her.

'I... I don't know, Dad.'

Cullen felt the sickening feeling in his gut again. Amy had been fine for almost two years now. The anxiety had developed in her final years at school, creeping through her like a metastasising cancer without anyone noticing, until it had taken hold. It had taken over a year of medication and therapy, plus a huge amount of support from her family, for Amy to recover.

Amazingly, though, throughout all this, she had still managed to excel in her exams, gaining a place at Bristol.

But the immense strain of supporting Amy had nearly broken Cullen's marriage. It had been the worst of times. And he would do anything to not go back there.

'Talk me through what you're worried about.'

'Well, it's just... I don't know... it sounds overdramatic...'

'Just tell me,' Cullen soothed. 'If there's something bothering you, it's best to get it out.'

Amy took a steadying breath, obviously still unsure about vocalising her worries. Cullen had noticed, since her recovery, that she rarely told them about her day-to-day concerns. Often they found out about things after the event, such as when Amy and Natalie had gone a week without heating during a bitterly cold period. It was good that she could cope on her own, without Dad coming to the rescue. But he wondered whether it was more than his daughter just growing up. Maybe she was now averse to worrying her parents, feeling guilty at what her illness had put everyone through. And he would never want that. He always wanted to be there to help. It was his job.

'This might sound crazy,' Amy began. 'Just tell me if you think I've lost the plot. But the text message. I'm not sure about it.'

'How do you mean?'

'What if it wasn't from Natalie? What if someone else sent it?'

'You mean, if someone had taken Natalie...'

There was a pregnant pause. 'It sounds ridiculous, doesn't it?'

Cullen checked himself before replying. He didn't want to sound dismissive. Not least because of his wider worries of his daughter's state of mind. 'It sounds unlikely.'

'Yes, I know it's unlikely,' she replied, talking it through with herself as much as with him.

'It sounds like Natalie has had a very stressful weekend,' Cullen continued. 'From what you said, this was a big deal for her, and if it didn't go well, then I can see how she might have reacted the way she has.'

'You think?'

'This kind of thing happens all the time, people going missing, but in the vast majority of cases, they disappear of their own accord, for a reason, and mostly they come back.'

'Okay...'

'You don't sound convinced.'

'Oh, I don't know...'

'Natalie's lucky to have a friend who cares about her. And when she does come back to Bristol, I'm sure she'll really appreciate your support.'

'Right...'

Again, something didn't feel right. He wasn't going to leave the conversation here. 'Is there anything you haven't told me, Amy, that might be important here?'

'Maybe.'

'Then you'd probably feel a lot better if you spat it out.'

'Okay. It's just that I didn't want to get people into trouble, you know, if I'm not right... it's her boyfriend, her ex-boyfriend, Jack...'

Cullen left a space for her to continue. He was finally getting somewhere.

'I think something happened before they broke up. Something bad.'

'Go on...'

'I can't prove anything, and Natalie wouldn't talk. We fell out about it, actually. So I decided to leave it, because it's her own business, I guess, and the important thing is that they'd split up, so I figured, you know, she was okay.'

'You're not explaining yourself properly, Amy.'

But it was quite obvious where this was going.

'Natalie changed over the last few months. She became really withdrawn. You know she's a really good badminton player, one of the best in the university first team? Well, she just quit. A month ago, right out of the blue. The team were in the finals of the Inter-university Championship, and she'd been so excited about it, but suddenly she just quit. No proper explanation. Just said she'd got fed up with it.'

'Maybe she had?'

'She also stopped going to the gym. Stopped swimming too. Then she stopped coming to the pub. For the past two weeks, after breaking up with Jack, I could see the old Natalie coming back. She was brighter, more optimistic, looking forward. This weekend was part of her new future.'

'You think their relationship was abusive?'

'Jack's quite a strong character. He has strong opinions about lots of things, thinks he's always right. I must admit, I never really took to him, but I trusted Natalie's judgement. She seemed to know how to handle him, and could put up with his speeches about politics and life. But as things went on, I started to suspect he was controlling her.'

'And that's what you confronted her about?'

'Yes. She denied it. Said I should mind my own business.'

'So you let it drop.'

A pause. 'Yes. Until three weeks ago. When I saw the marks on her body.'

5

Previous Friday evening

NATALIE WASHED off her misgivings over the strange 'ways of working and living' by hitting the shower, enjoying the power and warmth of the water for a good twenty minutes. It was the best shower she'd ever had. And by the time she had dried and changed, she was feeling better again about the whole experience. Maybe the policies weren't about control; maybe they were about ensuring fairness with the assessment process – removing opportunities for help during tasks. If everyone had their smartphones in their possession throughout the weekend, they could be misused in a number of ways.

The room phone rang.

'Hello. Natalie speaking.'

'Hi, Natalie. It's Tabitha here. Just checking all is okay with you.'

Natalie brushed a strand of hair from across her face.

They certainly liked to keep tabs on you here. 'Yes, fine thank you.'

'Great. See you downstairs in five minutes.'

~

NATALIE EMERGED into the lounge area, directed by the receptionist. The group of people, all holding full champagne glasses, turned their heads as she entered. She did a quick head count – it seemed she was one of the last to arrive.

Damn.

Tabitha moved across from the group. 'Natalie, you look *lovely.*' She looked her up and down in a way that made Natalie feel a little uncomfortable. 'Really lovely.'

'Thank you.'

'Here.' Tabitha handed her a drink and linked arms with her. 'Let me introduce you to some of our other guests.' She led Natalie over to one of the groups, interrupting the conversation. 'Hi, everyone!' she beamed, as the chatter shut down immediately. 'This is Natalie. She's another guest of Sir Kenneth's for the weekend.'

The three people, two men and one woman, said their hellos.

'Right, I'll leave you to get to know one another.' Tabitha smiled and drifted away to the other group.

All eyes were on Natalie. 'So,' she said, 'you're all here for the assessment experience?'

'We sure are,' the smallest one in the group said. He shook Natalie's hand firmly, and fixed her with a hard stare. 'My name's Krishna. Krishna Chatterjee. Founder and CEO of KC Communications.'

He said it as if she should have recognised him or his company, or both.

'We've been featured on BBC and in The New York Times,' he continued, sensing her ignorance. 'Named as one of the best startups in the mobile communications sector. We've won several awards,' he added, as if this would jog her memory.

Natalie thought she saw the woman who was standing opposite her exchange a sly, knowing smile with the gentleman to her left.

'Hi,' the woman interrupted with an outstretched arm, leaving Krishna open-mouthed. 'Samantha Townsend. Pleased to meet you, Natalie.'

'You too.'

'Ben Black,' the man to her left said. 'Good to meet you too.'

'So,' Krishna continued, undaunted. 'We design communication applications for mobile devices, with a focus mostly on the Indian subcontinent, where there are massive growth opportunities. We're helping to connect people, build relationships, new ways of working and living.'

The phrase rang a bell.

'We're part of the exciting global transformation in communication technology. But it's technology with a purpose, a vision.'

'Krishna's created a dating app,' Samantha said, another hint of a smile behind her cat-green eyes.

'A relationship facilitator,' Krishna corrected. 'Among a range of other applications. The app *Vicinity* facilitates relationship building across virtual and real-world settings, dissolving the boundaries between social-media and physical social interaction.'

'It enables users to hook up with people in their nearby vicinity,' Ben explained. 'Picks out likeminded people nearby and matches up couples.'

Ben and Samantha had obviously already heard Krishna's spiel.

'Based on our sophisticated algorithm,' Krishna added. 'It's complex but simple at the same time.'

'Sounds good,' Natalie said. She turned to Ben and Samantha. 'How about you two?'

'I've developed an online clothes business,' said Samantha. 'It's early days, but we're growing strongly.'

'And I'm in the exploration business,' Ben said. 'I help people to fulfil their ambitions, travel to far-flung corners of the world, climb Everest, swim with sharks, that sort of thing. I facilitate high-risk adventures, make sure everyone comes back safe and sound. A modern-day travel agent, I guess. I don't want to be too pretentious about it.'

'Sounds good.'

'Well, I do a lot of exploring myself, so I like it.'

'What like?'

'North Pole. Everest.'

'Dangerous stuff, then?'

'It can be. Crossed the United States last year on a bicycle, nearly got decapitated by a juggernaut that clipped my cycle helmet with its wing mirror at sixty miles an hour.'

'It's all for charity,' Samantha clarified.

Ben smiled. 'Yes, my trips, and the ones I set up, they've all got a charitable component to them.'

'That's great. So what's the scariest place you've experienced?' Natalie asked.

'This place ranks quite highly,' he joked, looking around. 'Scares me stiff.'

'No need to be scared,' Krishna jumped back in. 'Just be focussed on the tasks at hand.'

The three others weren't sure what to say to that.

'You've all done so much,' Natalie said. 'What about the others, have you met them?'

Samantha nodded across to the other group of four, two men and two women in the far corner, to whom Tabitha was chatting to. 'Susie Strachen, a Scottish entrepreneur with an online craft site, annual turnover of half a million, apparently. Matthew Hayes, city trader. Penny Houghton, she's the youngest, just seventeen, but created a baby-naming website that's big in China. And then Russell Cave, he's into death.'

'Death?'

'End of life with a difference.'

'Sounds intriguing.' She looked across at him. 'He doesn't look like an undertaker.'

'He runs a service that offers bespoke burials and cremations. You want your ashes blasted into space, or buried at the bottom of a deep ocean trench, Russell's your man.'

'So there's money in that?'

'Oh, yes. There's always money in death. He's got lots of high-end clients all around the world.'

'So how about you, Natalie, what's your background?' Ben asked.

She'd been dreading the inevitable question, ever since Krishna had regaled the group about his exploits. Now, having heard that each of the other candidates had similar amazing entrepreneurial back-stories, she felt like a fraud for being among them.

'I'm at Bristol City Uni. Studying marketing. Just coming to the end of my first year.'

The three waited for the punchline, but there was none.

'So what's your story?' Ben tried.

Natalie shrugged. 'Well, I'm doing a summer internship with Aardvark Animation – you know, they made all those stop-motion movies? They've got one out at the moment, Crazy Cats. It's about, well, cats.'

Ben nodded politely. 'Sounds good.'

'But what about your achievements?' Krishna blurted out. 'You must have done more. To have got this far, to be one of the eight, you must have done something to...'

'I came top in one of our first-year modules,' she said, regretting the words as they'd left her lips. It sounded so lame.

Krishna looked incredulously between the other two.

'You don't have your own business?'

'No.'

'Never?'

'No.'

'She must have done more,' Krishna said to himself. 'It doesn't make any sense otherwise.'

'Maybe she just wrote a killer personal statement,' Samantha said, offering Natalie a supportive smile.

Krishna shook his head, as if struggling to compute what he'd just heard.

Natalie didn't know how to respond. She was, however, quickly turning from embarrassed to angry. Who was he to dictate and question how someone had been selected? The reality was, however it had happened, she *had* been chosen.

'I don't know why I was selected,' she said finally, deciding against a combative response. 'I'm just really happy to be here.'

'And we're happy you're here, too,' Tabitha said, approaching from behind.

Natalie had no idea how long she'd been standing there, and whether she'd caught any more than the final flourish of their conversation.

'As are we,' Krishna got in quickly. He smiled at Natalie. 'I'm so looking forward to the experience! So tell me,' he said, turning to Tabitha, 'will Sir Kenneth be in attendance over the weekend?'

'Probably not,' she replied. 'He'd hoped to be here, but something has come up. I'm afraid you might have to make do with me.'

There was a micro-expression of devastation before Krishna recovered. 'That's such a pity. But I do hope to meet him soon.'

'The winner, whoever he or she is, will meet Sir Kenneth very soon, certainly,' Tabitha replied.

Krishna smiled as if she were talking about him and brightened, seeming to forget about Natalie's lack of credentials.

The group moved on to polite chat. Natalie sparked up conversation with Samantha and Ben, while Krishna, to Natalie's relief, moved over to the other group.

Soon they were called over to the adjacent dining room. It was another amazing space. The large table was set with gleaming cutlery and everyone found their places, which had been designated with name labels. Natalie breathed a sigh of relief as she saw Krishna pulling out a chair on the far end, too far away to be in danger of engaging her in conversation. By chance, Samantha was seated next to her, and Ben opposite, with Russell Cave on her other side. She nodded a hello and was about to strike up conversation when Tabitha, who was seated next to Ben, chinked her glass.

'Just very briefly, on behalf of Sir Kenneth, I'd like to

welcome you all again to New House. It's been absolutely wonderful to meet you all, and I'm really looking forward to getting to know you better. I do hope you all have a wonderful time over the next thirty-six hours or so. I'm sure you will! Cheers!'

Everyone toasted with the drinks that they had carried through from the other room.

'Enjoy your meal!' Tabitha added, as they all sat back down. 'We've brought in the award-winning, Michelin-starred chef Sanjay Deedie and his team, who have prepared a most amazing array of Indian dishes.'

'Do you know,' Russell Cave whispered conspiratorially from Natalie's left, 'it didn't used to be called New House. Sir Kenneth renamed it shortly after the purchase, a few years ago.'

'Oh, right,' Natalie said, as one of the servers began handing out the starters.

Russell leaned in a little closer. She could smell his woody cologne. She spotted Tabitha looking over, before the relationship manager resumed her conversation with Penny and Samantha. 'Used to be called Grove House. Home of the politician, Thomas Sinclair, and his family. Ring any bells?'

'No. Should it?'

'It was big news in the eighties. But I'm guessing you're quite a bit younger than me.'

'I wasn't even born in the eighties,' Natalie replied.

Russell nodded. 'I was, but only just. Maybe it's because I'm just naturally drawn to the macabre. I read a book about it.'

'About what?'

'About the mass murder that took place in this lovely house.'

6

'Tell me about what you saw.'

'Well, like I said, it was three weeks ago. I'd just got up, went into the bathroom, thought it was empty. But Natalie had forgotten to lock the door. She was just getting out of the shower, and I saw bruises all along the top of her right arm.'

'Did you ask her about it?'

'Later on that evening.'

'And what did she say?'

'She said it had happened a couple of days before, when she took a bad fall during a badminton match.'

'But you weren't convinced?'

'Not really, no.'

'Why? Sounds like a plausible explanation.'

'She didn't look convincing at all,' Amy replied. 'It was something in her eyes, like she was willing to tell me the truth, but she just didn't know how.'

'So what happened then?'

'Well, I let it drop. I wasn't sure what to say, really. We got caught up in watching that new police drama on Netflix, *Dragon Fire*.'

Cullen shook his head. *Everyone* back at HQ was talking about the show. He'd heard enough from their descriptions not to bother – a battle-scarred police detective, haunted by the disappearance of his daughter ten years earlier, takes on a serial killer nicknamed *The Dragon*.

Why did all police detectives have to be basket-cases?

'But then Jack called.'

'And?'

'Natalie went upstairs to take it. But I could hear them arguing through the floorboards. I crept up the stairs, listened from outside her room. She was sobbing, saying over and over that she was sorry, begging him not to end their relationship. I crept back downstairs, waiting to speak to her, but she didn't come down.'

'So what did you do?'

'I spent the rest of the night stewing over it. Didn't sleep too well. The next morning, over breakfast, I asked her what was going on. She said nothing, so I took a deep breath and let it all out, what I'd been thinking, and what I thought was going on. I said I thought Jack was a control freak, a bully, and that he'd caused the bruising.'

'What did she say?'

'She denied it at first, but then she just broke down, crying her eyes out. Then she told me everything. How Jack's character had changed in the last few months, how he'd become more controlling, wanting to know where she was going, who she'd been with.'

'And the bruises?'

'She still denied that they had anything to do with him.'

'So then what?'

'I tried to convince her to break it off with him. Like I said, I was no fan of the guy from the start, so after hearing that, I didn't really want her anywhere near him.'

'How did she react to that?'

'She listened to me, nodded in the right places, but by the end of the conversation, the tears had dried up, and the rose-tinted glasses were back in place. She was in love with him. She thought it was just a rough phase, that he'd go back to how he was in the early days when they'd just got together. I was pretty angry, but I didn't know what else I could do.'

'That kind of thinking happens all the time, with relationship violence.'

'I nearly challenged Jack directly, to tell him I knew what was going on, that I'd seen the bruises, and give him an ultimatum to break it off or I'd call the police.'

'You didn't though, I hope.'

'No. I decided that it might put Natalie at risk, because he'd know that she'd told someone.'

'And it would put you at risk, too.'

'I know. So I just decided to keep a really close eye on things, hoping that Natalie would see sense. And then, two weeks later, she just came out with it – she'd broken it off. She said she'd decided it was time to move on, focus on the future. She seemed much brighter, more optimistic. That's when she told me about being selected for the *Brand New* recruitment event. I couldn't believe it, after how she'd been. I was over the moon, of course.'

'You don't know what prompted her change of heart?'

'No idea. I didn't really care, though. I was just so glad that he was out of her life.'

'But now you're worried that he might have something to do with where Natalie is?'

'Yes, I know you probably think I'm overreacting.'

'I think you probably are,' Cullen replied. 'But I do understand.'

There was silence.

'Could you arrange for a missing person's alert to go out?'

'I'm sorry, Amy, but we can't launch a missing person's enquiry if the person isn't missing.'

'But she *is* missing.' Amy sounded exasperated.

'You don't know where she is, but that isn't the same as her going missing.'

'Dad.'

'Look, Amy, I do understand. But there's nothing the police can do.'

'Can't you make the decision?'

'Like I said before, a missing person's investigation, in the vast majority of cases, would be outside the remit of my team. Something like that in this area, it would be taken by London and the South East Division. So it would be their decision.'

'Could you pull a few strings?'

'Amy, we have no proof that anything has happened to Natalie.'

'But Jack...'

'What you've told me about Jack is another reason why she might have gone to ground. She's obviously had a very stressful few months, culminating in this weekend. The London guys will think exactly the same, if they were to do their risk assessment. I'm afraid it would never meet the criteria to escalate things.'

'Is there something *you* could do?'

'How do you mean?'

'I don't know, do what you normally do, investigate things, find out the answers.'

'But I've told you, it's not...'

'I mean unofficially, Dad.'

'And do what?' But even as Cullen said the words, he was already playing through how he could help. He could, with luck and some effort, confirm whether Natalie had boarded the train at London Paddington. He was good friends with Anthony Braddock, the head of the CCTV Operations Centre at Victoria. He could ask a favour, get them to look back at the recordings.

'I don't know. Look at the cameras at Paddington at the time her train was boarding?'

Cullen couldn't help but smile. 'I could...'

'Please, Dad.' She sounded as if she were fourteen again.

Cullen thought it through. The train was approaching the next station. He could jump off, board the next train back to Waterloo and head over to Victoria, giving Anthony a call en route to warn him.

'It might not be that easy,' he replied. 'Paddington is very busy, it might be hard to pick her out on camera, even with a lot of effort.'

'Could you just try?'

The train would be at the next station in under a minute. A couple of fellow passengers stood up and made their way to the doors.

'What if we do confirm Natalie boarded the train?'

'Well, it means she didn't stay in London, like the text message said.'

'But it doesn't mean it couldn't just be Natalie lying about where she'd gone.'

'No, I guess not...'

Cullen was running out of time to make a decision. If he were to get off, he could kiss goodbye to accompanying Sarah up to Wigan. But then he thought again of Amy's battle with anxiety. He couldn't risk it flaring up again. He just couldn't. Sarah of all people would wholeheartedly agree with that.

'Okay,' he said. 'I can pull a few favours, try to get a look at the cameras.'

'Thanks, Dad! Thank you. Thank you. You're the best.'

'I can't promise anything,' he said, as the train came to a halt and he slipped out of the doors, heading straight for the bridge. 'As I said, it might not be that easy to spot her. And I can't ask them to look for very long. Just a few minutes is probably all we can expect, and that's a big favour.'

'I know, I know.'

'Can you send me through a few photos of Natalie? Head-shots and full-length photos, as good a quality images as you can get. Just so they know who they're looking for?'

'I've got loads of photos on my phone they can look at.'

Cullen glanced up at the departure board, only half taking in what Amy had just said. The next London-bound train was in just five minutes. 'I don't understand. Just send two or three through.'

'No need,' she replied. 'I'm on the way into Paddington now. I'll meet you at the CCTV place.'

7

'Hey, Dad!'

Paul Cullen turned to see Amy striding towards him. Her smile was muted, and he could see the concern on her face as she brought her face close for a hug.

'This is a surprise,' he said. 'A *nice* surprise.'

'Are you mad with me?' she said, pulling back from the embrace. 'Coming here out of the blue like this?'

'It's always great to see you,' he replied, dodging the question. 'But what about your studies?'

She shrugged. 'There are no lectures this afternoon. And I can catch up with this morning's on video.'

'They record the lectures?'

'Yes.'

'For students who'd prefer to stay in bed, nursing their hangovers?'

'Well, maybe. And those who are sick, or...'

'Worried about their housemate?'

Now she smiled properly, with those pearly white teeth. 'Exactly.'

'I guess that's okay, then.' Cullen gazed at his daughter. Should he admit his concerns about her anxiety, and whether the fact that she had just hopped on the first train to London on a whim was a symptom of something that he should be worried about?

Because he was worried.

'I know it seems a bit crazy,' Amy said, seeming to read his mind. 'That I've dashed over here. But it was just instinct really. I felt like I *had* to do something, to find out where Natalie is, to find out what's happened to her.'

'But you don't know...'

Amy simply continued. 'After I'd spoken to Jack, I was just brooding in the house, worrying, not knowing what to do. And before I'd thought too much I jumped on a bus and headed for the station. I knew I'd be in London in under two hours.'

'And here you are.'

'Yes, here I am. So...' She turned her attention to the building they were standing outside. 'What is this place, exactly? I Googled it, of course...'

'Of course...'

'But there isn't much information on the Transport Police website.'

'We don't want to give away all our secrets,' Cullen replied.

'Good thinking.'

'This is the National British Transport Police CCTV Headquarters,' he stated. 'All those cameras you see at train stations, across the country, thousands of them – any camera on the country's rail network, including the London Underground – well, the footage from them can be analysed here.'

This was obviously what she wanted to hear. 'Great. So we can see whether Natalie got on the train at Paddington.'

'Not necessarily,' he cautioned.

'What do you mean?'

'Just because there is footage, it doesn't mean that we'll be able to spot her.'

'But surely if...'

'We can't ask them to spend very much time on this,' he said. 'And that's even if they agree to look for us in the first place.'

'Oh. But...'

'I put a call through to my contact there, just after we spoke. He said he'd see what he could do.'

'Right...'

Cullen felt slightly guilty at deflating her expectations so effectively. But it was necessary. There was a strong likelihood that even if Natalie had got on the train, they would fail to spot her among the crowds.

'It's okay, Dad,' Amy said, processing what he had said. 'We can only do our best. Shall we go in?'

'Yes, let's keep our fingers crossed.'

They would indeed need luck on their side. Maybe with hours of scrutiny, they could be more confident of an outcome, but that simply wouldn't be possible, even pulling a favour from a friend.

∼

'DETECTIVE CHIEF INSPECTOR PAUL CULLEN,' he said at the reception. 'And this is my daughter, Amy. She's doing some work experience, shadowing her dad. Aren't you, Amy?'

Amy glanced up at him and then smiled nervously at the

receptionist as Cullen handed across his ID. 'Yes. It's all very interesting,' she added.

The young receptionist smiled back politely, before examining Cullen's badge. He knew a few of the reception staff by name but he didn't recognise her. Maybe she was new, or a temp? She passed the badge back with another smile. 'How can I help, Detective?'

'We're here to meet with Anthony Braddock,' Cullen replied.

'Of course.' She picked up the phone. 'Hello. Detective Chief Inspector Paul Cullen is here to see you.' She replaced the handset. 'He said he'll be along in a few minutes or so,' but it might be longer. We've been having some problems this morning with the swipe card access across the building, locking people out, locking people in. Still teething troubles from our opening, I'm afraid. It's been one problem after another.'

'Still,' Cullen said, looking around at the impressively decorated reception area, 'it looks a lot better than the old place.' It was the first time he'd been in the new British Transport Police CCTV Headquarters since it had opened a month ago.

'I can't argue with that,' she replied. 'When we moved over last month I transferred from one of the back offices. Now, they were pretty unpleasant to work in. At least here I get to see daylight.' Just then the phone shrilled. 'Sorry,' she said to them, one hand reaching for the handset, 'you can wait over in the sofa area if you like. I'm sure Anthony will be with you shortly.'

Cullen and Amy took a seat across from the reception desk. The sofas were angled towards a flat-screen TV that was showing a promotional video about the new building.

'Are you sure this is okay?' Amy whispered. 'Me coming in here?'

Cullen nodded. 'I told Anthony you'd probably be with me.'

Amy nodded, seemingly soothed. 'I've been to better movie showings,' she quipped, as they watched a sped-up version of the construction of the building. 'Do you think they bring around popcorn?'

'The bosses are obviously very proud of their new temple. Want to show it off.'

'What was the old place like?'

'One of the ugliest buildings in London. Prince Charles even cited it once.'

'So this is an improvement.'

'On first impressions. Although,' he said, watching as Anthony Braddock struggled to swipe through the access turnstiles to get to where they were sitting, 'at least the doors opened in the old building.'

'Is this Anthony?'

'Yes.'

'You know him well then?'

'Well enough to get a favour out of him. He's a decent guy. Helped me out a lot on a number of cases. He loves his technology. Last time I spoke with him, he was very excited about the new stuff they'd have at their disposal once they moved in here. Maybe not so much now...'

Anthony Braddock approached. He looked flustered but his face brightened as he proffered a hand. 'Paul. Great to see you again.'

Cullen took his hand. 'And you. This is Amy, my daughter.'

'Pleased to meet you,' Braddock said. 'So, you like the new place?'

'Very swish,' Cullen replied. 'I hear you've been having some teething problems.'

'You could say that. But all's running smoothly in our new CCTV Hub. It really is a fantastic place. State of the art. Just wait until you see what we can do. Absolutely first-class.'

They followed Braddock through the swipe-access turnstiles and into the lift.

'It really is state of the art,' Braddock repeated, as the lift ascended. 'A real change from what we were used to. I think you'll be suitably impressed.'

'I'm sure we will,' Cullen said. 'And we're really grateful for your help.'

'Really grateful,' Amy added.

The lift swooshed open on the third floor.

'This is the National Railways CCTV Hub,' Braddock explained to Amy, leading them down the corridor. 'We have access to over thirty thousand cameras across the rail network. There are eight and a half thousand cameras on the London Underground network alone.' He led Cullen and Amy up to a main door. 'Fingers crossed this works,' he said, holding his badge up to the security panel. It flashed green on the first attempt. 'Thank goodness.'

They entered a large room, flanked by television screens. Along the side of the wall were banks of equipment. It reminded Cullen of a recording studio. Two workers perched on seats turned to greet them.

'So, this is it,' Braddock said to Amy, looking suitably proud. 'The heart of the operation to monitor the National Rail network.' He gestured to the screens. 'These are all live feeds.

Euston, King's Cross, Liverpool Lime Street, Manchester Piccadilly, Leeds, Birmingham New Street. We can bring up a live digital feed for any of the cameras on the national network, just by searching the database and selecting.' He turned to one of the consoles. 'We can also bring up a map of any of the stations,' he explained, as a map of the London Underground came up on one of the screens. 'And from the map, click onto any of these icons, which are all cameras. So we can chop and change angles and locations instantly, with a click of a button, which is particularly useful if we're tracking an offender in real time. This is Baker Street on the screen now. Last week we got reports of a pick-pocketer, with a description. We identified him and tracked the guy through the station, and were able to direct officers to make an arrest before he exited. That's just one example of how good this new system is.'

'That's cool,' Amy said, although Cullen could sense the impatience in her voice. 'So, Paddington?'

Braddock didn't pick up on Amy's hint. 'Look,' he said, like a kid on Christmas morning, 'you can zoom right in, with this little stick here.' He clicked onto a live feed from the entrance to Baker Street station, and zoomed right in on a young guy who was just passing through the barriers. The picture quality is just superb.'

Cullen and Amy exchanged a glance.

'So, Amy's friend, Natalie,' Cullen began, 'she was supposed to catch the eight thirty-five train from Paddington to Bristol Temple Meads last night.'

'Of course, of course,' Braddock replied, looking a little crestfallen that his guests weren't taking him on. 'Sorry, I can get a bit carried away by all these toys. Right, let's get down to business. Please,' he said, indicating to two chairs to his right, 'do take a seat.

'After you called, I took the liberty of retrieving the recording from last night at Paddington. As well as the live feeds, we can also bring up recorded footage for any given timeframe over the past few weeks. There's a vast amount of data stored on the system.'

'Thanks, I appreciate it.'

'I actually did a quick run-through of the footage. Well, Gary here did. The platforms are busy, I'm afraid. There was the big demonstration about health service funding cuts on the afternoon, and a lot of people were heading back at that time, it seems.'

Cullen nodded. The BTP had been on alert over the weekend, in case there was any trouble. It was unlikely, given that most of the marchers were healthcare workers, but these things had sometimes been infiltrated by extreme groups out to take more direct action.

'It just means that it might be that much more difficult to spot your friend,' Anthony explained. 'But, with any luck, and a keen eye, hopefully we can confirm whether she got on the train.'

Amy shuffled towards the edge of her seat, her eyes trained on the screen. 'Thank you. I'm ready.'

8

'As I said, you use the joystick to pan around, and zoom in and out,' Anthony explained, as Amy gazed up from the chair with Cullen sitting beside her. 'The buttons on the dashboard take you forwards and backwards in time. You can slow down the footage with the button on the right. Feel free to have a play. Any problems, let Gary or myself know; we'll be just outside.'

Amy nodded.

'Thanks, Anthony, for the big favour,' Cullen added, as Braddock went to close the door.

'More than happy to help,' he said. 'Fingers crossed you spot your friend, Amy.'

And with that the two men left.

'Okay,' Amy said, reaching for the play button. Cullen noticed that her hand was shaking ever so slightly. 'Here we go.'

The operative, Gary, had paused the footage at 8pm, some thirty-five minutes before the scheduled departure time of the train to Bristol. That seemed a sensible starting point to capture anyone who had boarded.

The camera that they were looking at was of the main concourse, pointing towards where one of the two banks of departure screens were located and where most people chose to wait until their train was announced as being ready for boarding. Opposite and out of sight was the second bank of screens, next to Platforms 6 and 7, where another group would be congregated. It was unlikely that Natalie would have chosen to wait there, as the Bristol train usually departed from Platforms 1 to 3 and she was a frequent enough traveller to know that. But they had that footage ready for viewing in the background, should the first recording not show anything.

They knew, though, that the train had departed on Platform 3 that evening. So the first camera, which also panned to take in the ticket barriers to that platform, should show whether Natalie had boarded the train.

Cullen watched on, letting Amy take control. She'd laid her phone on the table in front of them, showing a recent photo of Natalie, for Cullen's benefit. He'd met Natalie only briefly. At least with the photo it gave him more of a chance of being useful, and he did have a talent for spotting people in crowds, whether it be on screen or in the flesh.

'YOU'RE DISAPPOINTED?' Cullen said as they emerged into the bright spring sunshine.

'Yes.'

'And still worried?'

She nodded. 'I still don't know what happened to her.'

'Unless she was telling you the truth,' he tried, not wanting to risk sounding as if he was downplaying her concerns – even though he believed there was more than likely a non-sinister explanation for all this. 'Not seeing Natalie getting on the train, it backs up what the text message said about staying in London.'

'But the message before that, she was about to board the train.'

'About to,' Cullen countered. 'She wasn't on board. Maybe she changed her mind. Maybe someone called her just after she sent that text, offered her a place to stay?'

'You're probably right,' she conceded.

Cullen wrapped a fatherly arm around her. 'You don't look convinced.'

'Well, it's just... I thought the CCTV footage would provide the answers. But it hasn't really proved anything.'

'It's rarely that easy.'

'I mean, that platform, it was so busy, we can't be sure she didn't get on that train, can we? We might have missed her.'

'We might have. But we had a good look.'

Suddenly she had a thought. 'That platform, can't you get at it from the other side, from the Bakerloo Line? We didn't check the cameras from that direction. She might have boarded the train that way.'

'But if she was coming from West London, where you said the event was, then she would have caught the Circle Line.'

'Unless she came from somewhere else, from another direction?'

'Well, she could have done, but...'

'Can we go back inside, ask them to take a look at the footage from that other direction?'

'I... I really don't think...'

'If she *did* go that way, then it would show her, I'm sure of it.' She gazed up at him expectantly, in the way that brought him back to those early years, when as a toddler she could persuade him to do almost anything with just that look.

'Amy... you need to...'

'Need to what? Need to calm down?'

Oh no. Cullen felt sick as he saw that familiar defensive reaction in his daughter's face. 'Look, Amy, I didn't...'

'It's *not* like last time,' she protested, shrugging off his attempt to place a comforting hand on her arm. 'I'm anxious for good reason, Dad! I'm not just making this up, it's not just something out of my head.'

'Amy, please...'

'No, Dad, she's in trouble, I *know* she is. She wouldn't just disappear like this. Jack's done something. Taken her. Maybe worse... I don't know.'

Cullen reached out again. His daughter was spinning out of control. 'Please, Amy, you just need to sit down, think things through rationally, take a moment. You're not being...'

'Rational?' she snapped. Her face collapsed into itself, as if she were fighting with thoughts. Cullen had seen it before, and it broke his heart. Again he reached for her. But again, she slipped away, stepping back towards the edge of the pavement, dangerously close to the road.

Cullen backed off, hands held up. He needed to retreat, to give her some space. To his knowledge, she hadn't been this bad for some years. How he wished Sarah were here now. 'Amy, I'm here to help,' he soothed. 'I'm your dad.'

'Then *help* me,' she replied, her eyes filling with tears. She thrust a finger towards the building. 'Go back in there, tell them to get the other footage from the station, tell them to get the cameras from on board the train, the cameras from Temple Meads, whatever it takes.'

'We need to wait,' he said. 'If Natalie still hasn't reappeared in a few days, or if there becomes more reason to worry about her safety, then I promise I'll do all I can.'

She shook her head.

'We'll be able to bring in all the necessary resources to find her,' Cullen continued. 'We'll put out a national alert, her image will be distributed across the country. But we can't do it yet. It's too early. Particularly because of the text message.'

'But we're wasting time!'

'There are just too many people who go missing every day. Most of them reappear soon after. They would never sign it off. And we can't do anything without official clearance.'

It wasn't the answer she wanted to hear. 'But can't we just have a quick look at the other footage?'

'It's not that easy, Amy. You saw for yourself. Looking through all that footage, it's a major job. Anthony did me a big favour, letting us go in there, but I can't ask him to do any more. And if Natalie is still in London, which we've got no real reason not to believe, we still won't find anything, no matter how hard we look.'

Her face hardened. 'Well. If you won't help me, then I'll just have to do this on my own.'

And with that she set off, head bowed, down the street.

'Amy! Please, come back!'

She didn't turn around. And Cullen knew better than to follow.

9

Amy was sitting at the far side of the coffee shop. She glanced up as Cullen approached and smiled apologetically.

'I'm really sorry.'

Cullen slid into the seat, heartened that Amy looked better already. She'd called him, directing him to the Starbucks just down the road, apologising and asking for another chat. 'It's okay, Amy, you don't need to apologise.'

'No, I do, I do. Just turning up out of the blue, disturbing your work, demanding you investigate.' She exhaled loudly as she played with the spoon in her frothy coffee. She fixed him with those eyes again. 'I'm scared, Dad.'

'Scared of what might have happened to Natalie?'

'No. Well, yes. But I'm scared about, you know, this.' She gestured towards herself.

'You're worried about your anxiety coming back?'

She snorted, again playing with the froth. 'It never goes away, Dad. Never. Yes, it retreats. It's *controllable*. But it's still there, lurking, waiting to come out. Sometimes I kid myself that I'm cured. You know, like I'm in remission from cancer.

Except that mental illness isn't like that. I can manage it, but it's *always* there, with me.'

'You've done so well,' Cullen said. 'Since those really bad times. Me and your mum, we're so proud of you, what you've achieved, in the face of that illness.'

Amy looked off towards the distance. 'I've been so good for a long while. But this thing with Natalie, I feel like I'm slipping back into quicksand.'

'I'm here to help,' he offered. 'Me and your mum, we'll always be here.'

'I know.'

'I'm sorry I stormed off,' she said. 'I just needed a few minutes on my own. I found a little park around the corner, did some of my breathing and visioning exercises. It really helped.'

'That's great.'

She nodded. 'Do you think I've lost the plot? Coming here, accusing Jack Morton of kidnapping my friend, wanting my dad to save the day?'

'Me saving the day part I can understand,' he said, trying a joke. He was relieved that it garnered a smile from her. 'The rest, I think it's a case of holding off for a few days, for the reasons I outlined.'

'I know you're right...'

'But you've still got those bad vibes.'

She shrugged. 'I'll be fine. As long as Natalie does turn up.'

'Maybe you need something to take your mind off things,' Cullen said. 'How about we have a day out around the city? The weather's good. We could do whatever you like. The touristy thing. Maybe go for a cruise down the river? Head over to Greenwich? Whatever you like. We could go for a nice lunch somewhere too. Now you're here, it would be a shame not to take advantage.'

'But what about your work?'

'I'm on a day off,' he said. 'Actually, a week off.'

'Oh? But why aren't you...'

'With your mum? It's a long story.'

He explained what had happened that morning; the guy and girl on the tube, the suspected assault and subsequent chase out of the station, leading to the horrific collision on Euston Road.

Amy shook her head as Cullen finished his account. 'You should have said, Dad. All the time I was badgering you about my worries and you had all this to contend with.'

'It's okay.'

'But are you okay? What you witnessed, what you were involved in, just a few hours ago, it's pretty horrific. It must have been awful.'

'I don't want this to come across as sounding cold, Amy, but in my career I've lost count of the number of scenes I've come across that are up there with what I saw this morning.'

'I know.'

'Yes, it was shocking at the time, and I've thought about it a lot this morning – but it's more from a dispassionate view, a detective's perspective, trying to understand why the guy took off like that. The emotional side of things, I'm not thinking about him, his family, his friends, the terrible impact that this will have had on them.'

Amy looked on.

'You know, when I think about it, how I've been hardened against stuff like that, it's actually quite disturbing. But it has to be like that, otherwise I wouldn't be able to do this job. It's the only way of staying sane.'

'I understand. So what now?'

'I'm not sure.'

'But they can't just stop you from working. It wasn't your fault.'

'Technically they haven't stopped me from working. They *asked* me to take a holiday.'

'You didn't have a choice though, did you?'

'Probably not, no.'

She shook her head again, her mind seemingly taken away, at least momentarily, from her concerns about Natalie's whereabouts. 'It's so unfair.'

'It's process,' he said, dismissing the topic. 'I've learnt not to let things like this worry me unduly. Anyway, it's given me an opportunity to spend a day with you.'

Amy suddenly had a thought.

'When I called. You were on a train back home, weren't you?'

Cullen nodded.

'You were going to travel up to Wigan with Mum...'

'Seeing as I wasn't wanted at work...'

'And I stopped you, convinced you to turn back. And now Mum's driving all the way up there on her own.' She looked troubled again.

'Amy, it's fine. That was always the plan. If it hadn't been for this morning...'

'But it would have been such a good opportunity, for you two to...'

'Your mum will be fine. I'm going up there at the weekend.'

Finally, only partly satisfied, she nodded.

'So, how about it? A day in the city, you and me?'

'Okay,' she smiled. 'That would be lovely.'

THEY HAD A GOOD DAY, heading over to Greenwich and enjoying the sunshine, and then lunching at a lovely bistro before taking a cruise back to Waterloo Bridge.

Beswick called just as they were disembarking.

'Hey, Boss, I have some news about the fellow who had an argument with that HGV this morning.'

'Go on,' Cullen said, stepping over the boat's edge onto land.

'It's interesting.'

Cullen moved away from the crowds, with Amy in tow. 'So who is he then?'

'Tyrone Banks.'

'Should I know him?'

'Not particularly. He's not got any form with us. But the Met know a lot about him.'

'How so?'

'Criminal gang member. Not a leader, but has form for GBH, drug-running, and various other charges – most didn't stick because of suspected witness intimidation.'

'That's interesting.' Cullen thought on this. The guy's background could certainly explain why he had reacted the way he did. He would be primed for reacting quickly to the presence of the police.

'So the bottom line is,' Beswick continued, 'you've probably done society a great favour this morning.'

'*I* didn't throw him under that truck,' Cullen shot back defensively.

'I know, Boss, I didn't mean...'

'It's okay,' Cullen conceded. 'I know you didn't.'

'You're worried about reprisals?' Beswick said, reading the silence.

'Maybe. Do you know what gang?'

Amy shot him a concerned look.

'The Craz-e Crew.'

Cullen knew of them. Based out of North London, but with tentacles that stretched across the capital and beyond, they were a relatively new but fast-growing gang.

'Maybe you should get out of London for the time being?' Beswick suggested. 'Go up to be with Sarah.'

Cullen met Amy's gaze. A thought had come to him. 'Not a bad idea.'

'You've got a week off. Take advantage of it,' Beswick continued. 'I'll keep you updated on progress. The Super isn't talking, of course, but you've got a lot of friends who are more than happy to pass across information.'

'That's good. I appreciate it.'

Cullen ended the call, deciding on his course of action. He wasn't going to risk worrying Amy with the news, but he wouldn't need to.

'Amy. You're still suspicious of Jack Morton?'

'Yes.'

'How would you like me to pay him a visit?'

10

'Tell me about Jack,' Paul Cullen said across the table to Amy as the train they had boarded forty minutes ago sped across the countryside towards Bristol.

'He's a researcher at the university.'

Cullen was a little surprised. 'It's okay to date students, then?'

'It happens,' she replied. 'I know a couple of students who have dated staff.'

Cullen shook his head. 'I thought all that died out in the seventies.'

Amy smiled. 'None of the relationships involving staff and students have lasted long, or ended well.'

'I bet. So, this Jack. He's of course quite a bit older than you and Natalie?'

'A few years. He's in his mid-twenties. Twenty-five, I think Natalie said once.'

'How did they get together? Please tell me he wasn't her teacher.'

'No, no. Natalie's doing marketing. They met during Freshers' week at one of the student club nights in town.'

'Were you there that night, when she met Jack?'

'Yes, there were four of us; we'd met in Hall.'

'And Jack. Was he there with friends?'

'I don't think so.'

'So Jack was cruising around Freshers' events looking for girls.'

Amy hadn't quite thought of it like that before. 'Well, yes, I guess maybe he was. It sounds quite predatory, when you put it like that.'

'Indeed.' Cullen thought on something. 'Does Jack have a history of dating students?'

'I... I don't know. Natalie never told me anything like that. But I don't suppose Jack would volunteer that kind of information, would he?'

'No.'

Amy stared out of the window. 'You know, ever since I really started getting better, I was so scared about the anxiety returning.' She turned to look at her dad. 'But at this moment, I really hope that my anxiety is the explanation, and that Natalie is somewhere safe with friends.'

Cullen longed to hug his daughter, the way he had done when she was five, soothing her after a fall. Instead he just touched her arm briefly across the table. 'This morning, you said that you'd never really taken to Jack. Tell me more about why that was the case.'

'I think once you meet him, you'll understand,' she replied. 'Let's say actions will speak louder than words.'

THEY CAUGHT a bus from outside Bristol Temple Meads' impressive station entrance.

The time was just gone six.

'So we're just going to turn up at his place?' Amy asked.

'Never underestimate the element of surprise,' Cullen replied. 'Sometimes it's the most effective weapon.'

'He should be back from university by now,' Amy confirmed. 'Natalie was always going over to his place around this time of day.'

'Good. Let's hope he's kept the same habits.'

The bus pushed through the city-centre rush-hour traffic and roadworks. Bristol was a vibrant city under a significant amount of redevelopment, signified not only by the works on the road but also by the numerous cranes adorning its skyline. Cullen didn't know the city particularly well – work rarely took him across to this part of the world – although his awareness of it was better since Amy had started university there.

'If we get off here,' Amy directed, 'it's just a couple of minutes up the road.'

As they approached Jack's place, Amy filled Cullen in.

'Jack lives in a converted warehouse. I've been there once. It's pretty cool. Must be worth a fortune. But he just rents.'

They turned right and then left up side roads. Still within sound and smell of the city centre, Amy stopped.

'There it is, just on the right.'

The place was in a row of similar industrial unit conversions. It had a front door but no windows, with a shutter-style wall covering the rest of the low-level property.

'Interesting place. C'mon, then, let's see what Jack has to say about himself.'

Cullen strode up to the door and pressed the bell.

No answer.

He pressed again, and this time added a firm knock.

There were sounds. Activity behind the door.

Another knock.

And then the door opened.

Jack held the door partly open. He looked at Cullen, wary, before spotting Amy.

'Can I help you?' he asked, still keeping the door half-closed. He was wearing a comfy t-shirt and joggers. His short but trendily messy hair was so blond that it was almost white, and he looked younger than mid- to late twenties. It was clear that he could blend in, even at Freshers' events.

Cullen had considered how to play this, given that he wasn't on official police duty. But there was a fine line between abusing his position and simply stating his job title, and he was more than willing to walk it.

'Detective Chief Inspector Paul Cullen,' he said, producing his ID card. 'I was hoping to have a quick chat about Natalie Long.'

'Why? Has something happened to her?' His shock looked slightly forced, but it was sometimes difficult to read these things until you got a real sense of the person you were dealing with – their mannerisms, ticks, the micro-expressions that could give away so much more than you would ever believe.

'Is it possible to have a quick chat?' he repeated.

Jack thought for a second. 'Yes, sure, please do come in, Detective.'

They followed him through the open-plan living-room space into the adjoining kitchen. Cullen noticed the staircase on the right, which had to lead to the bedroom.

'Do take a seat,' Jack said, gesturing to the wooden table and chairs.

Cullen pulled up a chair. 'Nice place you've got here.'

Out back a set of patio doors looked out onto a small but pleasant garden area. The feature flooded the place with light, compensating for the absence of front windows. It was an ingenious design, making the most of what was actually very small square footage.

'Thank you,' said Jack, who was in the kitchen with his back turned to them. 'Just renting, but I try to add my own personal touches as I can. Can I make you both a drink?'

'I'm fine,' Cullen replied.

Amy shook her head. 'It's okay, thanks.'

Jack poured himself a filter coffee that was already in the pot and slipped into the chair opposite them. He looked at them both in turn.

'So, Detective Cullen, how can I help?'

'I'm investigating the whereabouts of Natalie Long. I was hoping you could shed some light on her movements. I understand that until recently you and Natalie were an item?'

Jack flashed a look at Amy before turning his attention back to Cullen. 'We dated, yes.'

'And you split up two weeks ago?'

Again he looked at Amy. 'Yes, we did.'

Amy held his stare.

'Natalie has gone missing,' Cullen explained. 'She was supposed to board the train back from London last night, but didn't arrive home.'

'I know,' he said. 'Amy told me this morning.'

'There was a text message, purporting to be from her, this morning,' Cullen revealed. 'But there is reason to believe that the message might have been sent by someone else. And we've been unable to make contact with Natalie, either before or since that message was sent.'

'I'm sure it's nothing to worry about,' Jack replied.

'That's not what Amy thinks.'

'Well, she doesn't know...' Jack pulled back from releasing the whole of the sentence.

'Doesn't know what?'

Jack hesitated.

'Jack, if you've got any information that might be useful for this case...'

'Amy doesn't know what I know,' he said finally.

'Doesn't know what?'

'Doesn't know about Natalie's state of mind,' he revealed. He fixed Amy with a stare but he continued to address Cullen. 'She thinks she knows Natalie, but she really doesn't.'

'I know she was suffering from your relationship,' Amy blurted out, unable to keep quiet any longer. 'And I know how happy she seemed when she ended it.'

Cullen put up a hand to quieten her. His daughter reddened, clearly knowing she shouldn't have raised the tension. The more personal this got, the less good would come out of it.

Jack shook his head. 'I'm afraid Natalie wasn't straight with you. I was going to tell you this morning.'

'Tell her what?' Cullen asked.

'Natalie didn't break up with me. I ended the relationship.'

Amy shook her head.

'I did,' he continued, calmly. 'I had to end it, because it was best for the both of us. I tried to make it work, I really did. But ultimately, I decided that ending it was the only way.'

'The only way of what?'

'The only way of trying to get through to Natalie that she needed help.'

'You're lying,' Amy shot back.

'Amy,' Cullen intervened. 'Please.'

Again, she conceded.

'Needed help with what?' Cullen directed at Jack.

'With her obsessive behaviour,' he replied. 'With her paranoia. Things were okay at first. They were better than okay – they were amazing. I really thought we had a future. But things started to feel wrong.'

'Like what?'

'She started questioning me about where I'd been, who I'd seen. One afternoon, I'd had a tutorial with a female student, and Natalie was waiting for me afterwards. She'd been hanging around the department, had seen the student go into my room, and had waited for an hour to challenge me. She started shouting at me in the corridor. I had to take her into my office, try to calm her down.'

Amy shook her head.

'There were plenty of witnesses,' he responded. 'They saw what happened. It was really quite embarrassing.'

Cullen processed what Jack had just said, all the time scrutinising the guy for any ticks that might give away whether what he was saying was fact or fiction.

'Tell me more about your relationship – the difficulties with Natalie.'

Cullen saw Amy flash him a look, as if surprised that he was seemingly going along with Jack's side of the story. But she should have known him better than that.

'Well,' Jack replied. 'Like I said, things were good at first. We were really happy. There were no signs of what it would turn into.'

'So apart from the happening at the university, what else gave you concern about Natalie's behaviour?'

Jack dragged a hand across his face, before shaking his head. 'I feel bad about telling you this, I really do.'

'Just tell us.'

'Okay. After what happened outside my office, we argued. I said she couldn't do that – that it might cost me my job. She seemed to understand, said she knew she was being silly, and that it would be different from now on.'

'But it wasn't?'

'For a week or so, it was. I thought maybe we'd turned a corner. But one night she came around to the apartment, accusing me of all kinds of things – sleeping with other students, other staff members. I tried to talk things through with her, tried to get her to face up to her mental health issues. I begged her to book an appointment at the health centre, see a GP or one of the student counsellors, but she just couldn't be calmed. So I ended it there and then. Told her to leave. I feel bad, but I just couldn't take it anymore. I thought maybe the shock of the breakup might be enough to push her into taking action to help herself.'

'And did it?'

'I don't know. Maybe it did. I hope so.'

'I'm sorry, but what you've just said about Natalie, I don't recognise any of it.' Amy looked at Cullen now. 'That isn't the Natalie that I know.'

'She's very good at putting on a front,' Jack said. 'I don't mean that in a bad way. I just mean that outwardly, to people other than me, she's fine. Absolutely fine. I've seen the way she is with others, and to be honest, it amazed me how different she was, how different she is. It's how she was with me in the early days of our relationship, and maybe that's the real Natalie, the person she is meant to be – if it weren't for her illness.'

'Did you not think of telling her friends? Of talking to Amy about it, trying to get support?'

'I did. But... to be honest, I wasn't sure how you'd react, Amy. I know you weren't too keen on me, didn't think we were a good fit. Natalie told me as much. And as Natalie seemed so fine outwardly, I thought you'd probably just speak to her about it and that would then make things worse. It could have just pushed her away from others.'

Amy listened in silence.

Jack looked back at Cullen. 'Look, maybe in hindsight I should have spoken to Amy. Or another of her friends. Even tried to get in touch with her brother. Especially with what's happened now.'

'With what's happened now?'

'Well, with her going missing.'

Cullen nodded. 'Do you think Natalie is in danger?'

'Maybe from herself, yes.'

'Did she give any indication to you that she was at risk of harming herself?'

There was a pregnant pause. 'No.'

Cullen held his stare.

'Well, that night, in our apartment, when I said I was ending it, she said something like, "I'll disappear off the face of the earth, and then you'll be sorry".'

'And you took that to mean...'

'Well, at first I thought she meant she'd move away, disappear, but later that evening I did wonder whether she meant something else.'

'That she'd take her own life?'

'Yes.'

'But you still didn't tell anyone.'

'No.'

'What about the bruising?' Amy said. 'The bruising on her arm?'

'The bruises? Natalie told me she took a heavy fall at badminton. Wait a minute, you're not suggesting...'

'Amy isn't suggesting anything,' Cullen cut in, 'but if you feel that the bruising is something of interest to the investigation...'

Jack looked aghast. 'You think I did it?'

Cullen waited for him to say more, giving him enough rope.

'You think I'm some kind of violent woman beater?' He laughed bitterly. 'Man, you couldn't be more wrong. I would *never* do anything to hurt Natalie, or any other human being. If you really doubt how she got those bruises, then I'm sure any one of her badminton teammates can give you your answer.'

'I'm just exploring all possibilities,' Cullen replied calmly.

Jack shook his head, obviously still smarting from the accusation.

'My priority,' Cullen continued, 'is to make sure Natalie comes back safe and well. I have to ask these questions. We owe it to Natalie.'

Jack nodded.

'Where do you think Natalie is?' Cullen asked.

'I really have no idea. I told Amy that this morning.'

'Are you worried about her?'

'Yes, of course I am. Despite how things ended, I still care about her. And I really hope she's okay.'

Cullen made to stand. 'Well, if you think of anything else that might be of interest to our investigation, then do please give me a call, however insignificant it might be.' He passed Jack his contact card.

'Thanks, I will.'

'WHAT DO YOU THINK?' Cullen asked Amy as they walked back down the road.

'I really don't know,' she said. 'Everything he said about Natalie, like I said, it wasn't the person I knew. Or thought I knew. Now I'm really confused, and I don't know what to believe. Maybe I got Jack wrong. How about you? Do you believe him?'

Cullen stopped. He turned back to look at Jack's apartment. 'I'm not sure if he's telling the truth or not about his relationship with Natalie. But there is something.'

'Something?'

'Did you not hear it?' he asked cryptically.

'Hear what?'

'The noise from upstairs.'

'No.'

'It was just the once. Hardly audible. But I'm pretty sure there was someone else in there. And in five minutes we're going to come back and pay them a visit.'

12

Previous Friday evening

'WHAT? YOU'RE JOKING.'

This time it was Russell's turn to glance across at Tabitha. Satisfied she was still in deep in conversation with Samantha and Penny, he continued. 'Deadly serious. I'd invite you to check the facts now on Wikipedia, if we hadn't had all of our phones taken away from us by the Gestapo.' He smiled mischievously.

'So what happened?'

'Thomas Sinclair was an up-and-coming politician, just entered the Cabinet, and tipped as a future Prime Minister. Very ambitious and power hungry. He was also fabulously wealthy, inherited the family tea company, which went back to the height of the Empire. Friend of the Royal Family, too. Anyway, rumours began to circulate that he'd been seeing other women. He denied it, saying that it was the opposition running a smear campaign. But the rumours didn't go away.

And then the press got the evidence that they'd been hoping for – two of the women came forward with a tell-all story, to be published the following day. When he got the call that evening, Sinclair knew the game was up. He called the police just half an hour after hearing about the breaking story, admitting to what he'd done.'

'Which was?'

'Systematically and coldly annihilating his whole family, one by one. His wife and two daughters, aged five and eight. All shot with the same hunting rifle. The children killed while they were sleeping. His wife had put up a fight, but she never had a chance. The police found him with a fatal gunshot wound in the room that we've just had drinks in.'

Natalie's skin prickled at the thought.

'He was sitting at the piano. On the stand, instead of music, he'd left a suicide note. In it, he refused to accept blame. He said that he held the press, and those working with them, accountable for what had happened. He was a really nasty piece of work.'

'Oh my goodness,' Natalie said, trying to come to terms with what she'd just heard. 'What a horrible story.'

Russell nodded solemnly. 'You can see why Sir Kenneth renamed this place, and why he doesn't talk about the house's history in the welcome pack.'

'Definitely.'

'But no doubt he got a bargain on this place. I'm sure it was a great piece of business.'

FOR THE REST of the evening, Natalie couldn't quite shake off thoughts about the grim tale that Russell had recounted.

After the meal, which was wonderful, the group retreated to the bar, where free drinks flowed. But it was noticeable that all of them remained restrained in their consumption of alcohol, most likely mindful of the need to have a clear head in the morning for the first task.

Natalie had a good chat with Penny, who seemed lovely and down to earth. She had dreamt up the idea of naming Chinese babies as part of a school project, and things had just taken off almost from day one. She said modestly that it was a case of being in the right place at the right time, but just as with Samantha, Ben and even the annoying Krishna, Natalie couldn't help but marvel at their exploits.

'So what do you do, Natalie?'

'I'm at uni, in Bristol. Studying marketing.'

'Cool.'

As with the others, Natalie knew she was waiting for more of a story, but Penny was too polite to press.

Natalie looked across at the others. 'I wonder why some of the people here want a job at Brand New. They all seem to be doing so well on their own. You included.'

Penny took a sip of her non-alcoholic lemon drink before answering. 'It's strategic,' she said candidly. 'Something to take me to the next level, a training ground for a few years, before I set off on my own again. I don't want to work for the company for the rest of my life, or even more than a few years.'

'So it's a means to an end?'

'Exactly. A strategic business decision. I imagine it's the same for everyone else here. How about you?'

'I went to a talk by Sir Kenneth at a book festival a few months ago,' Natalie replied. 'The place was packed, there were hundreds there. Sir Kenneth had everyone in the palm of his hand. He was just so inspiring – everything he's done in his career, and the way he thinks about branding, it just made the subject seem so exciting. He's worked all over the world, helped to build the biggest brands on the planet. But he's ethical with it, like how he's transformed the way politicians view green energy with his campaigns for environmental charities. I know he's over sixty, but his enthusiasm, the brightness in his eyes, he seems so young with it.'

'Sounds like you have a crush,' Penny teased.

Natalie blushed. 'Purely professional! To be honest, I'd been getting a bit disillusioned about my degree, wondering if I'd made a mistake. But sitting there listening to him, it reignited my passion for pursuing a career in the field. Afterwards, he was signing copies of his new book. I had a quick chat, and he mentioned about this opportunity – told me to keep my eyes open for the advert.'

'Wow, you were personally invited to apply!'

'Well, it wasn't quite like...'

'What's that?'

Samantha had overheard and joined them.

'Natalie got a personal initiation to apply from Sir Kenneth himself!' Penny said.

'Oh?' Samantha replied. 'How so?'

Natalie detected a coolness of expression that hadn't been there before.

'I just spoke to him at a book signing,' she explained, trying not to sound defensive. 'All he did was mention the opportunity was coming up.'

'So he asked you to apply?' Samantha said.

'Well, he said I should really consider it. I... I can't quite remember how he phrased it. I only spoke to him for less than a minute.'

Samantha nodded. 'Well, less than a minute or not, it's still a good thing. Well done you.' She seemed to thaw as she looked across to where most of the group had gathered. 'Just don't let Krishna know you've got a personal relationship with Sir Kenneth. I think he'll have a panic attack.'

'I wouldn't say I've got a…'

'It's okay,' Samantha said, touching her arm. 'I was only teasing.'

Natalie wanted to change the subject.

'What do you know about this place?' she asked the two.

'What? This house?' Samantha said.

'Yes. Do you know anything about the history of it?'

Both Samantha and Penny shook their heads.

Natalie hesitated.

Should she spread gossip, especially a story that had unsettled her and would no doubt have the same effect on others?

'C'mon, Natalie, don't hold us in suspense,' Samantha prodded. 'Spit it out.'

'Is this something Sir Kenneth mentioned?' Penny added.

'No,' she replied, 'no. You haven't heard about the murders here, involving the Sinclair family?'

'Murders?' Penny was aghast.

'It was a long time ago. Well, in the nineteen eighties.' Natalie recounted the story.

'How do you know this?' Samantha said, as Natalie finished with the revelation of the note left on the piano.

Penny looked spooked, standing there silently, cradling her glass.

Natalie wished she hadn't said anything. 'Russell told me, during dinner.'

They all looked across at him, just as he broke into a laugh whilst chatting with Ben.

'He's trying to freak you out,' Samantha said, 'to knock you off your stride. Maybe even to get you to leave the house completely. Watch out for him.'

'Do you think it's true, though?' Penny asked, still looking shaken. 'I mean, if that had happened, wouldn't we have heard about it? Wouldn't they say something to us?'

'Try not to worry,' Samantha said. 'I think it's more likely that he's just made it up. After all, we can't check the facts, can we? None of us have got access to the internet.'

'We could ask Tabitha,' Penny suggested.

'I wouldn't advise it,' Samantha replied. 'Either you'll come across as gullible for believing Russell's story, or you'll be pointing out that they've been keeping this from us. Both of those scenarios won't do your chances of winning this competition any good whatsoever.'

Penny thought on that. 'You're right. But it has really creeped me out.' She looked around at the walls. 'Now I know it, I don't think I'll be able to get it out of my head. It kind of makes it worse that I don't know whether it's true or not. Maybe I'll speak with Russell.'

'Don't,' Samantha stated firmly. 'Otherwise he'll know he's got one over you.'

Natalie wasn't sure whether she agreed about not approaching Tabitha, but she did think it wouldn't do any good to go back to Russell. 'I'm sorry I told you,' she said, her apology particularly aimed at Penny. 'I should have kept my mouth shut.'

Penny and Samantha didn't disagree.

∼

AN HOUR LATER, Natalie left the remaining members of the group who were still downstairs and retired to her bedroom. She tried to push away thoughts of the Sinclair murder story as she ascended the staircase to the second floor. But visions of blood flowing down the bannisters haunted her and she took her hand away, expecting to see red.

She reached her room and fumbled with the key, her imagination in overdrive, expecting a hand to snake around her from behind and clamp across her mouth. She pushed open the door and slammed it shut behind her. It was then that she spotted the folded piece of paper that someone must have slid underneath the door.

She retrieved it and read the cryptic message, scrawled in red pen.

You might fool the others, Natalie, but you don't fool me.

PART II

13

Previous Friday evening

NATALIE WALKED over to the table, and picked up the note again.

You might fool the others, Natalie, but you don't fool me.

She shook her head.

What the hell was that supposed to mean? And who had delivered it?

Putting it down again she paced the room, trying to not let it get to her. And surely that was it. Whoever had slid the note underneath her door was trying to put the frighteners on her.

Had one of the group left the reception dinner, climbed the staircase and deposited the note here?

And if so, who?

When she looked at the note again, it wasn't really as sinister as it first seemed. There was no threat. And yet, it *was* threatening. She placed it back on the table before sliding it out of sight, underneath the tea tray.

Deciding to put it out of her mind, she got ready for bed. It was already half past eleven, and the next day was surely going to be tiring, and one where she would need her wits about her – now for more than one reason.

As she brushed her teeth, she wondered if some of the others had also returned to their rooms to find similar notes. Or if it was just her. Maybe whoever had done it saw her as the softest touch, someone whom they could scare out of the way early on. She spat out the toothpaste and stared defiantly at herself in the mirror.

She was no victim. And she wouldn't be going anywhere.

FROM A DISTANCE, outside her dream, Natalie heard a noise. At first she thought it was just her imagination, but the knocking became more insistent, to the point where the dream faded and it was all that was left. An insistent knock on the door, increasing in frequency and intensity.

Natalie reached across to her watch and checked the time. It was half past midnight. She'd only got into bed just over half an hour ago. For a moment she just lay there, hoping the person would give up.

Who would be knocking at this time of night, for heaven's sake? And did they really expect an answer?

Then the thought came to her that there might be something wrong. Maybe it was someone from reception, coming to give her a message. Or maybe there was a fire in the house and this person was coming to rescue her, although there was no alarm sounding.

She sat up in the darkness as the knock sounded out again.

'Hello?'

She swung her legs out of bed and padded over to the door. Light leaked through the gap along the bottom. There was no security viewer, so whoever was on the other side was completely shielded from view.

'Hello?' she said again, her voice soft and nervous.

'Natalie,' the voice on the other side said, 'I need to speak with you.'

It took a second for her to place the voice. It was Tabitha.

Relieved it was someone familiar, and a girl, she flicked on the main light and opened up.

'Natalie.' Tabitha smiled apologetically as she examined her t-shirt and shorts bed-wear. 'I'm so sorry, did I wake you?'

'It's okay,' Natalie said, stepping back as Tabitha moved into the room without invitation. 'I'd only just gone to bed.'

Tabitha was well into the room, and looking around.

Natalie pushed the door to; the thought of leaving it open spooked her. 'Is everything okay?'

'Err, well,' Tabitha said, now more obviously searching for something. She moved past the bed. 'Is it okay if I just check the bathroom?'

'Check it for what?'

A tight smile. 'I'll explain in a minute.'

'Go ahead.'

'Is something wrong?' Natalie asked, as Tabitha emerged from the bathroom a few seconds later.

'Just a second,' she said, opening the double wardrobe, one door and then the other, peering inside at the space that was empty apart from an ironing board and some spare bedding.

'What are you looking for?'

Now Tabitha gave Natalie her full attention.

'We had reason to believe that you had... someone in your room.'

'Someone? Who?'

'Russell Cave.'

Natalie laughed at the suggestion.

'You do remember the house ways of working and living, Natalie, don't you? You agreed to abide by them.'

'I *have* abided by them,' Natalie responded, a little more strongly than she had intended to. Quizzed about boys in your room? It all felt faintly ridiculous – like something you might experience on a school field trip, where boys and girls with raging teenage hormones would try and sneak into each other's dorms.

'Who you have relations with on the outside is of course your own business, Natalie. But in here, there are ways of doing things. You agreed to abide by them,' repeated Tabitha.

Natalie tried to suppress her frustration. 'Why did you think that Russell was here with me?'

'You seemed very close to Russell during dinner. You appeared deep in conversation. There was obviously a connection between the two of you. A spark, maybe?'

Natalie decided not to mention Russell's revelation of the Sinclair family. 'I was sitting next to him, we had polite conversation, that's all. There isn't a spark.'

'When was the last time you saw him?'

'When we said goodbye at the bar. He stayed downstairs and I came back up to my room.' She wasn't sure why she had to justify this, but she did want to correct any misinterpretation, however much it really wasn't any of Tabitha's business what two grown adults did or didn't do. 'Haven't you spoken to him about this?'

'I tried. But he wasn't in his room.'

'And he isn't still downstairs?'

'No. Lights went out some time ago.'

'Well, I don't have a clue where he is. I swear.'

Tabitha just looked at her.

'I don't understand why you seem so sure something was going on,' Natalie pressed. 'You were really expecting to find him in my bed, weren't you?'

'We had our reasons,' she said cryptically.

'What reasons?'

Tabitha went to say something but stopped herself.

'Please, I have a right to know why you thought that, surely? You can see,' Natalie said, gesturing around the room, 'that there's no one else here.'

Tabitha nodded. 'There was a note. Left at my office.'

Now it was starting to make sense. Natalie took the other note from the desk and handed it to her. 'Like this one?'

Tabitha gazed at the message. 'Who sent this?'

'I don't know. Someone slid it underneath my door whilst I was downstairs at the reception.'

'I think the handwriting matches,' Tabitha revealed. 'I'd have to check, but I'm sure it's from the same person.'

TABITHA CLOSED the door behind her, taking the note with her. Natalie wondered whether she should have let her have it, but Tabitha had said that first thing in the morning she would take both notes to a staff meeting for discussion.

She did seem to be taking it seriously. Possibly more seriously than Natalie herself. But the people at Brand New did seem like a serious bunch.

Weirdly serious.

She hadn't had a chance to flick off the light when there was another knock at the door.

Tabitha must have forgotten something.

This time she didn't hesitate when opening. But she was shocked by who was smiling back at her.

'Russell?'

'Can I come in?' he whispered, a smile still playing on his lips. 'Before the Gestapo return and send me to solitary confinement.'

Instinctively, Natalie ushered him inside, closing the door softly.

'Russell, what the hell are you doing here? You know that...'

'Yes, yes, it's against the ways of working and living,' he said, making air quotes. 'No fraternising between the participants, and *certainly* no one creeping into other people's rooms. *Especially* of the... opposite sex... heaven forbid!'

Natalie looked properly at Russell. He was tipsy. But he'd only had a glass of wine during the meal, and she was pretty sure she'd seem him drinking Coke afterwards at the bar. Suddenly, though, she thought she could smell whisky. 'Russell, you know you can't stay here.'

'I know, I know.' He wafted away, turning three hundred and sixty degrees in the centre of the room. 'Nice place you've got here.'

'Isn't it just the same as your room?'

'Yeah. But I like what you've done with it.'

Natalie couldn't help but smile. 'You'd better sit down for a minute.'

'No need. Natalie, I want to show you something.' He held out a hand and smiled what was undoubtedly a handsome, if slightly drunken smile. 'Please, come with me if you want to live.'

She seemed to remember that was from a movie, but couldn't quite place it.

'Russell, I can't.'

'You can, you can.'

'They suspect something is going on between us,' she revealed. 'Tabitha came to my room just a few minutes ago, thinking you were in here with me.'

'Well, she was a few minutes too early then, wasn't she.'

Again Natalie couldn't help but smile. 'Where do you want me to go?'

'It's a secret.'

'I'm not sure I like secrets.'

'You'll like this one.' Suddenly he seemed to shake himself back into soberness. 'Just a few minutes. Tabitha won't be coming back. She's probably settled into her coffin for the night.'

Another laugh. Russell was actually a lot funnier than she'd first thought.

His charm worked and she relented without much persuasion. 'Go on then.'

'Fantastic!' he said, rather too loudly, apologising as Natalie put a finger to her mouth.

Natalie pulled on some trousers over her pyjama bottoms, and slipped on her shoes. Then she had a thought. 'We're staying inside the house, aren't we?'

'Yes, yes. *Right* inside the house, in fact. Come on.'

14

Cullen rapped on the door to Jack's apartment. Almost immediately, he heard a noise. But it was a good minute or so before the door opened.

'Detective Cullen.' Jack's cheeks were flushed. He looked as if he were trying to stay cool, but he couldn't hide his flustered expression. His t-shirt was now slightly off-centre, as if he'd just thrown it back on. And his hair was messy. He'd run a hand through it, but that seemed all.

It all served to strengthen Cullen's suspicions.

Jack pressed a hand against the doorframe, and Cullen wondered whether he was attempting to block the view inside. 'I didn't expect to see you again so soon.'

'I've just got a few more questions,' Cullen said.

Jack didn't move his arm. He surprised Cullen by twisting his mouth into a smile, as if amused by something. 'No Amy, then?' he said, peering past the officer.

'No, just me this time.'

'Then you'd better come in,' Jack said, retreating into the apartment. 'Do take a seat.'

'I'm okay,' Cullen said, remaining on his feet. 'I won't be long.' He let the silence settle as he listened out for any signs of the person he believed was upstairs.

'So, what can I do for you?'

'I'd just like to ask you a few more questions, if you don't mind.'

Jack looked as if he did mind. 'I'm going out in a few minutes, I've told you all I know.'

Cullen wondered whether now was the right time.

'Look,' Jack said, with a degree of irritation creeping into his voice. 'Am I an official suspect? If I am, shouldn't you be taking me into a police station, offering me a lawyer?'

'Jack, relax. You're not an official suspect. But you are someone who I think might be able to help.'

Jack shook his head. Then there was a flash of realisation. 'Can I see your ID again?'

'Sure.' He passed it across.

A smile broadened across Jack's lips as he examined the card and confirmed his suspicions. 'Paul *Cullen.*' He looked up, sufficiently satisfied to voice his accusation. 'You're Amy's father?'

Cullen sighed inwardly. This would not make things any easier. Maybe he should have left Amy outside during that first encounter. But no matter, it was too late now. 'That's correct.'

Jack swirled the ID card around his fingers, over-examining it front and back in a way that made Cullen want to snatch it back. 'So you're a detective in the British Transport Police?'

'Detective Chief Inspector.'

The annoying examination of the ID card continued. '*Transport* Police,' Jack mused. 'So *what* exactly do the British

Transport Police investigate? Leaves on the line?' He sniggered at his own joke.

Cullen refused to take the bait from the emboldened Jack, although he was sorely tempted to prick this guy's bubble. It was strange and interesting how Jack had suddenly come out fighting, and it was best to let it play out without too much provocation.

'Serious and organised crime on or connected with the transport network,' he replied.

He was well-used to having to explain to people what he did. If you worked for the regular police, people understood that. But the transport police was a different matter. They were a largely invisible thin blue line, often mistaken for regular forces, or just not noticed at all.

Cullen continued as Jack said nothing. 'Gang-related activities, terrorism, major railway accidents, murder, rape, serious assaults... missing people, where we have reason to believe they might be in danger or have come to harm.' He let the last part of the sentence hang in the tense space between them as they eyeballed one another.

Cullen plucked his ID card from between Jack's fingers and slipped it into his jacket pocket.

'I want to give you a chance, Jack,' Cullen said, seizing the moment to land a surprise blow.

Jack looked puzzled. 'A chance?'

'A chance to tell me the truth.'

There was a flash of something. Panic, maybe? Or guilt? For a moment, Cullen wondered whether Jack Morton was hiding something else, something that he hadn't yet even considered. He decided to give him some more rope and stayed silent.

'I swear, I haven't done anything to Natalie,' Jack

protested, running a hand through his messy hair. The bravado was gone for now. 'I haven't seen her since we split up, two weeks ago. I'm not responsible for her disappearance.'

Cullen just nodded. And there it was. A noise again, coming from upstairs. They both heard it. Jack couldn't help but instinctively glance towards the ceiling.

Their eyes locked and Cullen held the stare, issuing an unspoken challenge.

'Is it okay if I use your bathroom? Just upstairs, isn't it?'

Jack swallowed. He knew what was happening. The game was up. But he sprang a surprise on Cullen by agreeing to his request. 'Sure.' He managed to smile. 'Just upstairs, first door on the left. It's not a big place, you can't miss it.'

Cullen ascended the stairs, feeling Jack's gaze on him from below. He reached the top and moved straight past the open door of the bathroom, down the short corridor to the only other door.

He didn't knock.

The attractive girl, in bright pink bra and knickers, perched on the edge of the unmade double bed, smiled at him without embarrassment.

'Hi,' she said, brushing her sleek dark hair back over her shoulder. She looked as if she might be Spanish or Italian. No more than late teens. Probably a first-year undergraduate.

'Very sorry to interrupt,' Cullen said, averting his eyes as he examined the bedside lamp with mock interest. He thought back to what Amy had said about Jack's predatory behaviour at the university and wanted to warn off this beautiful young girl from the shark downstairs.

'It's okay,' she said, with a definite Mediterranean accent and a warm smile. 'Jack said he might invite a friend along.'

Cullen smiled tightly. 'Did he now?'

'He's not a friend,' Jack said hastily, standing at the doorway.

'Oh,' the girl said, puzzled. She pulled across her t-shirt and slipped it over her head, pulling her hair out from underneath the material.

As she reached for her jeans that had been dumped on the floor, Jack placed a foot over one of the legs. She glared at him, but pulled back, arms crossed.

'This is Detective Chief Inspector Paul Cullen. He won't be disturbing us for long.'

'Do feel free to put your jeans back on,' Cullen said pointedly.

Jack released his foot and the girl dressed, much to Cullen's relief. He was no prude, but he really didn't feel comfortable with her sitting there half-naked, and his entrance feeling like some kind of bizarre interlude in whatever games they were in the middle of.

'I'm investigating the disappearance of Natalie Long,' Cullen said, as the girl perched back on the edge of the bed. He spotted her eyes flick momentarily to Jack and back to himself again.

'She's a student at Bristol City University,' Cullen continued. 'Are you?'

The girl nodded.

'Do you know Natalie?'

'No,' she said, far too quickly.

'It's a big university, I guess,' Cullen quipped. 'Thousands of students. I just thought, well, Natalie and Jack here, I understand they were dating until recently.'

She swallowed. 'I know of her, but I don't know her. We never met.'

'You've never met,' Cullen said, correcting the tense.

'That's right,' Jack said. 'They don't know one another.'

'How long have you known Jack?' Cullen directed back to the girl.

'Since September. He's my...'

'We met at the university,' Jack cut in. 'In the department where I work.'

Cullen ignored Jack. 'He's your lecturer?'

Her face gave him the answer. 'It isn't what you think,' she said, her face suddenly hardening. 'He's not taking advantage of me. I'm not a child. Our relationship, what we have, it's serious.'

They *sounded* like the words of a child. And, despite her show of bravado, there was no doubt that she was being taken advantage of by Jack. 'You're in a relationship?' he repeated.

'Of course,' she said, bristling. 'You think I sleep with anyone?'

Cullen thought of the mention of the 'friend' coming over to join in the fun. 'How long have you been seeing one another?'

'Look, what's this got to do with Natalie disappearing?' Jack said.

'How long?' Cullen repeated.

'Two months,' she said.

'Interesting,' Cullen noted. He looked at Jack.

'Look, I know what you're thinking. I cheated on Natalie, yes, I admit it. But that doesn't mean I have anything to do with what's happened to her.'

'It means you're a liar.'

'We're all liars,' Jack shot back.

'It also means you didn't really care all that much for Natalie, did you?'

He actually reddened at that.

'She was just another one of your conquests.'

'I think you should go.'

'I haven't quite finished yet, Jack. Just a few more questions. About your whereabouts over the past few days.'

'Tell him, Gabby,' Jack said. 'Tell Detective Cullen where I was at the weekend.'

'He was with me.'

'All weekend?' Cullen studied her face for any tell.

'Yes, all weekend. Friday evening until Sunday evening.'

Cullen turned to Jack. 'Details.'

'Jack took me away for a romantic weekend,' Gabby said. 'It was amazing.'

'We drove down to Devon,' Jack added. 'In my VW Camper.'

'You stayed at a campsite?'

He nodded. 'Just south of Paignton.'

'Name?'

'Cliff Top View. If you want, you can give them a call, they'll have details of the booking. I've got the number.' He went to pull out his mobile phone.

'I may well follow that up,' Cullen said, 'If I do, I'll look up the number.' He turned to Gabby. 'Sorry to disturb you. I'll leave you to your... but I might want to speak to you again.'

She nodded as Cullen exited, with Jack close behind him as they descended to the ground floor.

'Thank you for your assistance, Jack,' Cullen said, stepping out onto the pavement. 'I'll be back in touch.'

Jack took up his blocking-the-doorway position again. 'I've told you everything I know. And as you heard, I was in Devon over the weekend. Why would you need to speak to me again?'

'I thought you might be interested in hearing any news about Natalie, seeing you were so close?'

'Yes, yes, of course.'

'And if you remember anything that could help in our enquiries, then don't hesitate to get back in touch.'

Jack nodded.

'One more thing,' Cullen added, just as Jack was about to close the door. 'The friend Gabby mentioned, the one she was expecting to join you both, is that person a member of the university teaching staff too?'

'That's *none* of your business,' he replied, stony-faced, shutting the door with a thud.

Cullen stood there for a few seconds, mulling over his thoughts, before heading back to meet Amy.

15

Previous Friday evening

NATALIE FOLLOWED Russell out of the room and down the stairs, back towards reception. The lights were dimmed but still on, so they could see where they were going. But that also meant that other people could see them.

'What if there's someone on the desk?' she whispered, acutely aware that if they were caught together, then that would be the end of their weekend experience at New House. Tabitha would naturally assume that there had been something going on between them, and that the note writer had been telling the truth.

'There isn't,' Russell said. 'Trust me.'

Natalie wasn't sure she did trust him. After all, she'd only met him for the first time just a matter of hours ago. So why had she agreed to jeopardise a chance of a lifetime, just because he had come to her room and asked her to?

It felt too late now to turn back.

'Just around here,' Russell directed, as they reached the base of the staircase.

Thankfully, the reception desk was indeed unmanned.

Natalie followed him past the desk, along a corridor that stretched off to the right and past several closed doors.

He stopped as he reached a panel. 'The book was right,' he announced.

'Book?'

'This book,' he said, producing a tatty paperback entitled *Murder in Mayfair: The True Story of the Sinclair Massacre*.

Natalie grimaced at the cover, which depicted the house they were currently residing in drenched in blood.

Suddenly she longed to be tucked up in her bed.

'I like to do my homework,' he continued. 'Found this book online. It's a very interesting read.' He flicked through the pages for effect.

'Disturbing too.'

'Oh, yes, certainly disturbing in places. Anyway, the book mentions that Lord Sinclair had an office in a hidden top floor of the mansion, which was only accessible via a secret spiral staircase. The book gave the approximate location. I must admit, I did wonder whether Sir Kenneth might have had it sealed up, but he didn't. Watch this!'

Russell smiled as he placed his hands on either side of the wooden panel. A sharp twist and the panel swung around, leaving just enough space for a person to squeeze through sideways.

'Come with me,' he said, his eyes wide with excitement.

NATALIE HESITATED for a moment in the corridor, as Russell beckoned her again from just behind the panel. She glanced back towards where they had come from. All was quiet.

'Come on,' Russell cajoled. 'The longer you stay there, the more chance there is of someone coming along.'

'But...'

'The panel closes behind us,' Russell said, reading her mind. 'No one will know we've been here.'

Natalie glanced back again.

'Last chance,' Russell said. 'I promise it will be worth it.'

Finally Natalie relented. She had gone this far, after all. She slipped through the gap and found herself at the base of a wooden spiral staircase.

'Good man,' Russell said, as he pushed the panel back into place, leaving them momentarily in darkness.

'Can we get back out?' Natalie asked, as Russell flicked on the light, which blinked several times before illuminating the small space which they occupied.

'Yeah, no problem,' Russell said, whose body was just inches away from Natalie's in the confined space. 'You just do what you did to open it from the other side.'

She felt a strange sense of excitement, sharing this intimate space with a stranger. With her face almost touching Russell's, she smiled. 'What on earth have I got myself into?'

'Ah,' he said, smiling and tapping his nose. 'Patience, Natalie, you'll find out very shortly. Now follow me. We'd better stay quiet, as we're behind the walls and who knows which rooms we'll be passing.'

Natalie nodded and followed Russell as they moved slowly but purposefully up and around the tight staircase. There were no more lights, and conditions dimmed along the climb. Round and round they ascended in the gloom, before the light got brighter again and they reached the top. The bare bulb, hanging above a solitary door, was burning brightly.

'Here we are,' Russell whispered. Before Natalie could reply, he pushed open the door and held it open for her to pass through.

Natalie stepped into the room, whose lights were already on. It looked like a very posh study, all mahogany and leather, bordered by impressive, full bookcases. Over in the corner were a desk and some comfy chairs. And ahead of them was a bar area, with a variety of alcoholic beverages. The sloping roof was high enough for it not to feel oppressive like some modern-day loft rooms.

'Impressive, eh?' Russell said, striding over to the drinks. He swiped up a bottle of whiskey and glass, pouring out a generous amount.

'We really shouldn't be here,' Natalie said, all of a sudden feeling very uncomfortable. She stepped back.

'It's *fine*,' Russell soothed. 'Natalie, don't worry, *no one* is going to catch us.'

'It's not that. It just feels, well, it doesn't feel right, that's all.'

Russell handed her a whiskey. 'Here you go.'

She took it, but the weight of the glass surprised her and it nearly slipped out of her grasp. 'Oh my goodness.'

'Careful,' Russell said, 'that's one expensive glass of whiskey you've got in your hand there. A vintage. I'm a bit of a whiskey buff, and I couldn't believe it when I saw it. Tastes amazing too. Powerful, yet light. The second glass is even better than the first.'

So that's why he'd seemed tipsy.

He saw her look at the half empty bottle. 'I just had a

couple of glasses, Natalie. And it's not like the owner is coming back to claim it. Unless you believe in ghosts, that is.' He smiled as he sipped at his latest drink. 'Ahh, that's good.'

Natalie really didn't feel like drinking. She didn't even particularly like whiskey, unless it was drowned in Coke.

'C'mon, drink up!'

She took a mouthful. The burn was intense.

'See, told you it was good,' Russell said, seeming not to notice her face telling another story. He flopped down onto one of the chairs and crossed his feet at the end of straight legs. 'I was a little disappointed that there were no cigars up here. It says in the book that old Sinclair used to enjoy a cigar or three while up here, stargazing.'

'Stargazing?' Natalie checked again, but confirmed that there were no windows in this top-floor room.

'Oh, yes,' he replied, getting to his feet. 'Just watch this. The book explained how it worked.' He moved across to a gold handle fixed to the wall, and began winding.

Natalie heard a crack of a mechanism cranking into action, as the roof began to part from the apex, revealing the sky above. By the time the movement stopped, about three metres of roof had retracted, allowing the cool night London air to swirl in and transform the room into an outside space.

'It's best without the lights,' Russell said, flicking them off.

'Wow,' she said, transfixed by the sky that was now spread out before them. It was a clear night, and she could make out some stars, even with the light pollution. 'That's amazing.'

'Isn't it just,' Russell said, also gazing up at the heavens. 'The book says that Lord Sinclair was quite a keen astronomer. Supposedly he spent a lot of time up here on his own. He seemed quite the loner. Not really a family man at all. Rumour has it that he only really married so that he could have descendants to keep the Sinclair name alive.'

'But didn't you say...'

'They had two daughters, yes. They say he was desperate for a son, but after their first two, it just didn't happen for them again. I think that took a toll on them – or on him, at least.' Russell looked around. 'I can see old Lord Sinclair wallowing in his thoughts up here, away from the family he'd never quite wanted. Maybe when the time came, it wasn't that difficult to dispatch them.'

Natalie shuddered, and not just from the cooling air temperature. She wrapped her arms around herself. 'I can't imagine how anyone could do that to anybody, never mind your own family – your own daughters.'

'It wasn't a spur of the moment thing either,' Russell revealed. 'He'd planned it for weeks. The police found the notes he'd made over there in those drawers.'

Natalie looked over at the writing desk. 'No.'

'He'd kept a diary, documenting his thoughts and feelings – about the business, his family – which had become increasingly dark and disturbing. In the last few pages, he'd sketched out the plans to kill himself and take the rest of the family with him. He planned things out in meticulous detail. He knew which night, he knew how he was going to do it. He probably penned the suicide note in this very room.' Russell turned to Natalie and smiled, the light from outside casting shadows across his face. 'You're surrounded by history, Natalie.'

Natalie shuddered again. This room was really giving her the creeps. It was as if she could feel the presence of something bad. 'Why did you bring me here?'

Russell shrugged. 'You seemed interested in the Sinclair story at dinner. I thought you might like to see it.'

'Right.'

Russell took a step closer. 'And I wanted to take the opportunity to spent some more time with you.'

'More time with me?'

'I know we've only just met, but I really like you, Natalie. I want to get to know you better, you know, before this silly competition starts in the morning.'

He cupped her shoulders, and Natalie let him. The attraction was mutual, and she felt a frisson of excitement as their bodies connected. He brought his face closer to hers, and they touched lips tenderly, just holding the kiss underneath the stars.

'I'm sorry,' Natalie said, stepping back. 'I'm sorry, I really can't do this now.'

16

Cullen stepped off the bus halfway up Gloucester Road, a bustling artery running north to south through the very heart of the city of Bristol. Lined with all manner of businesses – grocers, coffee shops, pubs, delis, record stores – it reminded him a little of London.

Amy's flat was just off the main road, in the Bishopston area of the city. A once grand Georgian house, it was now decaying and sliced into two. But it was in a decent street, flanked by privately occupied homes that had obviously been more recently renovated. The area was a prime location for the thousands of students looking for accommodation within walking distance of the city centre campus.

It didn't come cheap.

Cullen rapped on the door. He'd spent the short bus ride thinking about Jack. He was no doubt a nasty piece of work, and he wondered what Natalie had ever seen in him. They didn't seem like a good fit at all. But there was the power thing going on, and that kind of dynamic, that power imbalance, could attract as well as ultimately ruin.

'Dad,' Amy said, as she swung open the door. He could tell from her expectant look that, deep down, she had been hoping he would return with answers. And it wasn't because he was a police detective. It was because he was her father – the one who should be able to make everything right again.

He was sorry to let her down.

'Any news?' she added, her face falling as her hope was clearly already fading.

'Let's just step in.'

Cullen followed her through into the living room and took a seat opposite her. Her expression was slightly more positive again.

'I didn't find out any more about where Natalie might be,' he said, right off. The last thing he wanted to do was to raise her hopes without foundation.

'Oh.'

The look of disappointment on his daughter's face: it got him every time.

She gazed down at the threadbare carpet.

'I was right, though. There was someone upstairs. A girl.'

He had her attention back.

'Oh, right.'

'A student,' he expanded. 'In his bed.'

Amy flashed him a confused look, as if to ask how he had found that out.

'Jack was being evasive, so I had to take matters into my own hands and do some exploring of his apartment.'

'So what happened?'

'The girl thought I was there for something rather more interesting.'

Amy realised what he meant. 'Oh my goodness.' She pulled a face.

'I didn't take her up on the offer.'

'Dad, that's just *wrong*.'

He nodded. 'You said he and Natalie split up two weeks ago?'

'Yes.'

'This girl has been on the scene for longer than that.'

'It wouldn't surprise me at all.'

'Why wouldn't it?'

'Just a gut instinct. Like I said, I've never taken to him. He seemed like the sort of person who would do that sort of thing, if he got the chance.'

'But it doesn't mean that he has anything to do with Natalie's disappearance.'

'No, it doesn't,' she admitted. 'But I've been thinking since I got home – he really didn't seem to care at all that she was missing. Not one bit of compassion. He just seemed so cold.'

'I agree. But it still doesn't mean he's guilty of anything. Apart from being a lowlife.'

That got a smile from her.

Cullen thought for a second. 'You still think Natalie might be in danger?'

'Yes. I really do.'

'Would you mind if I took a look in her room?'

'I thought you were never going to ask,' she said, jumping up from the sofa.

'Just one question,' he said, 'before I begin.'

'Go on?'

'Have you got any Earl Grey? I'm parched.'

CULLEN SAVOURED the mug of tea, complete with a couple of Rich Tea biscuits that were perfect for dunking, as long as you left them in the liquid for just enough time. Amy had her father's love for 'dippers', as they called them up North, and he was pleased she'd got a stock in the cupboard.

'More biscuits?' Amy asked, entering from the kitchen as Cullen scrolled on his phone. He was looking for any new stories about this morning's incident, but there were none.

'Better not,' he said, downing the rest of the tea. 'Right, point me in the right direction.'

They made their way up the stairs and to Natalie's room. Amy did a quick check first, in case there was anything embarrassing there, but once she'd given the all clear Cullen got to work.

'What are you looking for?' Amy asked as he started looking through papers on the untidy desk.

'To be honest, I'm not sure,' he replied, continuing with the search. 'Something, anything that might give any indication of where Natalie is.'

There was nothing of note. Lots of articles about marketing and branding. A lifestyle magazine. Some receipts for meals out, groceries, and the rail journey to London.

And buried under everything, a book.

New Horizons.

Cullen picked up the autobiography, its cover displaying a smiling headshot of Sir Kenneth New. The strap line read:

The secret of my success, in my own words!

He examined the back cover.

'Some preparatory reading for the weekend,' Amy said sadly. 'She was *so* excited about everything. She got that book a few months ago in Cheltenham at the book festival. Went to watch a talk by Sir Kenneth, and he was doing a signing.'

Cullen opened the cover to reveal Sir Kenneth's message on the inside front page.

Lovely to meet you, Natalie. You are truly delightful! I hope we meet again very soon!

'This guy sounds a bit much. Were you there?'

'No, she went with one of her course friends. It's not really my thing.'

He placed the book down on the desk. 'Or mine.'

'If you're into branding, then Sir Kenneth is the main man. I remember when Natalie got back home from meeting him. She was so excited – couldn't stop talking about his presentation and how nice he'd been during the signing. I teased her about having a crush.'

'And did she?'

'Maybe. Whatever it was, though, after that day she was desperate to work for his company, so when she got through to the final selection weekend, it was a dream.' She paused in thought. 'And now it's turned into a nightmare.'

'I need to talk to these people.'

17

Previous Friday evening

'I'M SORRY,' Russell said, taking a step back. 'I'm really sorry, I didn't plan for...'

'It's okay,' Natalie replied. 'It wasn't just you.'

They looked at one another, not sure about the next move.

'No, it *was* me really,' Russell said with a smile, trying to lighten the mood. He held up his hands. 'I won't spout any rubbish about misreading signs, I promise. It was my bad.'

'I just can't,' Natalie said. 'I'm sorry.'

'No, I understand. It's a stupid idea, fraternising with a fellow contestant. It's very sensible of you to put a stop to it.'

'It's not that.'

'Oh?'

'In other circumstances,' Natalie said, 'it would be different. But I've just come out of a difficult relationship, and I don't think I'm ready yet.'

'I understand.' He looked at her carefully. 'Someone hurt you? Whoever the guy is, he must be mad.'

Natalie laughed away the compliment, but could feel herself blush. 'He is mad, of sorts. He's also controlling and a liar.'

'Sounds like you're much better off without him.'

'I am.'

'Was it a long-term relationship?'

'Eighteen months. We met in the first week at university, at one of the Freshers' events in town. Hit it off straight away. I wasn't sure at first, he's five years older than me, a postdoctoral researcher...'

'A postgrad hanging around Freshers' events? Sounds dodgy and desperate to me.'

'I know, I know, thinking back, it is a bit weird. But at the time, I didn't question it. I know now that it should have been a warning sign. Looking back, I feel like a bit of fool, to be honest. He reeled me in, and I just let him. Then he really hurt me.'

'You don't need to tell me any more,' Russell said. 'I don't want to pry.'

'It's okay,' Natalie replied. 'You know, I haven't even told my best friend, Amy, the whole story. I haven't told anyone. Maybe tonight is the right time, here with you.'

'Only if you want to.'

'But you don't want to hear this, do you? I mean, you don't even know me, why would you want to listen to my problems, my relationship failures?'

Russell shrugged as they took a seat across from one another. 'Because I've had three glasses of this,' he said, holding up the glass of whiskey, 'and I'm a pretty good listener when I'm drunk.'

Natalie laughed. 'For a person dealing in death, you're a pretty funny guy.'

Russell raised an eyebrow. 'It helps to have a sense of humour where death is concerned. Otherwise it all gets just so *morbid*.' He knocked back the rest of the whiskey. 'So, Natalie, oh lovely one, do tell me some more about this total jerk of an ex-boyfriend of yours.'

'His name's Jack. Like I said, he's a postgrad researcher at the university. Not the same department, thankfully. He's a psychologist.'

'Oh, psychologist, you've got to look out for those.' He tapped his head. 'I dated a psychologist once. Never again.'

This elicited another laugh.

'What's this guy's name?'

'Jack. Jack Morton.'

'And especially, *never* date psychologists called Jack.' He pointed at her with his glass. 'Ever.'

'I promise,' she replied.

'Sorry, do go on.'

'Are you sure you want to hear this?'

'Yes, of course. Tell all.'

'Okay. At first he was amazing, the perfect boyfriend. For the first six months really, things couldn't have been better. He was kind, considerate, gave me space to be with my other friends. I was so happy. Maybe that's what blinded me to the truth of what was happening. I didn't even notice the change at first. It came snaking around me like quicksand, and before I realised something was wrong, I was up to my neck in it.'

'So he started getting heavy?'

'It started out as little comments. About who I was going out with, and when. You know, just little asides, snipes at my friends. I can see now he was trying to drive a wedge between us – especially me and my housemate, Amy. He really didn't like her, and I think it's because she saw through him – she could see what I took a lot longer to see.'

'I've met men like him. They see women as possessions. I bet he cheated on you, didn't he? More than once?'

'Yes, he cheated on me. More than once. I found out that he'd been seeing one girl for a few months behind my back.'

'But he still wanted you.'

'I guess.'

'Was the abuse physical, if you don't mind me asking?'

'No, it was never physical. But it hurt in other ways.'

'I'm sure it did.'

'You know, when I look back, I can't believe I didn't see what was happening sooner. What's that they say about boiling a frog: do it slowly and the frog won't even realise until it's too late. Well, that was me.' She smiled sadly.

'But you weren't boiled,' Russell said. 'You survived.'

'Yes,' she said, sipping at her own drink. 'I did survive. And now I'm free. Although I don't really feel that free in this place, with its weird rules.'

'Quite. This place is just so controlling. I can't really get over it, to be honest. It's like being at some kind of Victorian boarding school.'

'I thought the same.'

'I guess that makes us the really naughty pupils.' He grinned mischievously. 'What do you think they'd do if they caught us?'

'What, apart from throwing us out of the house?'

'You don't think we'd just get a warning?'

Natalie thought back to how Tabitha had looked when she was searching her room. 'I really doubt it.' She decided to tell Russell what had happened.

'I can't believe it,' he said, as Natalie had finished relaying the story. He blew out his cheeks. 'So, she knows I was out of my room. He ran a hand through his hair. 'She's probably searching for me right now. Or waiting to ambush me when I come back.' His eyes twinkled in the semi-darkness. 'Hey, maybe I should come back to your room instead. Just for tonight.'

'You're persistent,' Natalie noted. 'I'll give you that.'

'No, seriously,' he said, 'I feel a bit bad actually. I mean, first you had the interrogation from Tabitha, and then I come along and convince you to break the rules, which might mean the end of your dream job.'

'It's fine,' Natalie shrugged. 'I didn't need much convincing.'

'No, I suppose you didn't,' he reflected.

'I guess I felt the need to rebel,' she explained. 'I've just come out of a controlling relationship. I felt free and excited. And then I step through the doors of this place, and it's right back to being under someone else's influence. I think I needed this.'

'That's good then,' Russell replied. 'I don't feel quite so guilty now. But I am intrigued.'

'Intrigued?'

'About who sent the notes.'

'Yes...'

'Aren't you?'

'I haven't had much time to think about it really,' she said. 'By the time I found out about the note to Tabitha, you came along and took my mind off it.'

'So, you've got time now,' he said. 'Who do you think it is?'

'I...' Natalie hesitated. She'd only just met her fellow housemates. It would be pure guesswork, so it seemed totally unfair to finger one of them for the act. 'I really don't know.'

Russell smiled conspiratorially. 'Don't you?'

'No. Why, should I?'

He shrugged. 'I thought you'd have your suspects, that's all.'

'Why, do you?'

He surprised her by nodding.

'Really? Who?'

'Samantha.'

'What makes you think it's her?'

'Gut feeling.'

'What? And that's all? You can't point the finger at someone just because of a gut feeling. It's not...'

'Fair?' he cut in. 'No, it's not I suppose. But I still think it's her. No, I *believe* it's her. I just don't have any proof, yet.'

Natalie raised an eyebrow. 'Yet? You plan to turn detective, do you?'

'Something like that.'

'Go on, Colombo, what's your strategy?' she teased.

'Well, it's quite simple really. We match the handwriting with the note.'

'Tabitha has the notes.'

'Okay...' He thought to himself. 'Then either I try and retrieve the notes from Tabitha, or I'll ask Samantha, look her right in the eye and ask her if she did it.'

'That sounds like a really bad plan. The plan of someone who's had too much expensive whiskey.'

'You're probably right.' He put down the empty glass on the table next to him. 'I do think it's Samantha, though. Just watch out for her.'

'But she seems so...'

'Seems,' Russell said. 'She *seems*.'

'What do you mean?'

'I mean that you don't know anything about her, apart from what she's told you. You have no way of checking out the facts, because you can't get out of the house, and you can't connect to the internet to Google her. She could be telling you anything.'

Natalie thought back to something that Samantha herself had said after dinner – that they couldn't check the veracity of Russell's Lord Sinclair murder story because they hadn't got access to the internet. It was funny to realise how much everyone relied on the web to validate things, and it was only once you were denied access that it suddenly became apparent. 'Well, you could say that about any of us. How do I know you're who you say you are?'

'You don't. You have to take my word for it. But I *could* be lying. After all, a business giving people the funeral of their dreams, blasting their ashes into space. It sounds a bit unrealistic, doesn't it? I could have just made it all up, as part of the game.'

'The game?'

'Yes, the game. We're all playing to win, aren't we, Natalie? And the prize is a big one.'

'Well, I guess. But I hadn't thought of it as a game.'

'Life's a game, with winners and losers.'

Natalie thought on what he had just said. 'So are you telling the truth about your business?'

'Yes.'

'But you would say that, wouldn't you?'

'Yes, I would.'

'So why should I trust you?'

'You shouldn't. That's my point. You shouldn't trust

anyone in here, and that extends to me, and to Tabitha, and to anyone else.'

'I...'

'I can tell you're uncomfortable with that thought,' he continued. 'But you need to have your wits about you. You need to toughen up. Because this weekend is really going to test you. And you need to be ready. Here.' He passed her a card. 'My contact details. When we all get out of this strange place, I'd really like to see you again.'

Natalie held the card and smiled. 'I'd like that.'

18

Cullen caught an early train back to Paddington, armed with as much information as Amy could muster about Brand New, and what Natalie had in store for that weekend. It wasn't a huge amount, but Google had filled in the basic blanks with some background on the company, including its location. His plan was to pitch up at the company headquarters on the banks of the Thames, and just wait in reception, passive-aggressively, until someone agreed to see him.

It usually worked.

He'd also taken details of Natalie's friends and contacts in the London area. Anything that might help his informal investigations. Natalie was pretty well connected, so if she had indeed decided to hide out at one of their places, there were plenty of options.

His phone bleeped. It was a text from Amy. Yet another contact for possible follow-up. An old schoolfriend of Natalie's who had recently got a job in the City.

Cullen texted back a thank you. He was glad Amy had agreed to remain in Bristol. As much as she wanted to help, it was better if he was left to do this alone. He loved spending time with Amy, but she was a distraction that he could do without if he were to work at maximum efficiency. She understood that.

He stretched out as the train sped towards the capital. He'd woken early with aches and pains across his middle back, following a night on the sofa bed at Amy's place. The fold-out contraption had obviously not been designed for comfort, with springs like razor blades and a pungent musty odour that smelled like something dug out from the back of a dank cellar.

After a few minutes of thinking, he speed-dialled Beswick, unable to switch off completely from what was going on back at base. But maybe it was more than that. Beswick was his day-to-day confidant, and just because this current work in progress was unofficial didn't mean that he didn't crave the same input, the same means of bouncing ideas off someone.

It was how it worked.

'Tony, how are things?'

'Okay, thanks, Boss. Nothing really of note has happened since you left. But it *has* only been less than twenty-four hours.'

Cullen heard the smile in his voice.

'Just checking,' he said.

'You enjoying your time off?' Beswick asked, continuing the theme. 'Taking the opportunity to relax?'

Cullen laughed. 'Oh, yes, I'm having a lovely time.'

'You on a train?'

'Great powers of observation, as ever. I'm on my way back from Bristol.'

'Bristol? Ah, you've been to see Amy.' There was a pause.

'But you're coming back already?'

'Well, she doesn't want her dad cramping her style, so I thought I'd better make it a short one,' he joked.

'I know the feeling.' Beswick had two daughters, both at university: one at Nottingham, the other at Durham. Clever girls and, as was the case with Cullen, the first in the family to study at university.

'Actually the visit wasn't for pleasure,' Cullen revealed. 'Amy's housemate is missing.'

'Oh.'

'She was supposed to come back from London on Sunday evening, but didn't return.'

'And no contact since?'

'A couple of text messages, but Amy suspects that they're not from Natalie.'

'What makes her think that?'

Cullen noticed the woman across the carriage glancing across at him, so he moved off to the vestibule area, out of earshot.

'A gut feeling,' he said, now standing between carriages. Fortunately the space was vacant apart from him.

'No more than that?'

'She suspects Natalie's ex-boyfriend has something to do with it.'

'Why?'

'Because he's a controlling, nasty piece of work. And Amy thinks he might have been violent towards Natalie, shortly before their relationship ended.'

'She *thinks* he might have been violent.'

'Bruises on Natalie's arm. Natalie denied it, but Amy has put two and two together.'

'I'm still confused about why you were in Bristol. Especially if Natalie went missing in London.' There was silence on the other end of the line while Beswick thought through something. 'Oh, you haven't, have you, Boss?'

'I went to see the ex,' Cullen said.

He could picture Beswick shaking his head.

'I wasn't too heavy,' Cullen added, feeling defensive in front of his more experienced, if less senior, colleague.

'Permission to speak frankly,' Beswick said.

'Of course. Always.'

'You're off duty. Not just off duty, but on a leave of absence at the request of your senior officer. Can you imagine just how livid Maggie Ferguson is going to be if she finds out you're undertaking your own investigation?'

'It's not an investigation,' Cullen replied. Even as the words emerged from his mouth, his brain had already dismissed them as a poor excuse. What was he doing, if it wasn't investigating?

'You went to speak to the ex-boyfriend, to question him?'

'Informally.'

'Did you tell him who you were?'

'Yes.'

'You told him you're a detective with the British Transport Police and then questioned him?'

'Yes.'

'Then you're undertaking police business, Boss. You *know* that.'

Cullen ran a hand across his face, on one level regretting calling Beswick and letting him know what had been going on. But their relationship and trust ran deep, and it was for the best that he got Beswick's input. It was like a sense check. 'I hear what you're saying, I really do.'

'Sorry, I don't mean to be harsh. I know you're just trying

to help Amy. But I like you a lot, as a friend and as a DCI. And I don't want to see you get in deep trouble because you're not thinking properly.'

'I am thinking properly.'

'I don't think you are.'

Cullen leant back against the wall. 'Amy asked for my help, and I didn't feel able to refuse.'

Beswick chuckled. 'Boss, I've got daughters too, remember? When my daughters ask for help, I always give it.'

'Maybe you're right,' Cullen conceded. 'I went too far, talking to Jack.'

'Did you find out anything from him that makes you think Amy's friend is in danger?'

'Unfortunately not. Although I confirmed Amy's judgement that the guy is a nasty piece of work.'

'Maybe her friend – Natalie, is it? – has just gone to ground for some reason. Perhaps to escape this ex-boyfriend, if he was being physical with her?'

Cullen agreed. It was something he had definitely considered.

'Any other leads?'

'I thought you were warning me against carrying out my own investigations?'

'Not necessarily.'

'Meaning?'

'Meaning that I didn't say you shouldn't investigate this. Like I said, if it was one of my daughters, then I'm sure I'd be doing the same right now. I just meant to be careful. If Ferguson gets wind of this, you'll be for the proverbial high jump, even if she currently thinks the sun shines out of your backside. You know what a stickler she is for following orders.'

'She won't find out,' Cullen said, already thinking that Beswick was right, and that if he were going to pursue further lines of enquiry he would need to be very careful if he didn't want to risk his job.

'Are you sure she won't?'

'Why, you're not going to tell her, are you?' Cullen joked. 'You looking for some hush money?'

Beswick snorted. 'I could do with some. I was thinking more about the ex-boyfriend. He might contact the force, and it wouldn't take long for things to get back to the Super.'

'He won't,' Cullen replied with confidence. 'Jack won't be wanting to speak to the police.'

'As long as you didn't give him any reason to.'

'Of course not.'

'Anyone else you've questioned?'

'Not yet. I did pull in a favour from Anthony Braddock though.'

'How so?'

'He let us look at the CCTV from Paddington.'

'Us?'

'Amy door-stepped me yesterday, travelled from Bristol because she was so concerned about Natalie.'

'And Anthony agreed to let you look?'

'As a favour, yes. I felt bad asking him, to be honest. But he actually seemed to enjoy showing us the new equipment.'

'Well, he is a bit of a tech nerd. I assume it didn't turn up anything.'

'Nothing. We looked for a good couple of hours. But as far as we could tell, Natalie didn't get her scheduled train back to Bristol. She was booked on the eight thirty-five.'

'Did you check the onboard footage too?'

'No. Not yet, anyway. We just checked the cameras on the

main concourse. I didn't feel as though I could ask too much of Anthony. And to be fair, I think the onboard cameras wouldn't be much use, unless we got really lucky. There's eleven carriages to check, and with those new high-backed seats, it's not easy to spot people once they've sat down.'

'Understood. You haven't pushed for a missing person's alert?'

'It wouldn't get anywhere at the moment, not for at least another day. You know what it's like now, it just wouldn't meet the criteria.'

'Unless there's a clearer reason to believe that Natalie is in danger.'

'Which is why I went to Bristol.'

'So who's next on the hit list?'

'Natalie was in London to take part in a recruitment weekend for a company called Brand New. The last text message that Amy believes was from Natalie mentioned something about the weekend not going well. To be honest, it's the only lead I've got. Apart from a long list of friends and acquaintances that Natalie might have contacted or be staying with.'

'Brand New. Never heard of them.'

'They're a cool branding company.'

'That would be why then. Whenever I hear the word "branding" cows come to mind.'

'Indeed.'

'Do you need any help? I could call a few of the names on your list, if you like.'

Cullen nearly said yes, but then he thought that even that small favour would implicate his friend, if he were to be caught working while on leave. 'It's okay, Tony, thanks for the offer, but I'll handle this myself.'

'Thanks,' Beswick said. 'I know what you're doing. But the offer is still open, if you change your mind.'

19

Previous Saturday morning

NATALIE WAS WOKEN by the ringing phone. She turned over, still tired from her late-night adventures, and checked her watch. It was half past six precisely.

'Hello?'

'It's Sir Kenneth.'

She sat up in bed, startled by the surprise of speaking to Sir Kenneth New, and feeling very self-conscious that she wasn't dressed, even though of course he couldn't see her.

'Oh, hi, hello, Sir Kenneth.' She pulled the bedsheets around her.

'I'd like you to be down in the piano room for eight am sharp. I'll be there to tell you the plans for the day. Please don't be late. You don't need to bring anything, apart from yourself and a willingness to go the extra mile. At Brand New, we are looking for the extra special, the person who rises above the crowd, and I hope that will be you. Don't let me down!'

Natalie felt lost for words. Was Sir Kenneth really telling her that he hoped she would get the job? She thought back to how the group had teased her the night before about favouritism. She hadn't believed it for a second, but after what he had just said, maybe there was something in it. 'I won't let you down,' she managed to say. 'I'll do my best.'

'Eight am sharp,' he repeated. And then the line went dead.

Buzzing from the phone call, Natalie felt energised as she stepped into the shower. She thought back to the events in the night. The excursion with Russell, the hidden door, secret stair-case and secluded study with its opening roof: it all seemed like something from a fanciful dream. But it had been real. She mused on how she had felt when Russell had suddenly moved in for the kiss. A part of her had wanted it. Yet she'd been right to resist the temptation. It felt too soon after Jack – and she'd only just met this guy. Plus the situation was not ideal at all.

She'd definitely done the right thing.

But the question was, would she take him up on his offer and call him?

She thought not. Russell wasn't really her type.

NATALIE DRESSED and headed downstairs for breakfast, wondering whether Russell would be there.

He wasn't.

There were only two people in the small dining room, sitting together at a far side table: Samantha and Ben. Ben smiled as Samantha beckoned Natalie over. As she took a seat next to them, she replayed Russell's words about not being able to trust anyone in here and also remembered his suspicions that Samantha was behind the sinister notes. She shook off the thought.

'Sleep well?' Samantha asked.

'Yes, really well, thanks,' Natalie lied. In truth, she'd struggled to settle after returning to her room. The events of the night had unsettled her and her mind had raced until the early hours.

'That's good,' Samantha said, snapping off a piece of toast with her impossibly white teeth, before washing it down with a sip of tea. 'Ben here didn't sleep too well, did you?'

Ben shook his head. 'Awful.'

'He thought he could hear voices from behind the walls,' Samantha chuckled. She raised an eyebrow at Natalie.

Natalie looked across at Ben, who stifled a yawn. 'Voices?' She wondered, with some panic, whether he'd heard Russell and herself climbing the staircase – maybe it had run behind his bedroom. But she was sure they hadn't spoken.

Ben shrugged. 'I could hear voices. A man and a woman, I think. But they were muffled. I thought at first it was coming from next door, but I put my ear to the wall, and then a cup, and I couldn't make out what they were saying. It went on for a while though.'

Natalie felt herself flush. Maybe it had been their voices coming from the top-floor study, somehow making their way into Ben's room, perhaps through a ventilation shaft or along the pipework.

'Ben thinks it might have been the ghosts of Lord and Lady Sinclair,' Samantha teased, smiling mischievously at Natalie and then Ben himself.

Now it was Ben's turn to go red. 'I... I don't.'

'I blame myself,' Samantha said, taking another bite of her toast. 'After you'd gone to bed, I told Ben all the gory details about the Sinclair murders.'

'Oh,' Natalie said. 'I feel like it's my fault then. Sorry, Ben.'

'It's okay, really.' He waved it away, slurping his black coffee. 'Honestly, I'm usually up for a good ghost story. They don't affect me. But last night, with those voices, after the alcohol, it was spooky.'

'What was spooky?'

They turned as Penny approached the table. She looked really tired.

'Oh, Ben got spooked by the Sinclair ghosts,' Samantha said.

'Me too!' Penny said, taking a seat. 'I was awake for hours, scared to death.'

'Did you hear any voices?' Ben asked.

'No, should I have?'

'It's okay,' Ben said. 'Just checking.'

'Well, it looks like Russell Cave was very successful last night,' Samantha noted. 'You've got to hand it to him.'

'How do you mean?' Natalie asked.

'Isn't it obvious? He spun a tale to unsettle the group, and it worked! You don't think so?' Samantha added, obviously seeing that Natalie wasn't convinced.

'Maybe.'

'It's a pretty low trick,' Penny said.

'If that's what he was trying to do,' Natalie said.

'Of course that's what he was trying to do,' Samantha said. 'He put the frighteners on you all.'

'Not you, though?' Ben said.

'No, not me,' Samantha replied. 'I had a *wonderful* sleep.'

Ben yawned again, this time setting off Penny.

'So you don't think the story is true?' Natalie said.

'I don't know whether it's true or not, but I wasn't going to let it get to me,' Samantha replied.

The conversation paused as a waiter appeared and took Natalie's and Penny's orders.

Just as the waiter was leaving, Krishna appeared at the doorway. He made his way cheerfully over to their table.

'Hello, guys,' he beamed. 'You all ready for a busy day?'

The group nodded.

'You know,' he continued, 'I slept like a baby last night. And I'm now full of energy, ready for the fight.'

'Good for you,' Ben muttered.

Krishna frowned. 'Pardon?'

'I said, that's good.' Ben forced a smile. 'I'm very happy for you.'

'Oh, thank you.'

Krishna just stood there for a few seconds, watching the group. There were no spare chairs at the table.

'Anyway,' he added, 'best of luck today, guys!'

He turned and headed for the table near the door.

Penny watched him go. 'Wonder why he's so happy?'

Ben and Samantha grinned conspiratorially at one another.

Penny noticed. 'What is it?'

'He's probably still buzzing from that wake-up call from Sir Kenneth,' Samantha said. She looked in turn at Penny and Natalie. 'You got the calls too, right?'

'Yeah,' Penny said, 'but how...'

'It was a recording,' Ben explained. 'The message from Sir Kenneth, it wasn't really him. Well, it was him, but I mean, it wasn't live.'

'And it wasn't personal to you,' Samantha added.

'So you're not really his favourite,' Ben said, in mock pity.

'And that goes for Mr Smiley Pants over there.' Samantha put up a hand as Krishna smiled across at the four of them. 'He really thinks it was real,' she said.

'So did I,' Natalie frowned, feeling a little bit silly now. But then, why would anyone suspect that it hadn't been Sir Kenneth himself, there and then, on the other end of the line?

'How did you work it out?' Penny asked.

'It didn't feel right,' Samantha said. 'As soon as he started speaking, it just felt a bit wrong. I can't really explain it.'

'Are you sure,' Natalie said, 'that it was a recording?'

Samantha nodded. 'You received the call dead on six thirty?'

Natalie nodded.

'Well, so did I. And so did Ben. And you, Penny?'

Penny also nodded.

'And so did Krishna over there, you can bet. Did Sir Kenneth say your name in the call?'

Natalie thought back. 'No, he didn't.'

'Me neither,' Penny said, 'as far as I can remember.'

'Because it was a generic recording,' Samantha said. 'The reception must have an automated system that can ring up many numbers simultaneously, and play a pre-recorded message. They had it set to six thirty, loaded with the message from Sir Kenneth, trying to make us think that we were receiving a personal wake-up call from the man himself.'

'And that we were all his favourite,' Ben added.

'But why would they do that?' Penny asked. 'Why play a recording, pretending that he'd said you were his favourite?'

Ben tapped his head. 'They're messing with us.'

'Well, I think it's weird,' Penny said. 'And I don't like it. I might say something to Tabitha.'

'I wouldn't,' Samantha advised. 'Just keep quiet, let it slide. Unless you want to be ejected from the premises.'

'I still don't get why they would do it,' Natalie said.

Samantha shrugged. 'Maybe they're looking to see whether we'd talk to one another about it, and figure out what was going on.'

'What, you mean testing whether we'd work as a team?' Natalie said.

'Something like that,' Samantha replied. 'It's just a theory. But look at Krishna over there. He's not going to be telling anybody, that's for sure. He's very happy knowing what he thinks he knows.'

'And you're not going to tell him?' Natalie said.

'Maybe later, depending on how annoying he gets,' she laughed.

They turned as Krishna was joined at the other table by Susie and Matthew. Russell was the only one of the eight who still hadn't appeared.

Probably got a sore head, Natalie thought, *after all that high-end whiskey*.

'You know much about Matthew?' Samantha enquired, eyeing the city trader with interest.

'Had a quick chat with him last night,' Ben said. 'Works for UGT doing foreign currency trading.'

Samantha shook her head. 'I don't really understand why he'd want to go into the branding industry.'

'Said he fancied a change,' Ben said. 'He's been doing that role since graduating, and wanted to try something new.'

'Brand new,' Samantha joked. 'What I don't understand is

how on earth did he get selected for this? Eight people out of all those entries, and he's one of them – someone with no background whatsoever in branding or marketing. It just doesn't make sense to me.' She looked around the table. 'Any theories?'

'Family connection to Sir Kenneth?' Ben joked. 'Maybe he's his nephew, or something.'

'Nepotism, yes possibly,' Samantha mused. 'I'd wondered that myself. Can't see the likeness though,' she joked.

'He could just be a wildcard,' Penny tried. 'Someone to throw in the mix, chosen at random, almost.'

Samantha nodded. 'Could be. I can see Sir Kenneth doing something like that – thinking out of the box.'

'You do have to wonder how any of us got chosen,' Penny added. 'I mean, yes, we've all done things, impressive things, but so have a lot of people. We're not that special. So how did we get picked out from all those thousands of people? It must be luck to a large extent.'

'The harder you work, the luckier you get,' said Ben, pointing at her with a shard of toast before popping it in his mouth.

'I agree,' she replied. 'But it still could have been any other number of people who got picked.'

'Except for Natalie,' Samantha stated.

Natalie looked up from her cereal bowl. She knew what Samantha was alluding to.

Samantha smiled. 'Remember that only one of us, to our knowledge, was personally invited to apply by Sir Kenneth.'

'True,' Ben nodded.

'To our knowledge,' Penny said, coming to Natalie's aid. She smiled at Samantha. 'Maybe you were invited too.'

'I wasn't really invited,' Natalie added. 'He mentioned it to me, that's all.'

Samantha held up her hands. 'Okay, okay. I'm teasing. I promise I won't mention it anymore. Back to Matthew though... any more theories?'

'Maybe he's not who he says he is,' Natalie thought out loud, not quite meaning to vocalise her thoughts.

'Ah, now that's a good thought,' Samantha said, a smile curling on her ruby lips. 'You think he might not be a city trader at all?'

'We've only got his word to go on,' Natalie replied, feeling a little uncomfortable speculating about the honesty of a man she hadn't even spoken to yet. 'Like you said last night, Samantha, we can't verify anything people say without access to the internet.'

'He looks like a city trader,' Penny noted.

'Talks like one too,' Ben added. 'When he got started about currency fluctuations and exchange rates, he lost me. Maths was never my strong point.'

Samantha narrowed her eyes. 'He seems familiar. Maybe he's an actor.'

'What, an actor employed by Brand New?' Natalie said. 'To pretend to be an applicant?'

'Wow, now *you're* sounding a little paranoid there, Natalie,' Samantha said. 'I was just wondering why he seemed familiar, that's all. But your theory is a whole other level of weird. I like it.'

'I wonder where Russell is,' Ben said. 'We're all here except him.'

Penny glanced at her watch. 'Maybe we should see if he's awake? It wouldn't be good to miss this morning's briefing.'

'Except that we don't know his room number.'

'He's in Oak Room, on the second floor,' Natalie said without thinking. She blushed. 'He mentioned it to me last night,' she added quickly.

Samantha arched an eyebrow, but bit her tongue. 'Surely the wake-up call would have woken him,' she said finally.

'Unless he fell back to sleep,' Ben said.

'I'll go,' Natalie said, sliding out her chair. 'You're right, Penny, we shouldn't let him miss the briefing. If he is still asleep, he's got less than half an hour.'

NATALIE STOPPED at the other table as she made her way towards the exit.

'Have any of you guys seen Russell this morning?'

They all said no.

'Why? Something we should know about?' Matthew enquired.

'I think he's overslept,' Natalie explained. 'I'm going to check on him now.'

She headed for the stairs and made her way up to the second floor. Just a few hours ago, she'd wished Russell good-night on this patch of landing, before retreating to her own room for that fitful night's sleep.

She knocked gently. And then knocked again.

There was no answer.

'Russell,' she whispered. 'Are you awake?'

She knocked again, this time with more force.

Still nothing.

Then, without really thinking, she tried the handle and it opened.

'Russell? You awake?' she said, stepping into the room, leaving the door open behind her.

But Russell wasn't there. The main room and the bathroom were unoccupied.

Natalie looked on in confusion at the perfectly made bed. It looked as if it hadn't been slept in. Or it had been remade by a professional. She didn't have Russell down as the neat bed-making type, but you never could tell.

'He's gone.'

Natalie spun around, somehow stifling a scream. Tabitha was standing in the doorway, with her trusty clipboard.

'Sorry?'

'Russell left the house early this morning.'

'Oh.'

'He said on reflection he didn't feel that the opportunity was for him,' Tabitha explained curtly. 'So he asked to leave, and of course we didn't stand in his way.'

'Right.' Natalie looked at Tabitha for any signs that there was more to this. Had Russell been expelled from the house because he had broken the rules by leaving his room out of hours? Or, she thought with a shudder, did they know exactly what had happened that evening?

Maybe they'd been caught on CCTV.

Tabitha smiled. 'We only want people here who really desire to be here, Natalie. Sir Kenneth wouldn't want anyone to feel uncomfortable. Did you get his wake-up message this morning?'

'Err, yes, thank you. It was... a lovely surprise.'

'Yes, I bet.' The smile stayed for a second or two, before fading. 'Anyway, Natalie, I'd better get back downstairs, ready for the briefing. Don't be late!'

Natalie stood in the middle of the room as Tabitha left.

Something didn't feel right about the circumstances of Russell's departure. He hadn't given the slightest indication that he was planning to leave the house. And why did his bed not look slept in? That suggested he'd never made it to bed after they'd said their goodbyes. But even if he had decided to leave, would he have left in the middle of night, rather than just sleeping on it and leaving first thing in the morning? She fished his business card out of her pocket and gazed at the cell number.

If only she had access to a phone.

20

Paul Cullen strolled down the banks of the Thames. He'd alighted a stop early, to take advantage of the time to think by the riverside. London was a fantastic city, especially in the spring. Yes, the streets were busy and polluted. But among that busyness, dirt and grime, were oases of calm – the Royal Parks and the river in particular.

He sat facing the water as a rowing boat skimmed past, followed by several passenger craft. He watched the water swash against the banks, lost in thought.

He pulled out his phone and twisted it over and over in his hand, considering calling Sarah. He'd asked Amy not to tell her mum anything about Natalie's disappearance, as it would only worry her and she had enough to deal at the moment.

With Sarah's name on the screen, his finger hovered over the call button. It was ten thirty. She would probably be at the care home, and wouldn't want to be disturbed.

He slipped the phone back into his pocket.

He would call her later, when the timing was better.

Cullen set off towards the road. As he was waiting to cross, a lorry rumbled past, evoking the memory of the boy under the wheels.

He shook off the memory and crossed on green.

It wasn't good to look back.

IT WASN'T hard to miss the offices of Brand New. Right by the banks of the river, the huge building of glass and steel thrust its way up some twenty floors towards the sky. Cullen gazed up at the gleaming structure.

'There's money here,' he noted.

He entered reception as if he were meant to be there, striding over to the desk confidently and with a smile.

'Detective Chief Inspector Paul Cullen, British Transport Police,' he said, flashing his badge at the receptionist. She squinted at the badge as Cullen waited. 'I'm here to see Kenneth New.'

He might as well shoot for the stars.

'Oh,' she said, puzzled. 'You have a meeting with Sir Kenneth?'

The incredulous nature of the question wound him up more than it should.

'Yes.'

She began tapping away at her computer, her brow knotted, desperately trying to confirm what she'd just been told. Cullen enjoyed seeing how far he could get in these kinds of situations. It was amazing how much could be achieved by a police badge and a large dollop of bravado.

'I called this morning. It's about an incident at the weekend.'

That wasn't a lie. He *had* called the main number that was listed online for the company, but had given up at the point where he was asked to select from six options, none of which included informal police investigation.

She was still tapping away desperately. 'I... I can't see anything here on the system...'

In a few seconds she would call backup.

'Who did you say you were again?' she asking, picking up the phone.

Bingo. 'Detective Chief Inspector Paul Cullen. British Transport Police.'

'Detective Chief Inspector,' she said slowly to herself, punching in a four-digit number.

'It's about a potentially serious incident at the weekend,' he pressed, just to make sure.

She nodded. 'I'll get someone down to see you.'

He smiled warmly. 'Much appreciated.'

'Hi, it's Anne-Marie here at reception. I've got a police inspector here. He said he's got a meeting with Sir Kenneth...' She looked at Cullen, who had stepped back from the desk but was still within earshot. 'I'm not sure... could you send someone down? No, I don't think so... thanks, that's great.'

'Someone will be down shortly to see you,' she said, as Cullen examined the large sculpture that stood just to the right of the reception desk.

'Fantastic. Thanks so much. This sculpture,' he said. 'What's it meant to be?'

'That's by Oscar Ocado.'

Cullen was none the wiser. 'Oscar?'

'Ocado. The world-famous sculptor. Brazilian. He designed a series of sculptures for the Rio Olympics. This is one of them.'

Cullen looked again at the piece. It was red metal, gnarled and twisted around a black object at the centre. 'So what's it meant to be?' he repeated.

'It represents the potential of humankind.'

Cullen didn't see it.

'Amazing, isn't it?' she tried.

'I'm more of a Lowry man, myself,' he said.

She looked confused.

'You know, matchstick men and matchstick cats and dogs?'

Equally confused. 'Don't worry,' he said. 'It was a song my parents used to sing. About the artist D.S. Lowry.'

'Not heard of him. I'll have to Google it,' she said.

'HI, PLEASED TO MEET YOU.'

Paul Cullen rose from the comfy chair as the young lady approached with arm outstretched, a clipboard tucked underneath the other arm.

He took her hand. 'Likewise.'

'Tabitha Blair,' she smiled. 'I work with Sir Kenneth. I hear you have a meeting with him?'

It was clear from the way she asked the question that there was no doubt in her mind that such a meeting had not been arranged.

'I'd like to speak with Sir Kenneth,' he said, dodging the question. He showed his badge again. 'Detective Chief Inspector Paul Cullen, of the British Transport Police.'

She gazed at the details, her face serious. 'How can we help?' she smiled eventually, hugging her clipboard in a way that reminded Cullen of one of those package holiday tour representatives. She was about the right age too – probably early twenties.

'I'm looking for a young lady by the name of Natalie Long. We've been contacted by a family friend who is concerned about her whereabouts...'

It was clear from her reaction that she knew Natalie.

'I have reason to believe that she spent the weekend in London as part of a recruitment event with your company.'

She blinked several times. 'That's correct, yes. She was one of the eight contestants staying at our house in Mayfair. In fact, she won.'

21

Previous Saturday morning

NATALIE RETURNED DOWNSTAIRS, where the others were still chatting over breakfast. They looked up expectantly as she approached.

'So, was he asleep?' Ben asked.

'He's left the house,' Natalie replied, sitting down.

'What?' Penny said. 'He's left?'

'Gone.'

'How do you know?' Ben asked.

'Tabitha told me. She saw me up there, looking for him. Said he'd left in the early morning.'

'Well,' Ben said, blowing out his cheeks. 'One down, eight to go.'

'Did she say why he left?' Penny asked.

Natalie shrugged. 'Just that he'd decided it wasn't for him.'

'Well, I'm surprised,' Ben said.

'I'm not,' Samantha stated.

They all looked across at her for more of an explanation.

'I'm not shocked,' she reiterated. 'He seemed a bit head-strong yesterday. I couldn't really imagine him working in a company like Brand New, taking orders from Sir Kenneth.'

'Well, *I'm* still shocked,' Ben said. 'I mean, why go to all the effort of applying for this amazing opportunity, then being fortunate enough to get a place, and then just turn and walk before you've even given it a chance?'

'You'll have to ask him yourself,' Samantha said, 'if you ever get the chance to meet him after we get out.'

Natalie thought again about Russell's card, which was still in her pocket. It was frustrating, having his number but with no means to call. She'd thought about possibilities. The only phone she'd seen was the one at reception, but surely it would be impossible to call him from there during the day without being spotted.

'You okay, Natalie?' Samantha asked. 'You look very thoughtful.'

'I'm fine,' she said, still wondering about access to a phone. Tabitha would surely have a mobile on her, but that would be even harder to get to than the reception phone.

Unless she left it in her office.

Or maybe there was a landline in there.

'You're sad he's gone,' Samantha tried. 'I could see you two had a connection.'

Natalie smiled, but inside she was thinking again about the anonymous tip-off that Tabitha had received. 'I got on quite well with him,' she admitted. 'But we'd only just met.'

'I think he'd have been a strong competitor,' Ben mused. 'It's probably lucky for us that he's walked.'

'Maybe,' Samantha said. 'But we'll never know now, will we?'

'HI, GUYS!' Tabitha called out across the breakfast room. 'Time for the morning briefing. If you wouldn't mind coming on through to the drawing room, everything will be explained.'

They all made their way past the reception, Natalie sneaking a quick look at the phone behind the desk, before following Tabitha along the corridor towards the drawing room. There were a few long leather sofas placed in a semi-circle, facing an open fireplace, and above the fireplace hung a huge rural landscape painting.

'Please, do take a seat,' Tabitha instructed. 'Sir Kenneth will be along in a moment to welcome you.'

She breezed out the door as the group broke into hushed excitement.

'I just *knew* Sir Kenneth would be here!' Krishna exclaimed. His face was lit up like a child on Christmas morning. 'This is just an amazing moment, a pivotal moment in my life trajectory.'

'Oh, please,' Samantha muttered in Natalie's direction. Natalie didn't take her on, instead remaining silent as they waited for something to happen.

Suddenly there was a noise, a mechanism moving, and the landscape painting began to move slowly upwards.

Behind it was a flat screen.

'I knew it,' Samantha said. 'Sir Kenneth isn't here. We'll be watching him on TV.'

'He's obviously far too busy and important to put in an appearance with us plebs,' Ben said.

Natalie looked across at Krishna, who was sitting between Susie and Matthew. He was crestfallen.

'I don't understand,' he said. He twisted his neck to locate Tabitha, who had just re-entered. 'Is Sir Kenneth not here?'

'Oh yes,' she said, 'he's here.'

Krishna frowned as he saw Tabitha carrying a tray of headsets.

'Please,' she said, 'if you can each take one and put them on.'

The group of seven complied. Natalie adjusted the headset, which wrapped around the front of her head, covering her eyes. She was in darkness. And then suddenly she could see the room again. She turned and saw Samantha to her left, as if she were just looking through clear glass. But there must have been more to it. Although she'd never tried it before, the equipment looked like the virtual reality headsets she'd seen in shops.

'Please,' said Tabitha, who was now standing in front of them. 'Do not remove your headset before you have been told it is okay to do so. Anyone who does remove the headset in contravention of this will unfortunately forfeit their place in the house. Can you all just give me a thumbs up to indicate you understand this.'

Natalie and the others did so.

'Fantastic. And now, here is your special visitor!'

'Welcome everyone!' a voice said. It was Sir Kenneth, and it sounded as if he were behind them. Natalie turned and there he was, hands clasped behind his back, pacing around the back of the sofas like a headmaster stalking amongst his pupils. 'It's great to see you all.' He stopped in front of them, next to Tabitha, and smiled widely. 'Welcome again to New House!'

Natalie looked carefully at Sir Kenneth. Was he really there? Surely not, as it had to be the reason they were wearing the headsets.

But he looked so real.

Sir Kenneth opened his arms. 'I expect you're all wondering what we have in store for you today. Well, I'll let the lovely Tabitha explain more.'

Tabitha nodded and smiled at her boss. 'Thank you, Sir Kenneth. Today, guys, you will be working in teams, on a very special branding exercise. The nature of your task will be explained further when you arrive at the as-yet-undisclosed location. For security reasons, we need to keep the location and task under wraps. The teams will be as follows: the Red Team consists of Ben, Samantha, Krishna and Matthew; the Blue Team is Natalie, Susie and Penny.'

Natalie was quite relieved not to be in Krishna or Samantha's group. In fact, based on first impressions, she couldn't have chosen a nicer couple of people to be teamed up with. Both Susie and Penny, whom she knew best of the two, seemed like thoroughly lovely people.

'So,' Sir Kenneth said, clasping his hands together, 'I shan't delay you any longer. Good luck with the day ahead, and may the best person win!'

With that he strode out of the room.

'You can now remove your headsets,' Tabitha instructed.

They all did so, placing them back on the tray.

The seven looked across at each other.

Ben was the first to vocalise what everyone else was surely thinking. 'So, was Sir Kenneth really here, or was that...'

'Augmented reality,' Krishna interrupted. 'The AR headsets enabled us to see the real world, but overlaid by projected images.'

'So Sir Kenneth was a hologram?' Ben said.

'Similar,' Krishna said.

'They did it with Elvis,' Susie said. 'My dad and I went watching the show. Elvis was up on stage, in three dimensions, singing like he was still alive. It was pretty cool.'

'A hologram is generated by projections, whereas AR is computer graphics,' Krishna explained, obviously deriving great pleasure from demonstrating his knowledge to the others.

'Okay,' Tabitha said, cutting off the conversation. 'If you're all ready, we'll now proceed to the waiting vehicles. You're in for a very interesting day.'

22

Tabitha's face knotted. 'So, are you saying that Natalie is missing?'

'We've been unable to contact her,' Cullen replied, thinking that something Tabitha had just said didn't really add up from what he'd been told by Amy. 'So, Natalie won the event?'

'Yes,' she said brightly. 'Natalie did so well.'

Just then a group of four entered the building and milled close to them.

'Would you like to come with me? Somewhere more private.'

Cullen nodded.

They headed for the lifts and ascended to the top floor.

'Just through here, Detective,' Tabitha directed, as they skirted past offices and out into a restaurant area. 'This is the staff restaurant,' she said. 'Would you like a drink?'

'Tea, if you've got it. Earl Grey.'

She nodded and requested it from a passing member of staff.

'They'll bring it outside,' she explained, leading him out through a set of doors onto a wide expansive terrace. The space wasn't empty – about a quarter of the tables were occupied by what looked like business meetings, but it was quiet enough for them to have a more private conversation.

They headed over to a table on the far left.

Cullen took a few more steps onwards, admiring the view over the Thames. Off to the right was the Shard, and to the left Tower Bridge. New and old London, somehow blending together perfectly to form a cityscape that was both historic and futuristic.

'Nice view, isn't it?' Tabitha commented at his shoulder.

'Lovely.' Cullen scanned the urban horizon and took some deep breaths.

Natalie was out there somewhere.

But was she in trouble?

Was this informal investigation a waste of time, or her only chance?

He thought he knew the answer to that. But he hoped he was wrong.

He turned back and they took their seats. 'So what does winning mean?'

Tabitha went to speak but was interrupted by the arrival of the drinks. Cullen took the opportunity to check his mobile, in case he'd missed a text from Amy or Sarah. There were no messages.

'Natalie has been offered a contract with Brand New, initially for a three-year term,' Tabitha began. 'For the first year, once she's graduated, of course, she will be working closely with Sir Kenneth, shadowing him, learning from him. She'll get to travel the world, be in top meetings with senior executives of some of the world's largest and best-known companies. It will be an amazing experience. On top of that, she will also receive a golden handshake payment of fifty thousand pounds upon signature of the contract.'

'Sounds like an amazing opportunity,' he said.

'Yes, yes, it really is,' she enthused.

'You must have had a lot of applicants for something like that.'

'Oh, yes. Thousands.'

'So even getting to the shortlisted stage was a fantastic achievement,' he noted.

'Most definitely.'

'And there were eight of them, you said?'

'Yes. Eight candidates at New House.'

'New House?'

'Our property in Mayfair. It's where the candidates stayed over the weekend, and their base for the activities.'

Cullen nodded as if he didn't already know this. It was one piece of information that Amy had been able to provide with some certainty: the name and address of the venue where her friend had gone. Cullen hadn't found out much about it, except for the revelation that it had been sold ten years ago for six million pounds. He'd looked at it on Street View; the images were just a couple of years old, and the place looked palatial from the outside.

'The other seven people – I'll need their contact details.'

'Yes, yes, of course,' she said. 'I can get you those, no problem at all.'

'Excellent.'

Cullen ran through what he could remember from Amy's recounting of Natalie's text message. It hadn't resembled a message from someone who had just won the opportunity of a lifetime.

Either something else had happened. Something bad. Something that had overshadowed the amazing triumph.

Or maybe the text message, as Amy had suspected of the later messages, hadn't been from Natalie at all.

'Were you there over the weekend?' he asked.

'Yes. I was the relationship manager.'

'So you met Natalie?'

'Yes, I did. Such a lovely person. To tell you the truth, I was really pleased that she won.'

'And was Natalie pleased?'

The question seemed to take her by surprise. 'Well, yes, yes, I think so. Yes, she was pleased. Why?'

He certainly wasn't going to tell Tabitha about the text message's contents. At least not yet. 'Just trying to establish if there is any reason why Natalie might not have wanted to return home.'

Her brow furrowed deeply. 'I'm not sure I understand.'

Cullen shrugged, feigning an apparent lack of direction in his reasoning, trying to relax Tabitha and put her off-guard. 'I don't know, maybe something that upset her over the weekend?'

'I don't think there was anything,' she replied. She thought for a moment longer. 'No, nothing that I was aware of. She seemed happy. Really happy.'

'When was the last time you saw Natalie?'

'Just before she left the property. It was about, oh, I'm trying to remember. I think it was about ten thirty on Sunday morning.'

'You're going to have to be more precise than that,' he stated.

Tabitha stiffened, sensing that the questioning was more formal than she had realised. 'I... I'll have to think...'

Cullen thought back to Beswick's warnings. Yes, he would have to be careful. If he were to lay it on too heavy, there was a chance that the company would follow up his visit with a call to the police, to check what this was all about.

And it wouldn't take long for the news to get to Maggie Ferguson.

But it was a chance he was willing to take. He would just have to be clever with how he did this, and keep it relatively low-key and unthreatening.

'We just need to be clear about the timelines,' he explained. 'I need to put together a clear picture of Natalie's movements.'

She nodded, still thinking. 'Yes,' she said finally, 'it was just after ten thirty. Definitely.' She seemed satisfied and soothed by Cullen's explanation of his questioning.

'Could you put together a timeline of the weekend for me: what Natalie did, when, and with whom?'

'Yes, yes of course.'

'Thank you.'

'Do you really think something bad has happened to Natalie?' she asked.

'I don't know.'

Tabitha shook her head. 'I just don't understand it. She was *so* happy. I can't imagine there was any reason for her to disappear. It just doesn't make sense.'

'These things never make sense, until they do.'

'So you're going to speak to the other applicants?'

'Yes.'

'I can try and facilitate that for you, if you like. I can contact them, ask them to come and see you.'

Cullen was going to say no, but time was precious, and if they were offering to help with the logistics of getting some potential witnesses together in one place, then that would be a help.

'That would be helpful, thank you.'

'I'll get onto it now. Would you like me to ask them to come here?'

'No. I'll meet them at New House.'

'Okay...'

It could help to jog memories by conducting the questioning at the actual venue.

'I'd like to visit the house first,' he said. 'And take a look around. I also need to talk to the staff who were on duty, so if you could prep them in advance of my arrival.'

'Sure, I can do that. No problem.'

This was going quite smoothly, but still he wasn't sure whether Tabitha's assistance was quite as innocent as it seemed. She seemed almost too eager to please. Although this wasn't unusual – people often acted like that in the face of police questioning, and it was a rookie mistake to equate that with a conclusion that they had something to hide.

'I also need to talk to Sir Kenneth,' he added, returning to his original request.

'I'm afraid that won't be possible at the moment.' She smiled apologetically.

'Won't be possible?'

'He's on a flight to Sydney. A business trip.' She glanced at her watch. 'The flight left about an hour ago.'

Cullen went to say something but stopped himself. It was a fair assumption that the millionaire businessman would be flying first class, in which case he would surely be contactable – either via a satellite phone system or the onboard wi-fi. Long gone was the time when being forty thousand feet in the air meant being out of reach.

'I'd like to speak to him when he lands.'

He was intrigued that she hadn't suggested either of those options, but decided to let it lie. She was probably just protecting her boss, letting him make the journey undisturbed.

'That's fine, of course. I'll check when he's due to arrive.'

'That would be great. Was Sir Kenneth at the property over the weekend?'

'Yes, sort of.'

'I don't understand.'

'He appeared to the applicants virtually.' She noted Cullen's bemused expression. 'Through augmented reality. Sir Kenneth likes to use technology to make an impression, and he wanted to test out the new equipment we have at New House. It's part of our new enhanced communication system.'

'Sounds... interesting.'

She shrugged. 'It's quite a big thing at the moment.'

'Must have missed that,' he quipped, feeling the need to check his mobile phone again, but resisting the temptation. 'So, is there anything else you think might be pertinent to the investigation?'

'I don't think so, no. Like I said, I just can't understand why Natalie would want to disappear. She seemed so happy.' Her face darkened. 'But that would mean that something bad has happened to her, wouldn't it?'

Cullen never liked to speculate, particularly with those who were part of the investigation. Unless, of course, the speculation was a means to an end – testing out the person he was talking to, observing their reaction to different theories. You could tell a lot with this technique.

But there was no need to do this with Tabitha.

Not at the moment, anyway.

'We're doing our best to locate Natalie,' he said simply.

Except there was no 'we' really. Just him, without the backup of his team or the resources of the British Transport Police. It was far from ideal, and he wondered whether it might be worth testing out whether there was any appetite for putting out a missing person's alert.

Maybe he would contact Conner over in the Missing Persons team, test the water informally. There was always the possibility that he would sway them into doing something over and above the usual.

'I hope she's okay,' Tabitha said.

'So do I. In the meantime, if you could get me that time-line and contact the other applicants, that would be very helpful. Also let your staff know I'll be coming over to New House within the hour.'

THE SECOND CULLEN left the building, he was on the phone to Conner McCarthy at British Transport Police's Missing Persons Department. Detective Inspector Conner McCarthy was head of the unit that was dedicated to responding to cases of missing persons across the national rail network. It was a particularly busy aspect of the British Transport Police's portfolio of work, with hundreds of active cases stretching back years. Cullen had first met Conner during a secondment to the unit in his first year at HQ. It was varied and challenging work, dealing with anything from teenage runaways to abductions, and everything in between.

'Conner. Paul Cullen here.'

Conner had heard about Monday morning's incident. News had obviously gone around HQ, where Conner and the

Missing Persons Department was also based, like wild fire. He passed on his commiserations, offered support, and suggested that any investigation would surely be short-lived and would be found in the DCI's favour.

'Thanks, Conner, much appreciated.'

Cullen relayed the details of Natalie Long, including the relationship to Amy, and how he had been drawn in to conduct some informal enquiries. Of course, the more people who knew what he was doing, the greater the risk that word would get back to the Super. But he trusted Conner, having played five a side with him after work every Thursday for the past four years. The forty-two-year-old had a great left foot and was as fit as a professional, despite a penchant for Guinness. Cullen counted the always cheerful Dubliner as a friend, rather than just a work colleague.

'So I was wondering if there's anything you could do, to get the word out.'

There were a few moments of silence, which actually gave Cullen some hope. At least it wasn't an instinctive, flat-out 'no', which he had every right to expect. After all, he knew full well the usual procedure where missing people were concerned.

'I'm not sure, Paul,' Conner said at last. 'You know the protocol is really strict for these things.'

Cullen was only too aware. 'Understood. It's why I've held off until now.'

'You know what it's like, with austerity biting. It's all about protecting our limited and ever-decreasing resources – financial and human. Missing Persons have never been the best funded.'

'I know.'

'And with those latest cuts, we're having to really scale

things down for those lower risk cases. The bar is set pretty high these days, as you know.'

Cullen had explained the same to Amy, but he felt now, a day on, it was worth a try. 'I understand,' he said, not wanting to apply pressure and misuse his position.

'The trouble is, Paul, there are just too many people who go missing each and every day to throw out all the stops too soon. The good news is that most of them reappear on their own accord after a few days.'

'I did say that to Amy.'

Cullen understood that completely. Any investigation launched too soon could be a waste of precious time and money. And more seriously, too many scattergun investigations would take away public focus from those of the highest concern, those that they really wanted people to take notice of.

'What's your gut feeling about this, Paul? You've got a good instinct. Do you think Amy's friend is in danger, or do you think she's just gone to ground?'

'I think she's in trouble,' Cullen said without hesitation. 'That doesn't mean she hasn't disappeared of her own accord, but from what Amy's told me about her, it just seems out of character.'

'Well, if that's your gut feeling, you're probably right.'

'I hope I'm wrong, believe me.' Cullen checked the time. 'Look, Conner, I'd better be going – got a few leads to pursue.'

'Sure.'

'And sorry to bother you, but as it's involving Amy, you know, I felt like I had to try.'

There was another pause on the other end the line, and Cullen's hopes rose again. 'Well, I guess we could do *some-*

thing,' Conner said at last, 'given the fact that you suspect something is wrong here.'

Cullen smiled. 'That would be great if you could. Anything would be a help, as I'm on my own here. I've not even got Beswick for company.'

'We wouldn't be able to launch a full national alert,' Conner cautioned. 'There's no way we would get authorisation for that at this stage. But we could put out information to people in a more targeted, informal way – station staff and BTP officers at Paddington and Bristol Temple Meads, for example. We could also alert the national Missing Persons charities to circulate her photo and description. It couldn't be top of their priority list, but they could add it to their bulletins.'

'Thanks, Conner, I know it's a massive favour.'

'We won't be able to do much more than that, though, I'm afraid. We can't start looking at CCTV, for instance. It just wouldn't fly.'

'I understand,' he said, deciding not to reveal that he'd already done some looking of his own with the help of Anthony Braddock. 'Just remind me, when could this be escalated?'

'She went missing on Sunday, did you say?'

'Yes, last sighting was at half past ten, leaving a property in Mayfair. But her scheduled train from Paddington back to Bristol was only at eight thirty-five that evening.'

'And you've no idea where she went from the property?'

'No. Last contact from her was later that day, saying that she was just about to board the train. But Amy thinks that the message was sent by someone else.'

'If she's still missing at the end of the week, then we could get authority to launch a full-scale national alert. We can also access the CCTV across the rail network, try and see if we can pick Natalie up en route to Paddington, at the station, or on trains to Bristol. Let's hope she reappears by then.'

'Indeed.'

'But in the meantime, if you come across anything that you think raises the threat level, let me know and we can take things from there.'

'Thanks, Conner, you're a true gent.'

23

Previous Saturday morning

Tabitha paused at the reception, turning to the group.

'Very best of luck today to you all. We'll reconvene here in the drawing room at six, where the winning team will be announced.'

'But what about *who* wins?' Krishna asked over Natalie's shoulder. 'There can be only one winner, surely?'

Tabitha smiled. 'The successful candidate will be announced later this evening. The person will not necessarily come from the winning team.'

'I don't understand,' Krishna said. 'Surely the team that's triumphant must contain the...'

'We'll be making an overall assessment of you all, based on your performance over the day,' Tabitha said, cutting him off with merciless ease. 'We'll be seeking expert advice from the client, as well as judging from our own observations – both today and yesterday.'

'I *knew* they were assessing us over dinner,' Ben whispered to Samantha.

She smiled. 'Of course they were.'

'So,' Tabitha said. 'Are there any further questions?'

There weren't. Or at least none that people were willing to vocalise.

'Great. So, if you'll just follow me, the cars are waiting. The Red Team can take the front car, and the Blue Team the vehicle at the rear,' Tabitha explained.

The seven emerged into the morning Mayfair light, to be faced with two bullet-grey Mercedes.

'Nice wheels,' Matthew noted.

Natalie breathed in. It felt great to be outside; although they hadn't been in the house for even a full day, it had still felt like a long time.

'I hope you all have a lovely day,' Tabitha said, as the drivers of both vehicles opened the back passenger doors and gestured them inside.

NATALIE SLID into the plush leather seats and sat against the window, with Penny in the middle and Susie getting in last. The door was closed with a reassuring *thunk* and, ignition turned, the car growled into life.

'Any guesses as to where we're heading?' Susie said, as the car pulled away.

The driver, wearing white gloves, kept his eyes on the road, giving nothing away.

'Not got the foggiest,' Penny replied. 'But I'm happy with the team I'm in, so I don't mind where we go.'

Natalie smiled across to the two of them. 'I think we should do okay today, wherever we're headed.'

'Sorry, Natalie,' Susie said. 'We haven't really had a chance to speak properly yet, have we?'

'No.' Natalie shook Susie's hand across Penny's lap. 'Nice to meet you.'

Susie peered out the window. 'I'm looking forward to this. It's definitely going to be a challenge, we can be sure of that. We already know how the company likes to spring surprises.'

'They do,' Natalie agreed.

'It's a shame about Russell leaving,' Susie continued. 'I guess he'd have been in our team, if he'd stayed.'

'Probably,' Penny mused.

'I heard the commotion during the night,' Susie continued. 'Not sure what on earth went on there.'

Natalie had been people-watching out the window, but she suddenly processed what Susie had just said. 'What? You heard Russell leave?'

'I think so, yes. It sounded like him, anyway. He was in the room next to me.'

'You said there was a commotion?'

'Well, I suppose most things sound like a commotion at two in the morning when you're half-asleep. There were voices, a heated discussion, maybe an argument, I'm not sure. And then I heard the door close and it all went quiet. Later on, I heard other noises from the room, and in the morning we were told he'd left.'

'Did you recognise the other voice?'

'Oh yes. It was Tabitha.'

Natalie caught the driver glaring at Susie in the rear-view mirror.

Susie continued, unaware of the driver's interest. 'I'm one hundred percent certain it was her.'

THE MERCEDES ENTERED PICCADILLY, in the heart of London, turning right at the famous statue of Eros, skirting past Leicester Square and heading past theatres advertising the latest shows. The three girls craned their necks expectantly, trying to somehow spot their destination in advance of their arrival.

The driver hadn't uttered a word throughout the journey and, apart from that one moment in their earlier conversation about Russell, had kept his eyes on the road.

Finally the car slowed to a stop in a side street.

'EXCEL-ENT,' Susie said, looking at the sign on the building next to where the vehicle had stopped. 'Any ideas?'

'It's a media agency,' Natalie replied. 'Represents clients across a range of areas, film, TV, books. They're one of the best.'

Penny looked across at her, impressed.

'We covered them as a case study in our course last year,' Natalie explained. 'They're really into branding for their clients. You know, Harry Jones...'

Harry Jones was a young British heartthrob who had starred in a trilogy of vampire romance movies. He'd been tipped as a future James Bond.

'The actor? Wow, he's hot,' Penny said, before blushing at the thought that had escaped her mouth. 'They represent him?'

'Yes. They won an international branding award a couple of years ago for the work they've done with him. Took him from a daytime soap actor to an international superstar. He's got his own range of "HJ" clothing, aftershave...'

'I know,' Penny laughed. 'I bought a bottle. Smells pretty awful, to be honest.'

They all laughed at that.

The driver opened the door and ushered them outside. 'Just buzz through to reception and ask for Catharine,' he explained. 'She'll be expecting you. I'll be back to collect you at three. Best of luck to you all.'

They watched as the Mercedes drove off.

'So,' Susie said, her finger hovering over the buzzer. 'You two ready?'

'Ready,' Penny replied.

Natalie reached over and pressed the buzzer. 'Let's do this. Go, Blue Team!'

24

Tabitha had offered to organise a lift over to West London, sort out a taxi, but Cullen preferred to make his own way there and think during the journey. He'd told her to warn the staff of his arrival, but wanted to keep them on their toes as to the time he would appear.

He called Amy and updated her on the visit to Brand New. She still hadn't heard anything from Natalie, and was sounding worried again. But she was heartened by the news that there would be some kind of missing person's alert, even if it wasn't full-scale.

Cullen promised he'd let her know any new developments, and she did likewise. It was strange, but having put Amy off returning with him to London, he missed her company during the investigation. She'd make quite a good partner.

But he would *never* encourage her to follow in his footsteps.

Life was just too short.

He'd only just slipped the phone back into his pocket

when it rang out again. Maybe Amy had just remembered something.

It was an unknown number.

'Hello?'

'Detective Chief Inspector Cullen?'

He didn't recognise the voice. 'Who's calling?'

'Zack Carter, London Daily Post. I was wondering if you had a minute...'

'Depends what it's about,' Cullen cut in. He was annoyed at the intrusion, but it was important to keep the press on side, and he did actually have a couple of friends on the staff of the paper.

Zack, though, he wasn't familiar with.

'It's about what happened on Monday morning.'

'I'm afraid I can't comment,' said Cullen. 'There's an ongoing investigation, I'm sure you understand, Zack.'

'So there *is* an investigation? Is that an internal police investigation, Detective?'

Cullen tried to think calmly. 'Any death of this sort is automatically referred to the Independent Office for Police Conduct. It's a matter of course.'

Which you should know, he felt like adding.

'Are you suspended?'

'No.'

'Oh, I thought I heard that you...'

'Well, I'm afraid your sources are incorrect.'

'So you're still working as normal?'

Another pause. Another deep breath. 'I'm taking a voluntary leave of absence.'

'Oh, I understand.'

'Do you. Listen, Zack, I've really got to go.'

'We've been contacted by his girlfriend,' Zack revealed hastily, as if to keep Cullen on the line. 'Shazney Powell.'

'Oh.'

Ever since the event he had wondered whether she would want to tell her story to the press. He had expected it, even. But when that seemingly hadn't happened within the first twenty-four hours, he thought that maybe she would surprise him by keeping a dignified silence.

'She's very upset, DCI Cullen.'

'I'm sure she is.'

'She wants answers.'

Cullen had to resist the temptation to say the same himself. He wanted answers to why the guy had turned and fled in the way he had. He also wanted to know why the girl-friend had lied about the instigation of his chase. But he was aware that everything he was now saying was on the record, and he certainly didn't want this to play out in the papers. 'That's what the investigation is for.'

'Of course, Detective. She says that you pursued her boyfriend off the train without reason. Can you confirm this? There is a conflicting story that there was an assault, and that you were asked by Shazney to give chase.'

It sounded like his colleagues back at Force HQ were briefing behind the scenes on his behalf. Unless one of the fellow tube travellers had come forward as a witness. But it had all happened so fast, he doubted that the other passen-gers had had time to realise what was going on.

'I'm afraid I can't comment on the ongoing investigation.'

'We've been doing some background research on the deceased. It seems he was known to the police. Maybe that explains why he reacted the way he did when you gave chase.

Do you have any further information about him that might be of public interest?'

'Well, I can tell you what he looked like after he'd been crushed under the wheels of the truck,' Cullen replied, finally losing his patience.

'Sorry?'

'I can describe his face for you, if you like. And the way his body was twisted around the underside of the vehicle.'

'No, that... that won't be necessary, Detective,' the reporter said, sounding shocked and spooked.

'Tell me,' Cullen said, 'did she contact you, or did you make contact with her?'

'Well... we made contact with her.'

Cullen shook his head. 'She was there, just behind me, when he died. She saw *everything*. The impact from the bus, him fly across the road, the truck crunch over his body. She watched as I cradled his head. She stood there, screaming. That was just over twenty-four hours ago. Leave her alone.'

'We were careful,' Zack said. 'We know she's vulnerable.'

'It's been nice speaking with you.' Already, Cullen was slightly regretting the tone he had taken. 'Are you new on the paper?'

'First month,' he revealed.

'Well, I hope to speak to you again, in better circumstances. Do say hello to Trevor.'

Trevor Goulding would be his boss.

Cullen and Trevor went back a few years, ever since they'd met on a particularly brutal case of a serial killer who was targeting late-night commuters. It was the first big case Cullen had been involved in after he'd moved down from Manchester. Since then, they'd worked together quite closely and amicably in a symbiotic relationship that suited them both. Trevor got his stories, and Cullen sometimes got some very useful leads.

'I will,' Zack said, without missing a beat.

Cullen wondered whether Trevor had put Zack up to this, although it didn't seem like his style, especially with someone he knew as well as Cullen. Trevor was one of a dying breed of journalists who wouldn't trample over their grandmother for the next headline.

'Just one thing, though,' Zack added, 'before you go. If you don't mind.'

'I really must go, Zack.'

'It's about something Shazney said. Something I think you should really know about.'

PART III

25

Previous Saturday morning

'HELLO, CAN I HELP YOU?' The male voice had an unmistakable French accent.

'Hi, we're here from Brand New,' Susie said into the intercom.

'Great. Do come on up. We're at the top of the stairs.'

The three of them were buzzed through and made their way up to the reception desk. There the man they had spoken to on the intercom was waiting to greet them. 'Catharine will be along in a minute,' he said, as if they knew who Catharine was. 'If you'd just take a seat.'

They did as requested, waiting nervously on the blood-red sofa, wondering what lay in store.

A girl appeared from around the corner. 'Hi, lovely to meet you. I'm Catharine,' she said, shaking each of their hands in turn. 'Please, do follow me, and I can give you a quick tour of our offices.'

The three of them followed, throwing quick glances at one another. They passed along the corridor and then out into an open-plan office, filled with long desks where dozens of twenty- and thirty-somethings were working at computers. None of them looked up from their tasks.

'This is the main office hub here at EXCEL-ENT,' Catharine explained. 'It's where the day-to-day business of the company takes place.'

'Do you usually work on a Saturday?' Susie asked, surveying the full office.

'For the past six months,' Catharine said. 'We have Mondays off instead. It helps with avoiding the rush hour one day a week, and you also get a lot fewer emails, so it's a good day to just get your head down and focus.'

Natalie wasn't really focussing on what Catharine was saying. She was too busy looking at all the telephones and imagining taking the opportunity to call Russell and settle the matter once and for all as to why he left, or had had to leave, the house.

But would she get a chance to call him?

'Those guys over there,' Catharine continued, pointing to the far corner where there was a group of eight people, 'are our branding team.' The team were all hipster clothes and demeanour, just like everyone else in the room. 'They work across our whole portfolio, from some of the world's biggest film and TV stars.'

'Like Harry Jones?' Penny couldn't help but ask.

'Yes. They work with Harry.'

'First name terms,' Penny whispered to Natalie, who couldn't help but smile.

'The branding team will be helping to assess you today,' Catharine said.

Natalie was going to ask a question, but Catharine had already moved on.

'Our agents occupy a suite of offices just down here,' she explained. 'We've got twenty agents, who represent the very best artists in the entertainment industry. We also have an office in New York City, staffed by a permanent team who work across North America, both for our UK clients and our US and Canadian clients.'

As they passed one of the offices, which all had clear glass walls, Natalie thought that she recognised the man inside.

But she couldn't quite place him.

She didn't think he was an actor. A famous author, maybe?

'At EXCEL-ENT, we pride ourselves on our bold spirit,' Catharine said, stopping outside one of the offices. 'We like to keep moving forward, keep developing, keep growing. If you'd like to step inside the office here, Diana will be with you in a few minutes.'

Natalie gulped at the name.

'Can I get you a drink?' Catharine offered, 'I can do tea, coffee, mineral water.'

They ordered coffees.

'So, do you know who this Diana is?' Susie asked, as they waited in the office.

'Diana Saunders,' Natalie replied. 'It has to be her.' She looked across at the photographs on the wall. There was Diana Saunders on stage with Tom Cruise, receiving an award from the superstar actor. Another photo showed her sharing a joke with Hillary and Bill Clinton, cradling a glass of champagne.

Penny looked worried. 'Should I know who she is?'

'She's one of the founding partners of the company,'

Natalie explained. 'It was set up by a few agents who broke away from their former agency. Diana was one of what the industry called the "Fantastic Four", all of whom are still directors. They took a lot of clients with them, but attracted more, and they've been tremendously successful. You heard what she said about the New York office. Since it opened a year ago, they've poached quite a few big names from the States, right under the noses of the established agencies.'

'I can see why they were a case study on your degree,' Penny said.

'I must admit, I'd never heard of them,' Susie said. 'Anything else we should know about Diana Saunders?'

Natalie hesitated, before deciding it was safe to continue, as long as she kept her voice down and one eye on the door. 'Diana has a reputation.'

Penny frowned. 'Reputation?'

'For being ruthless. There is a story about how she poached a client, a young female actress, from under the nose of a fellow agent at a rival agency.'

'Doesn't sound too bad,' Susie commented. 'Par for the course.'

'Except that the fellow agent was her father, who was in hospital at the time, recovering from a heart attack.'

'Oh,' Susie said. 'I take it she doesn't get on with her dad, then?'

'Oh, I think she gets on with him fine. To her it was just business.'

'Nice,' Penny said. 'I'd never do anything like that to my family.'

'There's lots of other stories. She knows what she wants, and she goes and gets it.'

'Sounds like a scary character,' Susie said, her Scottish

accent seeming to become stronger. 'And we're going to meet her any moment.'

And right on cue, her face appeared at the door. She just observed them for a moment, her eyes narrowing, as if she were looking at specimens in a lab. She turned and said something to someone next to her, just out of sight, before entering the room with a flourish that swept a gust of cold air around their ankles.

'Diana Saunders!' she announced, pushing her dark-rimmed glasses up into her jet-black, tied-back hair. 'Well?' she said, looking down at them, 'aren't you going to stand up and introduce yourselves?'

Natalie was the first to get to her feet. She held out her hand, but Diana's attention had already been diverted to her ringing cell phone.

'Hi, Eddie!' she gushed. 'Of course, darling, no, not doing anything important. Always time for you.' She laughed in a flirty way and placed a hand over the receiver. 'Ladies, if you wouldn't mind stepping out of the office for a moment, I need some privacy.'

'I ALREADY SEE WHAT YOU MEAN,' Susie muttered across to Natalie, as the three were left standing in the corridor while Diana Saunders continued her phone conversation behind the closed door. 'She's certainly a force of nature, you can tell that straight away.'

'She certainly is,' Natalie noted.

'I wonder what our task is going to be,' Penny said. 'I'm not sure whether I'm looking forward to working with her or not. I get the feeling it could be either the best or worst experience of my life.'

That brought a smile from the other two.

'I think we'll be fine,' Natalie said. 'As long as we do whatever she says. Oh, she's off the phone.'

The door swung open. 'Do come in!' Diana instructed. 'No time to waste!'

They retook their seats, this time faced with the imposing figure of Diana Saunders, who was scrutinising them again from her luxury leather swivel chair. At the same time, she was playing with her cell phone, turning it over and over in her right hand, which could have been mistaken for a nervous tic if it had been anyone else doing it.

'Sorry,' she said, glancing at her cell phone, before placing it on the desk behind her. 'Had to take that call from Eddie. He's on set in LA, middle of a shoot, needed to talk to me urgently about some extremely important business we're currently in the middle of. Can't really say more than that, as it's highly sensitive, but everyone will hear about it in the fullness of time. It's going to be huge. The director was champing at the bit to get back to filming, time being money, you understand, but you know Eddie, he's his own man and Stephen knows that. He's too smart to upset his star asset, far too smart.'

The three of them were too wise to ask who Eddie or Stephen were. It seemed as if Diana just expected them to know, and to admit otherwise and reveal their ignorance would no doubt go down badly.

'Anyway,' she continued, 'Eddie might be calling back in a few minutes.' She twisted around to check her phone, as if she might have somehow missed a call from him. 'So we'd better get started before my boy calls back – we don't want any further interruptions, do we?'

They smiled back.

'So,' she said, 'you're three of Sir Kenneth's lucky people. And you really are very lucky, have no doubt about it. You've been given a once in a lifetime opportunity, I hope you understand that.'

They nodded.

'I've been good friends with dear Kenneth for decades,' Diana continued. 'The man is a genius, one of a kind. Intelligent, insightful, imaginative. Our respective companies work very closely together, to our mutual benefit. We've had many, many successes in the years, and I can't speak highly enough of Brand New. They are true boundary pushers. Global leaders. Have you met Sir Kenneth?'

'Kind of,' Natalie replied.

Diana arched a tattooed-on eyebrow. *'Kind of?'*

'He appeared via virtual reality. Well, augmented reality I think it was.'

'Ah,' she smiled. 'Sir Kenneth does love playing with his technology – especially when it allows him to be in multiple places at once. I think he's in the Caymans at the moment.' She thought for a second. 'Or maybe Hong Kong. Anyway...' She waved the location issue away. 'Let's get down to business.'

Just at that second, Catharine appeared at the doorway, peering in with a tray of drinks in her hands.

Diana looked slightly irked. 'Come in.'

'Sorry to interrupt, Diana,' Catharine said, handing out the drinks. Diana had a huge cup of black coffee.

'You've met my assistant, Catharine,' Diane said. 'Catharine started at the company eighteen months ago. I took her under my wing, as she has aspirations of becoming an agent, don't you, Catharine?'

Catharine nodded.

'It's a long, hard road,' Diana said, 'to become a stand-out agent, an agent who doesn't just get the deals done and look after their clients, but truly excels in this cut-throat industry. Isn't that right, Catharine?'

'Yes, Diana.'

Catharine left the room.

'She does make great coffee,' Diana said, sipping at the steaming hot drink. 'But I'm not sure she'll make a great agent. I've been thinking of letting her go.'

They didn't know what to say, but thankfully Diana was obviously the kind of person who quickly filled any silent space.

'So,' she said, 'your task for today. Let me explain a little bit of background. Here at EXCEL-ENT, we like to push the boundaries, to lead rather than follow. But, I'm afraid, we've been rather caught on the hop over the past few years regarding our literary direction. I've recently taken personal charge of our books department, to remedy the situation, and we've let a couple of people go, who frankly, didn't really take the opportunities that had been staring them in the face. A few years ago, I led the development of our own film and TV production company, and we've been very successful. We've worked with key strategic partners across the industry and have had big hits. You'll have heard of *Future Fears*, our groundbreaking dystopian series which recently broke streaming records.'

'I love that series,' Penny said. 'Really imaginative, and quite freaky.'

Natalie knew of it too, and had watched several episodes, although some of them, the more horror-centred, were a little bit too freaky for her persuasion.

'Well,' Diana said, 'I'm now turning my sights to the publishing industry, which, quite frankly, needs a bloody good shake-up. I'm sick of being beholden to the big publishers, with their measly contracts and excuses for not promoting our authors in a way that they truly deserve. Which is why EXCEL-ENT are launching our own publishing house. We already have the authors, we have the means of production, both electronic and print on demand, so now we turn to the branding. Which,' she smiled, 'is where you come in.'

26

Previous Saturday morning

'So, girls, here's your task. You have,' Diana checked her watch, 'just under four hours to create a branding vision for our new publishing house. And then you'll present your work to the team here at EXCEL-ENT for their assessment and feedback.' She smiled the challenge at them. 'Do you think you're up to it?'

'Yes.' Susie was the first to reply. 'We're up for the challenge, aren't we?' She turned to the other two, both of whom nodded.

'Great!' Diana said. 'Right, I shall leave you to it. You can have access to a computer each, in the main office. The branding team are moving out for the day, to give you some space. Catharine will be back in a few minutes to take you through.'

She was halfway out the door when Natalie called out.

'What about the client?'

Diana stopped. 'Excuse me?'

Natalie doubted herself for a second, but shook it off. 'The client,' she said. 'EXCEL-ENT. What are your priorities and values, what are your business goals?'

Just as Natalie was doubting herself again, Diana smiled and stepped back into the room, closing the door behind her and slipping back into her seat. 'I thought you might never ask. It's Natalie, isn't it?'

'Yes,' she replied, wondering how she'd known, given that she hadn't asked their names up to this point. Maybe the list the company had been provided with by Brand New also contained their photographs.

'Well, Natalie,' she said, seemingly intentionally ignoring the other two, 'as I said, I've had enough of the traditional publishing industry. Sure, I have some good friends there, some very good friends – Mark, Gabriella, Margot. There's a lot of passion, lots of people who love literature, love books, and love what they do. But it's not enough, Natalie.' Her eyes were on fire, burning with an unnerving intensity. 'I want to take things to a new level. I want our publishing house to be the go-to place for authors, for the world's top authors. People like King and Rowling, I want them knocking on my door, begging me to take them on.'

Natalie had pulled out the notebook and pencil that they'd each been provided with. ''Can you describe what you want the publishing house to be, maybe in three keywords?'

'Unique. Daring. Ruthless,' she replied without missing a beat.

'And the company name?'

'Nice try,' Diana replied. 'I'll leave that to you. So,' she said, finally addressing Susie and Penny again, who had been watching on rather despondently from the sidelines, 'have you got any other questions? If so, you'd better be quick, before Eddie calls back.'

'We can access the internet, can't we?' Penny said. 'I mean, at the house, we weren't allowed to communicate with...'

'You can have access to the internet for research and development purposes only,' Diana explained. 'Any attempt to communicate with anyone, for assistance or any other reason, will be reported to Brand New. I hope that's clear enough for you.'

'Yes, yes, I didn't mean...' Penny stammered.

'Good,' Diana smiled tightly. 'Any questions?' She directed this at Susie.

'Is this a real task?' she asked.

'Sorry?'

'I mean, are we really designing the branding for your new publishing company?'

Diana laughed. 'Oh my goodness, no. That will be handled by our branding team. This is an extremely important part of our development, so we don't want to take any risks by handing over responsibility to anyone less than supremely competent. Of course, any ideas you have will be considered by my team, in the event that there is something of value there.'

Susie looked to the others after Diana had exited the room. 'Well, she really knows how to instil confidence, doesn't she?'

THE REST of the morning flew by. The three of them worked in the corner of the busy open-plan office, powered by coffee from the swanky bean-to-cup machine that was installed around the corner, as the branding team moved out into some of the outer offices.

They divided the tasks up between them. Susie was great with graphics, so she took the lead in working on sourcing possible images for the publishing house logo. Penny, whose self-built baby-naming website had won multiple awards, went to work on designing the website concept. Natalie focussed on the company strap-line and mission statement, which could be used across multiple channels.

Thankfully, they'd decided on a name very quickly. In fact, the idea had been pitched by Natalie and agreed on by the rest of the team even before Catharine had returned to collect them from Diana's office.

Black Tiger Publishing.

It had been a spark of inspiration on Natalie's part, which was seized upon by the other two. Sometimes things just happened like that. A few weeks ago she'd watched a nature documentary with her housemate, Amy, that had focussed on the mysterious black tiger. It was a rare genetic variant, where thicker than normal black stripes almost obscured the colour underneath. A very impressive animal, it seemed to represent perfectly Diana's three key words to describe what they wanted their publishing house to be: Unique. Daring. Ruthless.

They could only hope that Diana and her branding team felt the same way.

The imagery was another matter.

They needed something bold but basic. A logo that would work on the spine of a book, as well as on a website and on giant posters. It needed to be simple but original. Fortunately, Susie was good. Within an hour of seeking inspiration from other publishers, and testing out ideas, she had four possible logo designs.

Of the four, one stood out. It was the head of a black tiger, face on, with bold thick black stripes and piercing yellow eyes, set on a futuristic, metallic silver background.

'That's perfect,' Natalie said, as soon as she laid eyes on it.

'I agree,' Penny said. 'Definitely the best of four really good logos.' She looked at Susie and smiled. 'Nice work!'

'Thanks,' Susie said. 'That one was my favourite, too, but I didn't want to sway you two one way or the other. How's the strap line going?' She looked over towards the computer screen where Natalie had been typing and deleting for the past hour or so.

'It's been harder than I'd thought.'

Natalie had looked at what other publishers were offering; many of the traditional companies didn't have a strap line at all. Some of the new players in the industry did, though: mostly the digital-only houses. They were generally savvier, but that was probably because they were new to the game and had to stand out to survive.

'But I've got something I think works pretty well,' Natalie added.

'So let's see what you've got,' Susie said. 'And I promise we won't laugh,' she added cheekily.

'Hey,' Natalie joked back. 'Okay. Here goes. *Publishing Reimagined.*'

She looked at the other two with some sense of trepidation as they were both processing it without giving away anything.

Finally Susie nodded. 'I like it.'

'Me too,' Penny concurred.

Natalie wasn't convinced. There was something about

their reaction that was muted somewhat. She wanted to see a spark of excitement in their eyes, but it just wasn't there.

'How about this one,' Natalie said. '*Publishing Without Fear.*'

'I prefer the first one,' Penny said.

Susie nodded. 'So do I.'

Natalie turned back to the screen. The rest of her attempts weren't as good, she knew that. 'Give me a few minutes, and I'll come back with something better.'

'Honestly, the first one is fine,' Susie said, looking concerned that Natalie might be feeling rejected.

Natalie got to her feet. 'No, it's absolutely fine,' she said. 'I'm just going to take a walk around the building, and I'll come back with the winner.'

Susie nodded, reassured that they hadn't hurt Natalie's feelings.

27

'Detective Chief Inspector?' the guy said, approaching Paul Cullen in the middle of a busy Leicester Square. He had stylised boy-band blond hair, gelled up into a high quiff, and very blue eyes. Dressed all trendy, in tight drainpipe jeans and a jacket, he looked as far removed from his old-time journalist friend Trevor Goulding as you could imagine.

He made Cullen feel very old.

Cullen nodded and grasped his hand, pumping out a workmanlike hello.

Was this the kind of person he would have to deal with from now on? Someone who looked like he could be his son?

'Zack Carter. It's great you could meet, thanks so much for obliging.'

He was stepping back and forwards on his tiptoes, rather like a sparring boxer.

'Don't mention it,' Cullen said, quite put off by the guy's energy. Maybe he was just nervous and would settle down in a minute or so? 'But I really can't talk for long.'

'No worries, no worries,' Zack said, still moving. He

glanced over his shoulder. 'Fancy a pint?' He nodded to the bar next to the Odeon Cinema.

Cullen was about to say no, just to be difficult, but he felt as if he could do with something. 'Just the one,' he said. 'But not there. I know a place around the corner. Better atmosphere. And better beer.'

'Sure, lead on, Detective!'

Cullen nearly tutted at that, but held himself back, instead mustering up a tight smile. They crossed the Square, dodging tourists out enjoying the spring sunshine, pointing with their smartphone cameras and consulting their guide books. This part of London really was tourist central, and English accents were a rarity, compared with the many North American voices, not to mention the dozens of languages that floated through the air.

Cullen led Zack down one of the arterial side streets and through the door of a narrow pub that was sandwiched between a currency exchange shop and a store selling tourist trinkets.

The Underground was a favourite haunt of Beswick, who had taken Cullen there on his first week after starting in the capital. Run by a railway enthusiast, the place was a haven for those with any interest in transport, especially of the rail variety. It was frequented by a lot of Cullen's older British Transport Police colleagues, while the younger guys, some of whom were not too dissimilar in age to Zack, tended to prefer the more fashionable bars of the West End.

The place was dark and quiet. Cullen recognised the handful of locals, most of whom gave him a nod as they entered. Quite a few of the older guys were former Transport for London employees: tube drivers, bus drivers, and conductors.

Cullen caught Zack wide-eyeing the framed London Underground posters adorning the walls and other paraphernalia, including an old tube station sign that ran across the top of the bar. He was probably wondering what the hell this place was about. It did look a bit like one of those antique centres that Sarah liked to drag him around.

'Paul,' the barman said, with a broad smile. 'Great to see you. It's been a few weeks, hasn't it?'

'About two.'

'Feels like longer. How's Tony?'

'He's doing fine.'

The barman looked across at Zack, who was hanging back just behind Cullen's shoulder. 'Is this a new...'

'No, no, Beswick and I are still very much together. No one's going to break us up. Well, apart from the Grim Reaper. Or Maggie Ferguson,' he added mischievously. He was amused by the thought of Zack here as his all-new, trendy sidekick.

'Thank goodness for that,' the barman said. 'I was beginning to worry for a moment. Thought he might have finally retired.'

'Not a chance,' Cullen replied.

The man laughed. 'He's been *thinking* about retiring for as long as I've known him.'

'He said maybe one more year, but I think he'll go on for a few years more.'

'Let's hope so.'

Zack looked more confused than he ought to have been by their banter. In fact, rabbit in the headlights came to mind. But then this old real Londoners' pub probably wasn't Zack's usual haunt.

Cullen smiled. 'This is Zack. He's a journalist with the Daily Post.'

'Oh, right.' The smile disappeared. 'I don't much like that newspaper,' the barman admitted as Zack looked back uncomfortably. 'Only one good use for it, and I have plenty of quilted toilet paper, thank you very much.'

'Oh,' he said, stepping back on his feet again. 'Well, that's, err...'

'He's yanking your chain,' Cullen said, cutting in to end the guy's discomfort. He was feeling a little guilty about Zack. 'Aren't you, Mickey?'

Mickey smiled. 'Not really, no. I've still not forgiven that rag after they ran that terrible false story a few years ago about my beloved Spurs. But hey, no point dwelling on such things! What can I get you? I take it yours is the usual, Paul?'

'Indeed.'

Zack looked across the pumps at the bar's selection. 'I'll have what you're having,' he said finally, as the barman filled a pint glass with something called *Northern Line*.

'You'll like it,' Cullen said. 'As long as you like strong beer.'

Zack nodded, but didn't look particularly convinced.

'Or we've got some Babysham,' the barman said.

'No, no, that one's fine.'

They took the drinks over to a table on the far side. Cullen nodded another hello to an elderly gentleman, Clive, who was nursing a pint and talking to a woman Cullen hadn't seen before. He'd known Clive for a few years, since Beswick had first brought him to the establishment, and this was the first time he'd seen him with a female. Tony had filled him in on his backstory; he had driven tubes for forty years and had the cough to show for it. But it was his wife of fifty-five years who had succumbed to cancer just a couple of years previously, and the guy was heartbroken.

Maybe Clive, who must have been pushing eighty, had moved on.

'So,' Cullen said, as they settled down. 'What was it that you've found?' He wanted to get straight down to business – after all, there were things to do, not least interviewing the staff at New House and possibly Natalie's co-applicants, if Tabitha had managed to get in touch with them.

'First of all,' Zack said, his voice still nervy, 'thanks again for meeting me. I really appreciate it.'

Cullen nodded.

Zack reached into his satchel and pulled out a tablet computer. He flipped open the cover and opened up the screen using his thumb print, before swiping through to what he was looking for.

'Trevor's on holiday, went away this morning to Tenerife, but yesterday, before he left, he asked me to look into what happened yesterday, you know.'

'Go on.'

'Well, I spent the afternoon trying to find out more about the guy... you know, the guy who died.'

He kept looking up at Cullen, as if expecting him to say something, add in more info. But of course Cullen didn't. He let the silence push Zack on.

'I did some informal investigations, but I couldn't really find out much about the guy. He doesn't seem to have a social media presence; nothing at all was coming up on internet searches.'

Cullen shrugged. If Zack was fishing for more information, he certainly wasn't going to get it from him. 'So you contacted his girlfriend.'

He was still irked by that action, and wanted Zack to know that it was still uppermost in his thoughts. It was out of order, really: an insensitive intrusion into the girl's grief at a most vulnerable time – although Cullen had to admit, it was also totally understandable from a press perspective.

Zack nodded. 'She was different. Really easy to find. Shazney is on all the main platforms. Has quite a big following on Instagram, where she posts about fashion and makeup. She's also active on Twitter, and her Facebook page is open access. I knew from the photos from the morning that it was the same person, so I dropped her a line.'

His nervousness had dissolved, replaced by something like pride for his achievement. It made Cullen want to cut him down a little, as in his mind he had crossed a line, meddling at such an early stage in an active investigation.

'Did Trevor authorise you to do that?' he enquired. It didn't seem like Trevor's style at all. He was usually much more aware of boundaries, given his experience in the profession and his respect for police investigations.

Zack swallowed. 'No. He was out of contact before the question arose. Simon did, though.'

Simon Hardacre. He was the deputy editor, working under Trevor. Cullen didn't get on particularly well with him. Simon was ambitious and ruthless when it came to digging for stories. He'd managed to rub people in the force up the wrong way, not only in the BTP but also Cullen's colleagues in the Met. On more than one occasion he'd threatened investigations through over-intrusive practices. Usually Trevor kept the guy in line, but when the cat's away...

'Simon should know better than to interfere with a police investigation,' Cullen stated, watching as the flush spread across Zack's neck.

He looked down at his pint, the bubble burst. 'I... I was just...'

'It's okay,' Cullen said, rather more quickly than he'd intended. As annoyed as he was, and as much as he did want to send a strong message both to the journalist and the newspaper, Zack was just a kid, not much older than Amy, if at all. Now he was faced with him, it took some of the fire out. 'You were just following orders.'

This got a subdued nod from the young journalist.

Cullen took a sip of his drink as he played through his options. He would take the softly approach. After all, it wouldn't do to burn bridges. The Post *had* been a help with various police investigations more than it had been a hindrance, after all.

Which gave him an idea.

28

Previous Saturday afternoon

NATALIE MADE her way out of the open-plan room, and down the corridor past the private agents' offices, waiting for inspiration to strike. She passed Diana Saunders' room, expecting to see the formidable woman staring back at her, wondering why she wasn't hard at work on the branding task.

But the room was empty.

And that's why she saw the phone on Diana's desk.

She felt Russell's card in her pocket, and suddenly the urge to take the opportunity that had been presented to her felt irresistible.

It would only take a minute.

She looked left and right. There was no one else in sight.

She slipped into the room and closed the door softly behind her.

She felt shaky and vulnerable as she grabbed the telephone receiver. Keeping one eye on the door, she dialled

Russell's mobile number hastily. Such were her nerves that halfway through she hit the wrong button.

Damn it!

Another glance towards the door. Then she started again, punching in the numbers, this time trying to not make a mistake.

The number entered, she brought the receiver up to her ear. It was ringing.

'C'mon, Russell, pick up, pick up.'

It rang through to the message service.

She left a quick message, saying that she'd give him another call when she could.

She turned again to look at the door, just as she was leaving her mobile number for Russell. Diana's assistant Catharine was there, watching her through the glass.

Natalie brought the phone down and placed it back on its base. She was expecting some kind of inquisition, but Catharine didn't enter the room.

She just walked away.

Flustered and full of nerves, Natalie wondered what to do. Should she follow her and try to explain?

She exited the office and followed Catharine back along the corridor. Thankfully there was no one else there.

'Catharine?' She got up to her shoulder, although Catharine didn't stop. 'Catharine, I'm really sorry. I shouldn't have used the phone, I shouldn't. I didn't plan to do it.'

Catharine continued walking.

'I just wanted to call my friend, she's not well, you see.' In her desperation, the lie came easily, although whether it was convincing was another matter entirely.

Catharine stopped and turned to her. 'I didn't see anything.'

'I don't understand.'

She moved closer, glancing left and right to check there was no one in earshot. 'I know what Diana says about me behind my back. I don't owe her my loyalty, or anything else. Your secret is safe with me.'

Natalie didn't know what to say. 'Thank you. I really appreciate it.'

'I'm leaving this place,' she said suddenly, under her breath. 'I've got my resignation letter in my bag.'

'Oh.'

'I've got a new job, with a reading charity. They work with schools.' Her face brightened. 'It will be such a relief to get out of this place.'

'Is Diana that bad?'

Catharine glanced around again. 'Worse. But up to now I've been too afraid to leave. Diana has such strong contacts in the industry, she could make things very difficult for me.'

'You know, the way Diana spoke to you,' Natalie said, 'it reminded me of how my ex-boyfriend treated me. It took me a while to draw up the courage to escape, too. I know how hard it is.'

This seemed to give Catharine cause for thought.

'Come with me for a second,' she said at last. 'This room is free.'

Natalie followed her into the vacant room, which housed two photocopiers, a printer and what looked like the mainframe computer system for the building.

'We should be okay in here for a minute,' said Catharine, against the hum of the equipment.

'What is it?'

'I want to warn you.'

'Warn me? About what?'

'About Sir Kenneth. You need to be careful of...'

Diana Saunders entered the room, cutting the conversation stone-dead. She eyeballed them both, but saved her fiercest glare for Catharine.

'Catharine, I need to speak with you in my office. Now, please.'

Catharine nodded, vacating the room while Diana held the door open, turning her attention to Natalie. She checked her watch.

'Better get back to the others, Natalie. Time is running out for you.'

29

Previous Saturday afternoon

'NATALIE, we wondered where you'd gone!' Penny said, smiling with evident relief as Natalie re-joined them in the office.

'Penny thought you might have decided to do a runner,' Susie quipped.

Penny nodded. 'When you walked off, you looked a bit troubled. I thought you might have decided to pack it all in. It would have been such a shame.'

'I just needed to have a think,' Natalie replied, distracted by the interrupted warning from Catharine about Sir Kenneth. What had she been trying to say? 'I was trying to think of a better strap line,' she said at last.

'So have you?' Penny asked hopefully.

Natalie shook her head, still not able to fully push aside thoughts of what had just happened. 'Unfortunately not.

Sorry,' she said, sliding back into her seat. 'We'll probably have to go with what we've already got.'

'I liked it anyway,' Penny replied. 'Publishing Reimagined.'

'Me too,' Susie said. 'Let's stick with it.'

Penny then ran through where she had got to with the website. She'd taken Susie's Black Tiger logo and the related images that she'd created, and populated a mock-up of the new publishing house's site.

'Wow, Penny. Diana is going to love this,' Natalie said, finally moving on from the experience with Catharine, as Penny scrolled through the pages, highlighting the features.

It looked stunning: stylish, modern, dynamic.

'Thanks,' Penny replied. 'I'm really pleased with it. It helps that your graphics are *so* good, Susie.'

'Thank you,' Susie smiled. 'You know, I think the three of us make a good team.'

Natalie smiled back, wondering if she should tell them about Catharine's warning. There was no way she could tell them here, or in the taxi back to the house, so it could only be done later.

'Just the pitch left to do,' Susie continued. She glanced at her watch. 'We've got less than an hour to get the presentation together.'

Natalie buried Catharine's warning. She owed it to the others to focus and do her best. 'We'd better get started then.'

An hour and twenty minutes later, the three girls stood in front of EXCEL-ENT's branding team and a selection of other company employees, including Diana Saunders.

She was standing at the back, texting.

The presentation was in one of the company's small seminar rooms, and it was packed. Natalie scanned the audience. Most of them were chatting amongst themselves. A number, like Diana, were deeply involved with their cell phones.

Natalie decided now was the time. Susie and Penny gave her the nod as she picked up the microphone. They'd decided beforehand that Natalie would do the introductions.

'Ladies and gentlemen...'

The chatting continued.

'Ladies and gentlemen,' she repeated, a little more loudly. She looked towards Diana, who still had her head in her phone. 'Thank you for taking the time to listen to our presentation today.'

Thankfully, the conversations were dying out as people started to focus their attention on her.

Natalie took a deep breath. 'We'd like to introduce you to Black Tiger Publishing. Publishing Reimagined.'

Penny showed the first slide, featuring Susie's striking Black Tiger logo.

'Unique. Daring. Ruthless. The black tiger is a rarity in nature.'

Penny flicked to images of black tigers in the wild.

Natalie glanced over at Diana.

She was watching.

She was interested.

'Familiar but strikingly different, the black tiger represents something different and exciting, standing out from the crowd. It has that wow factor. That's why we feel it is a perfect fit for your new publishing house.'

Natalie chanced another glance at Diana, who had put her phone down. She narrowed her eyes in concentration.

They certainly had her – for now, at least. The trick would be to maintain her interest.

'Publishing Reimagined,' Natalie said confidently. 'A bold message, that both conveys the core mission of the company but also signals a departure from what has come before, and what still exists in an industry that is in need of a disrupter. Boundary-pushing, Black Tiger Publishing will take on the traditional publishing world with imagination and flair, harnessing the latest technologies for the benefits of their clients and consumers. A publisher with a global reach, from London to New York and across the world, Black Tiger will lead through innovation and the dedication of its team.'

Diana was still watching.

'I'm going to pass you on to Susie, who will talk to you about the logo.'

Natalie stepped aside as Susie took the floor, with Penny switching the slide to a close up of the black tiger head. 'The logo is designed to be striking and instantly recognisable. The black-and-white head, with bright yellow eyes, works well at various scales, and is especially good on book spines. Complimenting the headline logo is a series of graphics for use in promotion and marketing activities, showing the black tiger in various poses. The graphics also form the basis of the website branding. I'll pass you over to Penny for more about this.'

Penny stepped to the front. 'Thank you, Susie,' she said, sounding natural and confident despite her younger age. 'This demonstration site illustrates some of the features that would form the core of Black Tiger's online presence. For example, on the home page the logo is prominently displayed, with space for featured books and a short introduction to the company. The pages behind this offer opportunities to showcase authors and their books, with links to all major sellers.'

Natalie, who had taken up position at the laptop, clicked through the various shots of the website's pages.

'The site would also enable readers to sign up to the company mailing list, which is very important these days for building brand loyalty and a real connection with consumers.'

Penny stepped back as Natalie returned to the front.

'We hope in this short presentation we have successfully conveyed our vision for the company, and how our use of language, visuals and web-design work together to communicate the ethos of the new publishing house. Thank you for listening. Are there any questions?'

As the three of them lined up shoulder to shoulder, not yet risking any demonstration of satisfaction, several hands went up.

Diana Saunders' was one of them.

'Who thought up the name?'

'It was Natalie,' Susie admitted. 'We all loved it as soon as we heard it.'

Diana remained poker-faced as she looked at Natalie. 'A fan of tigers, are we?'

'They've always been my favourite animal,' she replied.

'Mine too,' Diana revealed. 'I like the name. A lot.'

The girls couldn't help but smile. And that revelation gave them the confidence to deal with the half a dozen questions that came flying at them – from queries about the strap-line to technical issues relating to the website, all of which they dealt with like professionals.

'Final question,' Diana announced, just as a girl in trendy glasses was about to speak.

The girl thanked Diana with a nod, before turning to the three at the front. 'Hi. I'm Carmella Flurey, head of the branding team, and I just wanted to say, I think what you've managed to achieve in such a short space of time is really impressive. *Really* impressive.'

Now truly was the time to relax. 'Thank you,' they all said, maintaining their composure.

'Right!' Diana said. 'Thank you for coming, everyone – now back to work!'

As the room cleared quickly, Diana approached them. 'Well done, girls. That was most impressive. Most impressive indeed. Especially when you take into account the fact that you are all new to this. I must admit, you took me by surprise. I'll certainly be feeding back a very favourable report to Sir Kenneth and his team. Bravo.'

'Thank you.'

She made to leave the room, but turned. 'I hope you remember the document you signed at the beginning of the day. Everything you presented here – the name, the logo, the strap line, the website design – it all belongs to EXCEL-ENT now. We own the intellectual property. You have waived any right to financial or other commercial claims. Do you understand?'

They all nodded. Diana Saunders certainly knew how to sour the taste of victory.

'That's terrific,' she said, brightening again as she headed for the door. 'I'm glad we all understand the situation. I wouldn't want things to get difficult, not for three lovely girls like you.'

Her smile told the real story.

30

'Tell me a bit about yourself, Zack.'

Zack seemed surprised by the question. 'Me? Oh, well, like I said, I've just started on the paper.' He nodded, as if agreeing with himself. 'It's a good start for me, the Post has the biggest circulation of any non-national in the country. I feel lucky to have got the job.'

'Your first job?'

'Yes. Well, if you don't count when I edited the student newspaper at uni.'

'Which university?'

'Manchester.'

Cullen smiled. 'My home patch.'

'And mine,' Zack replied. 'Sort of. Actually I'm from your way. Well, across the hill – St. Helens.'

'Really?' Cullen hadn't recognised the accent. The town of St. Helens was just a short ten miles from Cullen's home town of Wigan.

'My family moved to Hertfordshire when I was ten,' Zack

explained. 'So I've lost the accent, pretty much. But I still have a lot of family there, and it still feels like home.'

Cullen's mood towards Zack softened some more because of their geographical connection. He had family in St. Helens, too. His mum's side lived in the borderlands of Billinge, a small town bridging the two much larger towns in the rolling hills of the Lancashire countryside.

'So I see you've done your homework on me,' Cullen noted.

'Of course.'

'You always wanted to be a journalist?'

Zack nodded. 'Ever since I was little.'

'Why?'

'Because I want to make a difference,' he said, without missing a beat.

Cullen nodded. 'In my experience, journalists fall into one of two camps. Those who make a difference for the right reasons. And those who make a difference for the wrong reasons. Which one do you want to be, Zack?'

'The first, definitely. Which is why I wanted to speak to you.'

'*Simon* wanted you to speak to me,' Cullen stated.

'No,' Zack corrected. 'He doesn't know about this.'

This was interesting. 'Isn't that a bit of a risk, being the new boy, going behind your boss's back?'

'Trevor knows.'

'I thought you said…'

'He's on holiday, yes. But I got in touch via WhatsApp. He said it was okay to speak to you.'

'You said you had something of interest to the police internal investigation.'

Zack nodded. 'Something that I think you should know. It

might be a big help for you. You see, when I spoke to Shazney this morning, something in her story, it wasn't right. And then I...'

Cullen held up a hand. 'Please, Zack, don't say any more.'

'But...'

'If you have anything relevant to the internal investigation, please report it directly to the British Transport Police. You'll have all the contact details back at the office.'

'Well, I will, of course, but I thought...'

'There are strict rules about these things, Zack. I really shouldn't even be meeting with you. Any suspicion of interference in the independent police complaints investigation could have serious consequences for me.'

'Then why...'

'Did I agree to meet you?'

'Yes.'

'Because I was interested to meet you,' Cullen said. 'It's always good to make contact with the new journalists in town.'

'Oh.'

'And I also wanted to make a polite request, which in my experience always comes across better in person.'

Zack looked pensive, as if steadying himself for a blow from the guy who seemed twice his size. 'Okay...'

'Please respect police investigations.'

Zack flushed again. 'I do, I do.'

'And if you really want to make a positive difference, be more like Trevor and less like Simon. One is a principled journalist who knows the line to tread between getting a story and respecting the work of those trying to bring people to justice. The other is a lowlife. I'll let you work out which is which.'

This actually got a smile from Zack. 'Understood. So you don't want to know about what I found out? I think it will help to explain what happened.'

'Of course I *want* to know,' Cullen said. 'And don't get me wrong, I'm not afraid of bending the rules in the right circumstances. But this isn't one of those occasions.'

'Okay.'

Cullen clarified. 'I've got faith in my colleagues to come to the right conclusions about what happened on Monday. It might take a little time, but that's fine. The wheels of justice sometimes turn slowly. I can wait.'

'And me telling you what I know could really mess things up, right?'

Cullen nodded. 'Mess things up is the right word. My boss would come down on me like a ton of bricks if she thought I was soliciting information for my own case. I love my job. I really do. So I don't want to screw things up by being impatient.'

'I understand.'

'That's great, thank you, Zack.'

They settled into a few seconds of silence. Zack sipped nervously at his drink, unsure about what he was supposed to do next, now that he had been cut short in telling his story.

'So you're taking some time off?' he said finally, unable to stomach the silence any longer. He seemed to regret the probing question as soon as it had left his lips. 'Sorry, I didn't mean to be nosey.'

Cullen thought about what he'd already done since Monday morning, and his plans for the rest of the day. It certainly couldn't be classified as taking time off. 'I'm keeping myself busy,' he replied.

Zack nodded, as the silence descended again.

That's when Cullen had an idea. 'Actually, there is something that you might be able to help with.'

Zack brightened. 'Oh, yes?'

Cullen paused, giving himself one or two more seconds to weigh up the pros and cons of telling the press, especially a journalist he'd only just met, about this. He decided any risks were minimal, while the potential benefits were massive. 'A girl has gone missing.'

'Oh?'

'She's a friend of my daughter's. Her name is Natalie Long. I think you might be interested in the story.'

Zack reached for his tablet computer. 'Is it okay if I...?'

Cullen nodded. 'Sure, go ahead.' He waited as Zack opened up the notepad app and tapped out Natalie's name.

'She's a student at Bristol City University, shares a house with my daughter, Amy. At the weekend, she travelled to London for a residential recruitment event. The last Amy heard of her were a couple of text messages, but she feels quite strongly that it wasn't Natalie who sent them.'

'What makes her think that?'

'The phrases. They didn't seem right to her.'

Zack nodded.

'The last message that she feels *was* from Natalie was one sent on Sunday afternoon, saying that she was about to board a train at Paddington, heading back to Bristol. She made reference to the fact that the weekend hadn't gone well.'

Zack was busy tapping away. He looked up for more information.

'Amy asked me to look into things.'

'But aren't you...'

'On leave, yes. This isn't an official police investigation. It's a concerned father, helping out his daughter.'

'Oh,' Zack said, puzzled. 'So the police aren't concerned?'

'It's too soon,' Cullen explained. 'Too many people go missing every day. They need to prioritise. I'm afraid unless there's a clear sign that Natalie is in danger, it's a matter of waiting for a few more days until the police will take things forward.'

'I see.'

'Which is why I'm helping Amy out.'

'Do you think Natalie is in danger?'

'Amy does. And that's enough for me to take it seriously.'

'Won't you get into trouble with your bosses if they find out what you're doing?'

'As I said before, I'm not afraid to bend the rules, or take risks, if I have to and the circumstances dictate it,' Cullen said.

'So how can I help?'

'I'd like some publicity, raise Natalie's profile, see if anyone comes forward with information.'

'You'd like us to run a story?'

Cullen nodded. 'I've initiated something on the rail network, using a contact of mine. They're putting up posters at stations on the route from Paddington to Bristol, and have alerted station staff. But without a formal police-led Missing Persons investigation being launched, that's the limit of what can be done.'

Zack looked perplexed. 'I could probably arrange for an announcement in the ads section.'

'I was thinking more about an article. I want something that a lot of Londoners are going to read, not just the ones perusing the classifieds.'

'I might be able to get them to place it next to the "Love on the Run" feature. A lot of people read that.'

'Maybe.' That feature, messages from London commuters declaring love for strangers they had come across on their journey, was popular. It was a frequent talking point among Cullen's team.

But was it enough?

Zack ran a hand through his hair. 'The thing is, I just don't think that Simon will run with the story. Not unless there's an angle to it, something to capture the interest of the readers. Like you say, people go missing in London every day. Is there anything else that might make it stand out?'

'The recruitment event was run by Brand New,' Cullen tried. 'There's every reason to believe that Natalie's disappearance is linked with what happened at that event.'

Zack nodded. 'It adds interest, definitely,' he said, tapping away some more. 'They're a high-profile company, that's for sure.'

'Do you think it will be enough for Simon?'

'Maybe.'

'Can you call him now?'

'Now? Er... I guess.'

'Excellent.'

'Shall I tell him all the details? You know, about your involvement?'

'Yes.'

Zack dialled through and, after thirty seconds on hold, was put through to the Deputy Editor. Cullen watched and listened as Zack made the case, against what appeared to be some resistance. Cullen did wonder whether revealing his involvement might be more of a hindrance than a help, given his history with Simon.

Zack brought the phone away from his ear and tapped on

the mute function. 'Simon said he would run the story, front page this afternoon, if we can report on your involvement.'

Cullen shook his head and smiled, imagining how the article would be framed. 'Detective under investigation launches personal crusade to find daughter's missing friend.'

Zack just looked at him, phone poised, waiting for a decision.

Cullen thought for a few more seconds. Without doubt, both the front-page splash, the undermining of police proto-col, and the fact that Cullen had gone off on his own mission while under orders to refrain from work activities would not go down well with Maggie Ferguson. But at the same time, it could be a chance worth taking, especially for a front-page story.

Natalie's photo on the front page would reach tens of thousands of people. It would be publicity that money couldn't buy.

And if Natalie were really in trouble, which was the working hypothesis, then it *was* worth a bit of an ear-bashing from the Chief Super.

'Do it,' Cullen said. 'Run the story however you like, as long as it's front page. I don't care what the headline is. But I want Natalie's face front and centre.'

Zack nodded, before relaying the information to Simon. 'He wants to speak to you,' Zack said at last.

Cullen took the phone. 'Simon. How are you?'

'Good, thanks, Paul. I just wanted to check that you're sure about this.'

'I'm sure.'

'Because I know from experience how you guys like to complain if you think we've stepped on toes,' he added.

'Only when it's warranted, Simon,' Cullen shot back.

'Well, we'll have to agree to disagree on that particular point, Paul. But you can understand how I wanted to hear it from the horse's mouth that the force won't come complaining after this hits the newsstands.'

'I understand,' Cullen replied. 'Trust me, you've got nothing to worry about on that score.' It wasn't the newspaper that would be in the line of fire after this story broke. It would be him, all the way.

'So Zack tells me that you're undertaking an informal investigation about the disappearance of this girl?'

'Natalie, yes.'

A low whistle. 'DCI Cullen. Carrying out unofficial police business, against the orders of your senior officer. Won't you get into big trouble for this?'

'Quite possibly.'

'We'll have to cover this in the story, you understand?'

'I understand. Do what you like, as long as you get it up on the front page.'

'You won't get any editorial oversight on this,' he stated. 'This will be our story, independent from others.'

'No stories are independent from others,' Cullen replied. 'But that's fine, I don't want to see what you're going to write – as long as Natalie's headshot is prominent on the cover.'

'Agreed. Is she good-looking?'

'Yes,' he answered, holding back on what he really wanted to say. He knew how things worked with the press. Any story featuring a pretty girl was much more likely to receive high-profile coverage than a story about a plain Jane, or worse, a guy. They saw it all the time when trying to get the press interested in investigations. Pretty faces shifted more newspapers, and it was no different for the London Daily Post.

'I assume you can provide the headshot image?'

'I'll send one through.'

'You'll need to be quick. If we're to hit the afternoon edition.'

Cullen had the selection of photos that Amy had sent over yesterday. He remembered that there was a good head-shot, but he'd also send through the two other full-length photos in case the paper was tempted to print more than one. 'I'll pass it through to Zack now.'

'Excellent. If you can just let Zack have as much detail as possible about the case, then we'll get the story in. Nice doing business with you, Paul.'

'You too.' Cullen passed the phone back. He didn't trust Simon not to screw him over in the piece, but that wasn't important. He could say whatever he liked as long as that photo appeared.

'Are you sure about this?' Zack said, as he cut the call to his boss.

'I'm sure.'

Zack nodded. 'I'd better get some more details then, and start writing up. We're under quite a time pressure if we're going to hit today's deadline. I'll try and write this as sympathetically as possible, but the final edit will be down to Simon.'

'I understand, Zack. Don't worry about me, I know what I'm getting myself into.'

'Okay, as long as you know what gets printed might not be exactly what I wrote. It's not my style to sensationalise.'

'Don't worry, Zack. I get good vibes from you. And I get it, Simon will put his spin on it.'

'Thanks. If it helps, I think you're going to be very pleased when you find out what I was planning to tell you. I reckon it will be a big help for that independent police investigation.'

'Well, do tell my colleagues,' Cullen replied, secretly desperate to know what this revelation was. It would be great to be back in the fray, with his team, doing the job he loved. But process was process. 'I'll wait to find out.'

Zack nodded his understanding. 'I'll call them straight after this. But in the meantime, are you ready for this?'

'Fire away,' Cullen said, wondering whether he should pre-empt the piece by letting Maggie Ferguson know personally about what was happening. It would probably be the most sensible thing to do. But it would no doubt ruin his afternoon plans of visiting New House.

Maggie Ferguson would quite rightly order him to stand down from his informal investigations, and he just wasn't prepared to do that.

31

Previous Saturday afternoon

THE CAR WAS WAITING for them as they exited the building.

'Well done,' Catharine said at the entrance. 'Best of luck with the rest of the weekend.'

She looked at Natalie as if she wanted to say something significant. 'Look after yourself,' was all that she said.

Natalie wanted to press her, but the car was waiting, and the others were standing next to her. She couldn't put Catharine in that position. 'Hope everything goes well for the future,' Natalie said.

They hugged.

'Just be careful of that man,' Catharine added in the embrace.

'WELL, THAT WENT WELL!' Susie said, as the car started off. 'I must admit, I'm still buzzing with excitement.'

'Me too!' Penny said, beaming. 'What a team we were!'

Just be careful of that man.

Catharine's words echoed in Natalie's head. But she couldn't say anything to the others, because there were no details. Did she really want to be responsible for all that disruption and upset, based on half-spoken warnings?

'You okay, Natalie?'

Natalie snapped back to the present situation. 'Yes, yes, I'm just a little worn out by the day, I guess.'

Penny and Susie nodded their understanding.

'I wonder how the other team have got on,' Penny said. 'We don't even know where they went.'

'Yes, it will be interesting to find out what happened,' Natalie said.

'I can't imagine Samantha and Krishna working together in harmony,' Susie said. 'She really dislikes the guy, and I just don't think he can see that he winds people up the wrong way.'

Natalie thought back to the previous evening and over breakfast, where Samantha's scorn for Krishna was unconcealed. She could only agree with Susie's assessment of what their working relationship would be like. Although surely they realised that any group disharmony must significantly harm their chances. Maybe someone like Ben would have managed to hold the peace for the good of the team. 'I guess we'll find out shortly.'

'I'm not supposed to tell you anything,' a voice said from the front. The driver was addressing them via the rear-view mirror. 'But my colleague radioed through while I was waiting for you guys. According to him, the other group have fallen out so badly, they had to call for an extra vehicle to take them back to the house in separate cars.'

'HI, GUYS! WELCOME BACK!' Tabitha was waiting on the pavement, her clipboard still clutched to her chest. 'Great to see you all!'

She was acting as if they'd been away for weeks, rather than a few hours.

'C'mon on in,' she said. 'If you could go through to the drawing room where we met this morning, we've got some refreshments for you. The other team are in there already. I'll be with you in a couple of minutes, where we'll be reporting back on the day.'

She didn't give them a chance to ask any questions. She was already striding back towards the house.

'Can't wait to find out what happened to the others,' Susie joked, as they entered the house. 'Must be something bad to have needed separate cars.'

Natalie had been wondering the same thing. 'Sounds like it.'

They made their way back to the drawing room, where three of the other four were indeed already present. Samantha and Ben were talking over near the table of tea and coffee, while Matthew was over on the other side, inspecting one of the paintings. He was the first to notice their arrival, and he smiled in a way that looked something like relief.

He met them just inside the door.

'Have you heard what happened?' he said under his breath.

'The driver said something about a falling out,' Susie replied. 'We don't know any more than that.'

He shook his head. 'Absolute disaster. Most embarrassing experience of my life.'

Penny's interest was piqued. 'Why?'

'Because of Krishna,' Samantha said, approaching them with Ben just behind her. 'He was even more of a nightmare to work with than I'd imagined.'

Natalie looked at Ben for confirmation.

'Total nightmare,' he said.

'Why, what did he do?' Natalie asked.

'Tried to take over,' Matthew said. 'Appointed himself team leader and wanted to do everything his way.'

'And when any of us suggested anything, he'd dismiss it out of hand.'

'But you didn't just take it, did you?' Susie asked.

'No, of course not,' Samantha said. 'We tried to reason with him, to *try* to get him to be a team player, for the good of us all. But Krishna isn't a team player.'

'Not at all,' Ben said. 'It's either Krishna's way, or the highway.'

'Where is he now?' Penny asked.

'Hiding out in his room,' Samantha smiled. 'At least that's where I assume he is. He came back on his own in the other car, so we haven't seen him since leaving the recording studio.'

'Recording studio?' Susie asked. 'What was your task?'

'We had to come up with a branding strategy for a boy band called *Young Gunz*,' Ben said.

'With a "z"!' Penny said. 'I know about them! There's four of them, from Liverpool, I think. They're going to be the next big thing.'

'Not if they follow our branding strategy,' Ben replied, deadpan. 'Not that there's a cat in hell's chance of that, of course.'

'No, I'm pretty sure they *won't* be taking forward our suggestions.'

'Was it really that bad?' Natalie asked.

'It was shocking,' Matthew replied. 'Like I said, one of the most embarrassing experiences of my life. We had to present in front of the band and senior executives from their record label.' He shook his head at the memory. 'I mean, during Krishna's opening address I was just wishing the ground would open and swallow me whole.'

'Krishna decided he was going to lead off the presentation,' Samantha explained. 'We tried to talk him round, but in the end, we were wasting so much time going around in circles, we just gave up and let him do it. Big mistake.'

'We thought with all the talk of him being this mega-successful entrepreneur that he'd do well, even though we didn't feel he was the best person to front things,' Ben added.

'But he wasn't good?' Penny asked.

Ben shook his head. 'Totally bottled it. He couldn't get his words out, he was stuttering and he didn't seem to be able to remember anything we'd rehearsed. I mean, I actually felt sorry for the guy, up there dying on his feet, but he brought it on himself. And he ruined things for everyone.'

'So what happened?' Susie said.

'He left the room,' Samantha replied. 'Virtually ran out.'

'Oh.'

'And we had to pick up the pieces. Except that by then we were rattled, and we didn't really get the introduction right. We did okay with the basics of the branding, the logo, the descriptions, but because of Krishna's influence a lot of the presentation was about the development of an app to promote the band's brand. We did okay presenting the basics on it, but because he wasn't there to answer any of the technical questions, we got absolutely hammered in the Q and A.'

Ben ran a hand through his hair. 'One of the guys in the audience was in charge of the band's current digital branding, and he just went in for the kill when he realised we couldn't answer the questions.'

'Sounds awful,' Penny said.

'That wasn't the worst part,' Ben explained. 'The private feedback that we got from the record company was just awful, really awful.'

'So,' Samantha said, 'unless you guys had a similar worst-day-of-your-lives experience, I'd say that I'm currently looking at one of the winners of this weekend's Brand New recruitment exercise. Because I'm sure as certain that it isn't going to be one of us.'

Susie, Penny and Natalie looked at one another, hesitating to confirm the news that the others were surely dreading hearing.

'We were sent to EXCEL-ENT, the media agency. Had to come up with a branding strategy for a new publishing house they're launching,' Susie explained. 'We got really good feedback.'

Samantha put up her hand. 'That's all we need to hear, I think. Congratulations – especially for not having Krishna on your team.'

Natalie wasn't sure that she liked Samantha's tone, and the insinuation that Krishna's presence, or not, was the sole reason for the outcome of both teams. It was maybe for that reason that she decided to say what she said. 'Do you know Krishna's room number? I'm going to go and see if he's okay.'

'You're what?' Samantha replied, agog.

'He needs to be down here for the debrief,' Natalie said.

'Room Two,' Ben said.

'Great.' Natalie looked at the time. 'We've got a few minutes until Tabitha returns. Should be long enough to convince him to come back down.'

'Rather you than me,' Natalie heard Samantha mutter as she headed for the stairs.

32

Previous Saturday afternoon

BY THE TIME Natalie had reached the door to Krishna's room, she was seriously reconsidering her decision to venture up there.

She didn't know Krishna, apart from those brief, rather uncomfortable conversations the previous night and at breakfast this morning.

Who was to say how he'd react to the intrusion?

And why did she think that she'd be the one to change his mind and come downstairs?

But she was here now.

Knock!

There was no answer and no sign of any movement behind the door.

Knock! Knock!

Still no signs of life.

'Krishna? It's Natalie. Natalie Long. I was wondering if

you're going to come down for the debrief.' She checked her watch. 'We've got about five minutes until Tabitha comes back.'

Still nothing.

Natalie glanced back towards the stairs, wondering whether she should just give up and rejoin the others. After all, Krishna was an adult – if he wanted to stay in his room, it was his right.

But she wasn't about to give up.

'Krishna. I heard things didn't go very well with the pitch. I just wanted to check you were okay.'

After a few moments of silence, the lock clicked from the inside and Krishna stood facing her. His face was puffy and his eyes swollen. If he hadn't been crying, he must have been close to it. 'I just want to stay in my room,' he said sadly.

Natalie tried to brighten the mood. 'C'mon, you can't just hide out here. It wouldn't be the same without all of us there. Just come down, even for a few minutes.'

'They don't want me, Natalie,' he replied. 'The team, they *don't* want me to be there, because they blame me for ruining everything.'

He turned and headed back into the room, leaving the door open for Natalie to follow.

'I think they're just still upset,' she said, as Krishna perched on the edge of his bed, his head in his hands.

She took the place next to him.

He shook his head. 'You know, Natalie, I was looking forward to this day so much. I thought it was going to be the best day of my life, the culmination of all my endeavours. But it was hell.'

Natalie tried to be diplomatic. 'I heard the team had problems.'

He laughed incredulously. 'Problems? Is that what *they* told you?'

She had to be careful what she said. The last thing she wanted was to worsen the situation – she was here to try to calm things down, not pour petrol on the flames. 'They said there'd been issues with the team, that's all.'

He shook his head. 'Oh, yes, there were problems with the team.' He looked directly at her, his eyes burning with intensity. 'They are racist.'

Now Natalie did regret voluntarily stepping into the situation, which it seemed she really knew nothing about. 'Racist?'

'They look at me, from India, and they think, oh, he cannot be the leader, it's best we put him to work, he can take orders from us.'

'I'm sure they're not racist, Krishna.'

He didn't look convinced. 'Natalie, I am a successful business entrepreneur, I have made millions from the companies I have created. I have achieved more than any of the others combined. And yet, I am not capable of leading the team! Why? Why would that be?'

'But I thought you did lead? Samantha said...'

'Huh,' Krishna interrupted. 'She was the worst of all. Samantha was obstructive, critical, a block on things all day. She set out to undermine me, using whatever means possible. She wanted to destroy my chances, because she knew I was the main threat. And I'm sorry to say she was successful. Her and that sidekick of hers, Ben.'

Natalie had come around to the idea that with Krishna being so angry and bitter, it was probably best for him to try and calm down in the privacy of his room. And it was time to leave, anyway, as Tabitha would be returning any minute. 'Maybe I should go...'

'The pitch, it was awful. I'd felt so under attack, for the whole day. But I thought I'd got through it. And then, as we were in front of everyone, about to present, I looked across at Samantha, and she just gave me a look, it was a horrible, mean look. It was something in her eyes, hatred or, I don't know, something awful. And it got to me. I couldn't concentrate, I couldn't remember the script that I'd memorised, I couldn't even speak. And I was just looking at all those people, those important people, key to my future success, and I couldn't do it. I *couldn't* do it.'

'I'm sorry, Krishna.'

'So I ran. I *ran* off. Out of the room. Like a coward. That's not who I am, Natalie. Not who I thought I was.' He looked towards his feet. 'I've brought shame on my family.'

'You haven't, Krishna. Look at everything you've achieved. You've done more in your life already than most people achieve in a lifetime. Your family must be so proud of you. And you'll bounce back from this, I know you will.'

For the first time since the beginning of their conversation, she seemed to be getting through to him, to be pulling him out of the mire.

'Won't you just come down?' she tried again.

He looked at her. 'Why do you care?'

Natalie shrugged. 'Because.'

He smiled. 'I'm sorry, Natalie.'

'Sorry? For what?'

He looked away.

'Krishna?'

'Maybe you'd better get back downstairs,' he replied, still with his face away from her. 'You don't want to miss the announcement.'

'Why did you say you were sorry?' she pressed. She had her suspicions as to what this was about.

Finally he turned back to her. 'This was a once in a lifetime opportunity for me. Sir Kenneth, he's a hero of mine. I've read all his books on the business. I would have done anything to work for him.'

Suddenly it made sense.

'I just wanted to scare you off, unsettle you.'

'The note in the room,' Natalie said. 'You wrote it.'

He nodded. 'I wrote the note, and slid it under your door. I did what I thought I had to do at the time.'

'What you thought you had to do? I don't understand, Krishna. You'd only just met me. Why do that?'

She stood up from the bed, stepping back a pace from him.

Krishna gazed up at her. 'It was just business, nothing personal.'

'Business?'

'I needed to gain the competitive advantage,' he said. 'I admit, when we first met, and you said you were still at university, I wondered why had you been chosen for this great opportunity. But when I heard you'd met Sir Kenneth, and he'd invited you to apply, I felt that I had to do something.' He looked at her with the pleading eyes of a child, as if she should somehow feel sorry for him.

'He didn't invite me, Krishna.' Frustration was building inside Natalie, and she wished she'd never told the group about her encounter with Sir Kenneth. After all, it had been nothing, no invitation, just a chance remark that he probably made to a dozen other people that day. And how many other people before and after that? 'All he did was mention the opportunity, Krishna. Nothing more than that.'

'I know, I know. But he told you face to face. The great Sir Kenneth New, he *told* you personally.'

Natalie shook her head. She wasn't getting through to him, and probably never would.

'I must admit,' he continued, 'I felt jealous. And also I was scared. I was afraid you'd take my dream away from me.'

'You didn't need to do what you did.'

Krishna shrugged. 'I did what I thought I had to do. I thought the note might be enough.'

'Enough for what?'

'Enough to unsettle you. I don't know, maybe I thought you might not sleep very well, and then your performance might not be too good the next day. Or maybe you'd decide to leave the house. I'm not sure. I was desperate. I wanted to win so badly.'

'It all sounds so pathetic,' Natalie said, rather more harshly than she'd intended.

Krishna surprised her by nodding.

'But you didn't stop at the first note. Why did you then involve Russell? Or did you just use him to get to me again?'

Krishna looked confused. 'I don't understand. What about Russell?'

'You told Tabitha that we were together, in my room.'

'No, I didn't.'

'She came looking for him. You'd told her and she came to find him.'

He stood up. 'I swear, Natalie, I didn't do any such thing. I sent the note. I've admitted that. But I didn't do anything else.'

She looked at him. Why would he have any reason to lie, having already admitted to having written the note?

'I didn't do anything else,' he repeated. 'Is that why he left the house, because of what someone said about him and you? Did he get thrown out of the house?'

'I don't know why he left.'

'Well, I need you to know that I'm telling the truth, Natalie. You do believe me, don't you?'

'Yes, I believe you.'

'Oh, thank you, thank you,' he said. 'That makes me feel so much better.'

Natalie wished she could have said the same. But she now felt a lot worse. Because accepting that Krishna was telling the truth meant only one thing – there was someone else in the group who was out to get her.

Someone waiting downstairs.

NATALIE CHECKED her watch again as she left Krishna's room. She was a few minutes late. But she didn't particularly care, given that most of her mental energy was directed towards the issue of who else had sought to undermine her.

She returned to the group, who were still waiting for Tabitha to return.

'No Krishna?' Susie asked.

'He wants to be alone,' Natalie replied. 'He's pretty upset about everything – disappointed with himself more than anything.' That wasn't really true, but she wasn't about to pass on his accusations of racism.

'Oh, well, it was good of you to try,' Penny said.

'I knew you wouldn't be able to convince him,' Samantha said. 'You were wasting your time. He wanted one thing, and he blew it. Now he's sulking.'

Natalie didn't really want to engage. She watched

Samantha and thought again about Russell's warning that she couldn't be trusted.

'Did you tell Tabitha about Russell and me,' Natalie said, surprising herself by vocalising her thoughts.

'Sorry?'

'Someone told Tabitha Russell was in my room last night,' Natalie continued. She had started along this road, so she might as well follow through.

Samantha smiled. '*Was* he? I just knew there was a spark. I could see it during the meal.'

'No, he wasn't. But someone told Tabitha that he was. She came to my room, looking for him.'

'Well, it wasn't me.' She didn't look offended. 'Why would I do such a thing?'

'You're lying.'

At first Natalie thought someone else was accusing Samantha, but the comment had been directed at her.

'You're lying,' Ben repeated. 'I saw you and Russell together last night.'

Natalie struggled to find the words to explain that it had all been an innocent situation. Russell *had* come to her room, but it was after Tabitha had visited with her accusations, and she hadn't invited him over. 'It wasn't anything,' was all that she could manage under the gaze of the other four.

Samantha shook her head. 'I see what this is all about. Shifting the blame and the attention from you to me. Well, Natalie, it looks like you've been well and truly caught out.'

Natalie turned to Ben. 'It wasn't what it looked like. Russell wanted to show me something.'

That prompted a juvenile laugh from Matthew.

'He wanted to show me the secret room. The top-floor study where Lord Sinclair lived.'

'I've heard it all now,' Samantha said.

'So it's true, then?' Penny said. 'The story about the Sinclairs, what he did, it's true?'

'I don't know,' Natalie said. 'All I know is that there's a secret staircase, just along the corridor, past the reception. It's hidden in the wall. You push in the right place and it swings open. And behind the wall is a spiral staircase, which leads up to a top-floor study.'

'Cool!' Matthew said. 'Can we go and check it out?'

'I'm afraid that won't be possible.' They spun around to see Tabitha standing in the doorway. 'Now if you could all take a seat, I've got a very important announcement to make.'

33

Cullen strode along Mayfair, feeling as much out of place as you could do. This was the most unaffordable area in the country, with the whitewashed mansion-style houses costing in the tens of millions of pounds. It was the home of the super-rich, some of whom – mostly from abroad – never set foot in the deluxe properties that they owned. For most it was an investment, and for some a money laundering exercise, profits from corruption and organised crime. And while the everyday London worker could barely afford to live within twenty miles of the capital, and thousands of others were sleeping homeless on the city streets, here were these temples to greed, standing empty.

The injustice and inequality made Cullen's stomach churn.

New House was particularly impressive, and at least it was inhabited and being put to good use. Cullen gazed up towards the entrance. It resembled a boutique hotel. The lights in the lobby glowed invitingly through the glass panelled door, beckoning him in. But as he climbed the ten steps up towards the front door, his thoughts were on Natalie Long. Just a few days ago, she had climbed these same steps, but now where was she? And was the secret to her disappearance held within the walls of this small palace?

Cullen entered and approached the reception desk. A young girl smiled warmly.

'Detective Chief Inspector Paul Cullen, British Transport Police.'

'Nice to meet you, Detective,' she said, unsurprised by his arrival, the smile remaining.

'I'm here regarding the disappearance of Natalie Long,' he explained.

'Yes, of course,' she replied, her smile vanishing just like the girl Cullen was searching for. 'It's really scary, to think that someone can just disappear like that. And someone who was here, who was one of the family.'

'You met Natalie, then?'

'Oh yes, I met all the applicants over the weekend. What do you think has happened to her?'

'That's what I'm here to find out.'

She nodded, realising that her question was probably inappropriate. 'Of course, of course. Sorry, I'm just a little bit shaken up about it all. I'll call Tabitha down.'

Tabitha had phoned Cullen just after he'd said his good-byes to Zack. She'd been trying to contact the other applicants, with little success. Of those who had spent the weekend at New House, only two were available to see him. The others, unsurprisingly, really, had already travelled back to various parts of the country – including one to Wales, and another to Scotland.

'Detective, nice to see you again,' Tabitha said, approaching from behind. 'The two applicants are waiting in the lounge. As I said, some of the others I haven't yet been able to make contact with, but another two have said they would be happy to speak by phone.'

'Thanks. I appreciate the effort.'

'Not at all. It's such a serious matter. I'm more than happy to do what it takes.'

'Excellent. Have you got the list?'

'List?'

'Of those who were here over the weekend,' Cullen reminded her. 'Applicants and staff. Including contact details – phone numbers, preferably.'

'Yes, sorry, of course. I'll draw it up while you're speaking to the two in there. Sorry, I totally forgot. But you'll have it before you leave.'

'That's great, thanks.'

The list was key. Outside of a formal investigation, there was a limit to which Cullen could put pressure on these people to speak to him. But he could certainly try his best to tease out any information that might lead to a breakthrough.

Tabitha led Cullen through into the impressive lounge area where two people, a woman and man, were waiting nervously in comfy armchairs.

'This is Penny and Krishna,' Tabitha said, as the two smiled back uncertainly. 'Penny, Krishna, this is Detective Chief Inspector Paul Cullen, who is investigating Natalie's disappearance.'

'It's okay,' Cullen said, aware of their discomfort. 'This is just meant to be a relaxed conversation with you both, to see if there's anything that might shed light on Natalie's whereabouts.'

Both nodded.

'I really appreciate you taking time out to speak to me,' he continued. 'It's important I build up as clear a picture as possible about what happened over the weekend.'

He noticed an interesting micro-expression flash across Krishna's face.

The guy was worried.

'I'd like to speak to you individually, if you don't mind,' Cullen explained. 'It will be easier that way.'

Again both nodded.

'You can use the sitting room upstairs, if you like,' Tabitha volunteered. 'It's free.'

'That would be great.' He turned back to the other two. 'Krishna, if you don't mind, I'd like to speak with you first.'

'Oh,' he said solemnly. 'Yes, yes, of course,' he added, jumping to his feet. 'Let's do this.'

Cullen pretended not to notice his unusual behaviour, but he could see Penny looking at him, clearly thinking something. 'Penny, if you make yourself comfortable, we won't be too long.'

'That's fine, no problem.'

'I'm sure the staff here will sort you out with a hot drink of your choice,' he added, noticing that the table in front of them was currently free of any such items.

'Of course,' Tabitha said. 'Someone will be in shortly.'

The three of them, Cullen, Tabitha and Krishna, made their way upstairs to the empty room. Tabitha arranged three chairs in a triangular shape while Cullen and Krishna watched on.

'If you don't mind,' Cullen said, 'I'd like to speak with Krishna alone.'

'Oh, yes, sure. I wasn't planning to stay.' She looked at the three chairs. 'I did that without thinking. So sorry.'

Cullen watched Tabitha excuse herself from the room.

She suddenly looked incredibly flustered. Gone was the cool and calm persona from their earlier meeting. That was interesting.

He turned his attention to the nervous-looking young man who was standing behind one of the chairs. 'Please, do take a seat, and we'll begin.'

34

Previous Saturday afternoon

THE SIX REMAINING contestants sat down as Tabitha readied herself at the front. She looked pensive. Maybe it was just because she wasn't looking forward to giving the feedback. But Natalie sensed that there was something else. A certain way she looked, it set her on edge for some reason.

She cleared her throat. 'Well,' she said, her face brightening so suddenly it just served to highlight how tense and unhappy she had looked. 'I trust you've had an enjoyable as well as a challenging day.'

Unsurprisingly, there was a noticeable difference in reaction between the Blue and Red Teams. Samantha, Ben and Matthew did nothing to hide their disappointment, almost grimacing at the thought of the day's events. Natalie, Penny and Susie meanwhile returned subdued but genuine smiles. And it was them that Tabitha chose to focus on.

'Blue Team,' she smiled. 'You were sent to EXCEL-ENT,

one of the premier agencies not just in the UK, but globally. You worked closely with Super Agent Diana Saunders, to develop a branding strategy for their new publishing house.'

The three girls nodded.

'You presented your strategy to the branding team at EXCEL-ENT, which included a name, Black Tiger Publishing, along with strap line, logo and website. I'm pleased to tell you that the feedback from the company was very positive. They reported on your professional approach to the task, your friendly natures, your first-rate presentation and your impressive response to questions from the team. Well done!'

Natalie couldn't help but smile broadly at her two teammates. Yes, Diana Saunders had told them to their faces that she had been impressed, and would reflect that in the feedback. But there was a part of Natalie that still doubted whether she would really pass on such praise.

'Thank you,' Natalie said, followed by Susie and Penny.

'You should thank yourselves,' Tabitha said. 'Again, very well done.'

She turned to the Red Team and her expression changed instantly.

There was bad news coming.

'Red Team, you were sent to Stonewood Studios, to meet the band *Young Gunz* and senior executives from their management team and record label. As with the Blue Team, you were tasked with developing a branding strategy.'

Samantha, Ben and Matthew nodded solemnly. They knew what was coming; or at least they thought they knew.

'You developed a logo, a promotional text and an app to promote the band's brand. This was presented to the band and their management at the studios. I'm afraid that the feedback from the band and their team was not good. Not good at all.'

'No surprises there,' Samantha muttered. 'Tell us something we don't know.'

Tabitha ignored her interjection, but there was a flicker of something on her face, maybe irritation, as her inner feelings leaked out briefly. 'The team reported back that the presentation went very badly, and you were unable to communicate your vision adequately.'

'Krishna walked out on us,' Ben said. 'He threw us under a bus.'

Again, Tabitha ignored the unsolicited input from the team. 'We received reports that a member of the team left the presentation. This was taken into account in the feedback. However the consensus was that the remaining team members could have remedied the situation, yet did not.'

Natalie saw Matthew shake his head in disagreement. 'We did our best.'

'Most seriously, we also received reports of bullying within the team.'

'Don't believe him,' Samantha said. 'The guy is a bitter, twisted individual. He's upstairs, crying that he blew his big chance, and he wants to take revenge on us.'

Tabitha blinked hard a few times, staring Samantha down. 'The reports came from the client.'

That stopped Samantha dead in her tracks. 'Oh.'

Tabitha referred to her clipboard. 'We had more than one report.'

'It wasn't like it looked,' Ben tried. 'If you'd have had to work with Krishna all day, I mean, you'd have done something.'

'He was driving us crazy,' Matthew added.

'Brand New prides itself on our values,' Tabitha continued, immune to their pleas. 'Sir Kenneth instils his own values of tolerance, equality and fairness across the company.'

'We agree with all of those,' Samantha said.

'Your behaviour today falls far short of that expected by Brand New. It also goes against the ways of working and living, as outlined to you, and agreed *by* you, when you arrived at the house yesterday. It is for this reason that the Red Team has been eliminated from the selection process, with immediate effect.'

Now Natalie knew why Tabitha had looked so pensive. She had been tasked with kicking them out.

'But that's not fair!' Samantha said. 'You can't...'

'Your bags have been packed,' Tabitha continued. 'They're waiting for you in the reception, where you can also collect your electronic devices.'

'What about Krishna?' Samantha said. 'Tell me *he's* not being allowed to stay. It should be him being kicked out, not us.'

'Krishna has voluntarily withdrawn from the selection process. He will be leaving shortly.'

'Of his own accord,' Samantha spat, 'while we're being thrown out in disgrace, our bags chucked onto the street.'

'Samantha, please,' Tabitha smiled.

'I want to speak with Sir Kenneth,' she said. 'He needs to know the truth about what really happened.'

'I'm afraid that won't be possible. He does, however, know about the situation, and is fully supportive of the decision.'

Samantha shook her head. 'You know, I'll be *glad* to leave this strange, strange place.' Another angry shake of the head.

'I mean, what is it with you people? With your "ways of working and living"? It's like some kind of cult.'

Ben put a hand across to try and stop her flow. 'Samantha.'

She brushed him off. 'Oh, get lost, Ben. You know you feel the same way as me about all this. The difference is, you're too much of a coward to say it.' She got to her feet. 'I'm out of here.'

Ben and Matthew looked to Tabitha for direction.

'It was nice meeting you both,' was all that she needed to say.

They both left without a goodbye.

'So,' Tabitha said, all smiles again. 'And then there were three.'

'MANY CONGRATULATIONS,' Tabitha said, as the three others looked on. 'And I must say, very well deserved. You really did make a very positive impression today, and I'm sure you've learnt that Diana isn't one to suffer fools.'

'Did the other team really bully Krishna?' Susie asked. 'It seems, well, you know, why would they do that, when they knew they were being observed and assessed?'

'As I said, we received multiple reports of their behaviour,' she replied. 'Including testimony from Krishna himself.'

Natalie thought about an alternative scenario. If she had been placed in the team, would things have been any different? Or would she now also have been ejected from the house in disgrace?

'Why did Krishna withdraw from the selection process?'

Penny asked. 'If he's the victim, and hasn't done anything wrong, why has he chosen to leave?'

'I think he's embarrassed by what happened today, at the way he walked out of the presentation,' Tabitha said. 'But I also think the experience, the bullying, has left him feeling vulnerable and he just wants to get back home.'

Penny shook her head. 'That's sad. It really is.'

Tabitha shrugged. 'To be honest, even if Krishna had stayed, he knew that he wouldn't have been in with a chance of winning.'

And that was the real reason he had chosen to leave, Natalie thought. For Krishna, it was more palatable to walk of your own accord, under the cover of being maltreated, than to stay and not achieve your ultimate goal.

'Can we say goodbye, before he leaves?' Penny asked. 'It might make him feel better about everything. You know, if he knows we're supportive.'

'He's already left, I'm afraid,' Tabitha replied.

Penny looked terribly deflated. 'Oh, that's a shame.'

'Krishna will be fine,' Tabitha said. 'He will move on. Which is what we all have to do now.' She looked at her watch. 'Evening meal will be in an hour, where the winner of the selection process will be announced. So please, in the meantime do take some time to relax. You're of course free to go up to your rooms. I shall look forward to seeing you shortly.'

'WHAT DID you think of all that?' Susie asked, lowering her voice, as they made their way upstairs. They'd decided they would take some time out in their rooms, before the final meal and the announcement of the winner. 'The way they just got rid of them all. It seemed a bit...'

'Draconian?' Natalie replied.

Susie nodded. 'They certainly don't mess around if you break the rules.'

'No, they don't,' Natalie agreed. 'I'm still wondering whether they found out about what Russell and I did, and that's why he disappeared in the middle of the night.'

Penny looked intrigued. 'You don't think it happened how Tabitha said – that he just decided it wasn't for him?'

'Not really. Especially after what you heard, Susie. I reckon that they found out we'd broken the rules, and told him to leave.'

'But not you,' Susie noted.

'No, not me.' Natalie had sought an explanation for that flaw in her theory. 'Maybe they don't know that I went with him. Maybe they saw him the first time he went up to the study, before he came to get me. Tabitha *did* go to his room, so she knew he'd left it at some point.'

'Or maybe they decided to cut you a break, because Sir Kenneth invited you to apply personally,' Susie teased.

'Don't...' Natalie replied.

'Natalie, I hope you don't mind me asking,' Penny said. 'But when you said Russell had shown you the secret study, what was it like? I think I'd have been really creeped out by it. Not sure I could have gone up there, to be honest.'

'I was okay at first,' Natalie replied, 'but I did get spooked after a while. Russell took it all in his stride, didn't seem fazed at all. He even had a book about the events involving Lord Sinclair. That's how he knew about the hidden staircase and the study.'

'So the story was true,' Penny thought out loud. She visibly shivered. 'There *was* a mass murder in this house.'

'I guess so, yes.'

'Makes you wonder why on earth Sir Kenneth would have bought this property, knowing the history,' Penny added.

'He probably bought it *because* of the history,' Susie said. 'Adds character to the building, maybe?'

Penny looked around. 'Now the others have gone, and there's just us three left, it feels even more creepy. I'm looking forward to getting out of here and back home.'

'I think we all are,' Susie agreed. 'I know I can't wait to get back to normal life. But for one of us, the victor, it's probably not going to be the last time we come here. Maybe that person will get the chance to ask Sir Kenneth in person about why he bought this place.'

Natalie thought again about what Catharine had said about Sir Kenneth New.

Be careful of that man.

Susie was right. At some point, one of them would surely meet Sir Kenneth face to face.

Should she pass on Catharine's warning? Even though there were no details?

'You okay, Natalie?' Penny was looking at her intently.

Natalie nodded slowly. She'd made up her mind. 'Can you both just come into my room for a moment? There's something I need to tell you.'

'What is it?' Susie said, as they stood facing one another in Natalie's room, the door closed to avoid being overheard.

Natalie thought about how to get the words out. Suddenly she felt unsure again about whether the fairest thing was actually to say nothing, flip-flopping about what the best thing to do was.

'I...'

What would she achieve by passing on Catharine's unexplained warning?

'I...'

She changed her mind. 'I just wanted to say to you both, I had a great day today, and whoever wins, I'll be happy.'

'Aw, thanks hun,' Susie said, giving Natalie a hug. 'I feel the same way too.'

'Me three!' Penny concurred.

The three of them embraced.

Looking over Susie's shoulder at the portrait of Sir Kenneth, still wracked with doubt, Natalie suddenly had a disturbing image of their potential future boss, lying on the bed, waiting for the winner to be announced.

Was that what the warning was about?

35

Cullen eyed Krishna across the space between them. The guy looked incredibly nervous. So on edge, in fact, that he wondered whether he'd somehow hit the jackpot here, and got a result. But still, he had to remind himself that this wasn't an official police investigation, and Krishna wasn't under caution.

'So,' Cullen began with a smile, going for bright and relaxed, which was difficult when faced with Krishna's worried expression, 'as I said, my name's Paul Cullen, and I'm a detective with the British Transport Police.' He needed to be careful with his words here. 'I've been asked to investigate the disappearance of Natalie Long, who I understand was a resident at this property over the weekend.'

Krishna nodded.

'Now, this isn't an official police interview. It's very much an informal discussion. Are you happy to continue on that basis?'

Again there was a nervous nod.

'It's nothing to worry about,' Cullen said. 'I'd just like to find out a bit about the weekend, anything that might have happened that might help with the investigation. My priority is to find out where Natalie is, that's all, so anything you could help with.'

Krishna's brow furrowed.

'It might be something that you think is inconsequential,' Cullen continued, maintaining the light and friendly tone. 'Anything at all.'

Krishna was busy chewing a fingernail.

'Tell me about what brought you to the house?' asked Cullen, trying a different tack.

Krishna seemed unable to answer even that question without some difficulty. 'I thought you would know all that,' he said at last.

'I know a little, but I want to hear from you.'

Krishna eyed him warily. 'I was selected as one of the final shortlisted applicants for the place at Brand New,' he said hesitantly.

'I hear it was a very tough selection process. Lots of applicants. You must have a very impressive CV, to get through to the final stage.'

'Yes, yes,' he replied, distracted, before bringing himself back into the moment. 'I'm a successful businessman.'

'What exactly?'

'Technology sector. I've developed several highly successful apps.'

'Sounds good,' Cullen replied, hiding the fact that he really wasn't that bothered with apps – that was more for Amy and her generation. He had a smartphone, but wasn't signed up to any social media platform. Partly that was due to security, but it was also because he found it all to be a waste of time.

'You might have heard of Vicinity, my dating app,' Krishna added, his expression brightening for the first time since they met.

'Not familiar with it myself, but then I am happily married.'

'It's been covered in the media a lot,' Krishna said. His expression darkened again, as his thoughts returned to the current situation. 'What do you think has happened to Natalie?'

'I have no idea,' Cullen admitted. 'Do you?'

'Me?' he said, shocked by the question. 'You think I've done something to her?'

'I meant, do you have any thoughts as to what might have happened to Natalie. I wasn't accusing you of anything.'

Krishna shook his head. 'No, I have no idea. Absolutely no idea, I swear.'

'And there's nothing you can think of over the weekend, nothing happened involving Natalie that you think in hindsight might offer any clues about her current whereabouts?'

Krishna put a hand to his forehead, pressing in the sides of his head.

'Are you okay, Krishna?'

'Headache.'

'Would you like me to get you a drink, see if one of the staff have any tablets?'

'No, I'm fine,' he said unconvincingly, bringing away his hand with a grimace.

'We can pause the discussion.'

'No, no, I want to get this over with,' he said.

'Get what over with?'

'I know why you asked to speak with me,' he said slowly.

Cullen suppressed his confusion and held his poker face. 'Why do you think that is?'

'Because of what I did.'

'Go on.'

Krishna looked directly at Paul Cullen, his face now determined to say something. 'Because I sent the note to her, trying to scare her off.'

Cullen sat forward. 'Tell me about it, Krishna.'

'It was stupid,' he spat out in evident self-disgust. 'Really stupid. I... I behaved terribly, because I was so desperate to win. I *really* wanted this. I was willing to do anything to achieve my dream.'

Willing to do anything.

The phrase hung in the air.

'I didn't mean *anything*,' he corrected quickly. 'I put things right with Natalie, I apologised, it was the last thing I said to her...'

His sentence trailed off, and again he put a hand to his head.

Cullen watched him. 'What did the note say?'

'It was just a stupid message, really stupid,' he said from behind his hand. 'Childish. I wanted to get Natalie out of the competition.'

'What about the other contestants?'

'How do you mean?'

'You didn't send notes to them also, try to undermine them too?'

'No.'

'Just Natalie?'

'Yes.'

'Why?'

'Well, because I saw her as the main threat.'

'Why was that?'

'Because she'd been invited to apply for the position by Sir Kenneth.'

Cullen thought back to what Amy had told him, how Sir Kenneth had asked her to apply when they had met briefly at his book signing.

'You thought she might have an unfair advantage?'

'Yes. She didn't have any experience, any track record in the branding arena. She was, is, still at university. That first evening, over drinks, I couldn't understand how she had been selected, out of all those applicants.'

Krishna had a point there. What were the chances that a current undergraduate with no track record in business would be selected as one of eight people, from the thousands that Tabitha had confirmed had applied?

Unless she *had* been picked out at Sir Kenneth's request...

'And then I heard about her relationship with Sir Kenneth, and suddenly it all made sense to me.'

'Relationship?'

'I don't mean it like that,' he said. 'I just meant, they knew one another, they'd *met*. Natalie said it was just the one time, and maybe that was true, but then again, maybe it wasn't. After all, she did win.'

'Do you think Natalie was always going to win?'

Krishna hesitated. 'Truthfully, yes I do. I think this was all one big set-up.'

'That must make you angry,' Cullen suggested.

Krishna knew where he was going with this. 'I was angry, but not with Natalie. My anger is with the company, for wasting our time.'

'Of course it's just a theory,' Cullen said. 'There's nothing to suggest it was a set-up.'

'Maybe.'

'So, the last time you saw Natalie was when?'

'At the house, just before I left, when I apologised to her for my stupid actions.'

Cullen nodded.

'You suspect Penny and I have something to do with Natalie's disappearance.'

'What makes you think that?'

'Because you've brought us both back for questioning.'

'No, you misunderstand. I intend to speak to *all* of you. It was just that the others couldn't make it at short notice.'

'Oh,' he replied. 'I thought…'

'As I said at the beginning, this isn't an official police investigation. Not yet anyway. But thank you for your time today, and I or one of my colleagues may want to speak to you again in the next few days.'

Krishna nodded. 'I hope Natalie is found safe and well, Detective. I'll be thinking of her.'

36

Previous Saturday evening

NATALIE SPENT the time before dinner thinking about the events of the past twenty-four hours.

Had it only been that long?

It had certainly been a very strange experience: one that had left her longing for a return to normality, for Bristol and her studies.

Free from the controlling influence of Jack.

She couldn't wait.

And then a sudden thought hit her. She was one of just three people left in the selection process. What if she were to win? Did she even want the job? If she didn't, how would she turn it down?

She lay on the bed, staring at the ceiling, her face deliberately angled away from the portrait of Sir Kenneth.

What if she won, but she didn't want the job?

The question kept whirring around and around, until it brought on a throbbing headache.

Should she leave now?

She looked towards the door, imagining traipsing down to reception with her case, picking up her cell phone, and leaving.

The thought felt good.

But then she would never find out if she'd won, and part of her wanted to know. She also didn't want to just walk out on Susie and Penny without explanation. It wouldn't feel right.

She wouldn't win, anyway. She felt sure that Susie or Penny would be placed ahead of her. And she'd be genuinely pleased for them.

She wanted to be there to congratulate them.

CONVINCED in herself that she should stay, Natalie changed for dinner and made her way downstairs and through to the dining room that this time yesterday had been filled with hopeful contestants. Now the room was deserted. Just a single, small table was set.

She edged warily into the room. She checked the time, and she wasn't particularly early. It was just a couple of minutes to seven.

But no Susie and Penny yet.

She stood alongside the table, leaning against one of the seat backs. It didn't feel right to sit down on her own. It was only after a minute or so of waiting that she noticed that the table was only laid for two.

She stared at the silver cutlery, lost in thought.

Maybe it was a mistake?

'Ah, Natalie!'

She turned to see Sir Kenneth New approaching. This time he was very much here in the flesh, and the sight of him walking towards her was a shock, for more reasons than one.

'Oh, hi,' she managed.

'Lovely to meet you again!'

To her relief he proffered a hand rather than going for something more physical. She took it and he shook it warmly, but thankfully not in a way that could be taken as being overly friendly.

Again.

He remembered.

'You look confused,' he smiled, releasing her hand. 'Please, make yourself comfortable.' He pulled out a chair for her.

She took the seat and tried to process what was happening as Sir Kenneth settled down opposite her, taking his napkin and laying it across his lap.

'Well,' he said, fixing his azure-blue eyes on her, 'I expect you're wondering what on earth is going on?'

'I... I'm a little bit confused, yes. Where are...'

'Susie and Penny have left,' Tabitha said, scaring the life out of Natalie. Somehow she'd managed to get within a few inches of her back without Natalie noticing she was even in the room.

'Oh. I thought we were all going to have dinner together.'

She saw Sir Kenneth prompt Tabitha with a look.

'I informed Susie and Penny about the results of the selection centre. They both asked me to pass on their congratulations to you.'

'Indeed,' Sir Kenneth said, smiling broadly. He opened up

his palms like a worshipper giving thanks. 'Many, many congratulations, Natalie.'

Only now did she truly understand. 'I've won.'

'Yes, you are our winner,' Sir Kenneth confirmed. 'Although we don't really like to talk about winners and losers in the company. We prefer to talk about those who have achieved their goals, and those who are on the way to achieving them. Those goals might not be the ones they believe they want or are striving towards. Susie and Penny, they are wonderful, wonderful people, but they weren't right in this case. And I only want people who are *right*, Natalie.'

Natalie was fizzing with thoughts. It almost felt like a prelude to a panic attack: the sense of spinning out of control, surrendering to the emotional vortex.

'Here are your menus,' Tabitha said.

Natalie managed a nod and then pretended to scan the list – the truth was she could barely focus on the words, such was her state of mind.

'I'd recommend the sea bass,' Sir Kenneth said. 'It's excellent.'

'Then I'll have that,' Natalie replied, with more of an instinctive reaction than a conscious decision. It was one less thing to think about.

'Excellent! Tabitha, we'll both have the sea bass. And do please bring us a bottle of my favourite white.'

Tabitha was back surprisingly quickly with the wine.

'Cheers!' Sir Kenneth said, as she poured out two glasses.

It seemed that the waiting staff from the previous evening weren't on duty this evening, leaving Tabitha to take on the role. 'I'll be back with the main course,' she said, leaving them alone.

Sir Kenneth watched her go right until she disappeared out of sight.

'Well, I must say, many, many congratulations, Natalie,' he said, finally shifting his gaze back to his dining companion. 'Your performance today was most impressive. I received the most fantastic feedback from my good friend, Diana. She really was impressed. Most impressed.'

'Thank you,' she said, 'but it was a team effort.'

'Yes, yes, of course, but a team effort still leaves room for individual brilliance to shine. And it did with you, Natalie.'

He held her gaze.

'To be honest,' she said, 'I don't think I did any more than Susie or Penny. Susie came up with the fantastic logo, and Penny created the web design, which was really impressive.'

He nodded, but didn't seem to be listening.

'I'd hoped that they might have been here for the meal, too.'

He was still nodding.

'It would have been nice to round off the weekend with them.'

Just as Natalie decided Sir Kenneth wasn't listening to her at all, he replied. 'We offered them dinner, but they said they preferred to leave.'

'Oh, right.' Natalie was surprised by how deflated and disappointed that news made her feel.

Sir Kenneth frowned, studying her face with an unsettling intensity. 'You seem a little subdued, Natalie. You've just won the competition. Of all those people who applied, so few were selected to come here, so very few, and of those, you are the one. Yet you appear melancholic. Is something the matter?'

'Well, it's just... it feels strange that Susie and Penny decided to leave, without saying goodbye. I thought...'

'Don't look back, Natalie,' he cut in. 'Just look forwards. Susie and Penny, that's what they're doing, looking forward, striving for their goals. Please don't see their decision to leave as a reflection on you, or your relationship with them. Because it isn't.'

'Okay.'

Except it wasn't okay. She was on edge, having a one-to-one meal with this man – the millionaire owner of one of the world's most famous companies. This tête-à-tête would no doubt have felt strange without the warning from Catharine, but with it, there was an added edge, an anxiety deep in her gut.

She was alone in this house.

With him.

'Are you sure you're okay, Natalie?' He had cocked his head, gazing into her eyes.

Be careful of that man...

'I just need the bathroom,' she managed to say, leaving the table and fleeing into the hallway.

Head down, she nearly ran straight into Tabitha, who was returning with more wine. 'Are you okay, Natalie?'

'I'm fine.' She didn't stop to chat.

INSIDE A CUBICLE she sat there for a few minutes, still in a state of mild panic.

What the hell was she doing here, in this house, with its weird rules and horrific history?

'I don't want this job. I don't want this job.'

Not for the first time today, she fantasised about escaping back to Bristol. Back to her studies. Back to normality. She should have left when she'd had the chance, right after they'd got back from EXCEL-ENT. It would have been easier to go then, blending in with the others who were ejected so unceremoniously. No one would have even noticed.

To leave now would be so much more difficult. How could she do it?

'I've just got to ride it out, just for tonight.'

She started to relax, to think more logically. This wasn't some kind of initiation into a cult, it was a selection centre for a job at a reputable business.

There was a way out.

Next week she would inform the company that she'd had a change of heart, and would politely decline the job offer. They would express their disappointment, but would quickly move on and forget her. Maybe they could approach Susie or Penny, and give one of them the job instead.

Yes, that's what she was going to do.

She exited the cubicle and was shocked to come face to face with Tabitha.

'I was worried about you, Natalie.'

'I'm okay.'

How long had she been standing there.

What had she heard?

'I thought you might be feeling sick.'

Natalie forced a smile. 'To be honest, I had some cramps, you know, that time of the month. But I'll be okay.'

'Oh, you poor thing.' She placed a hand on her arm. 'Will you be okay? Maybe you should go and lie down. I could tell Sir Kenneth you've gone to rest. He'd understand.'

'It's okay.'

'Great,' she said, brightening. 'I guess you've got to ride it out, just for tonight.'

I've just got to ride it out, just for tonight.

She *had* heard.

BY THE TIME she'd returned to the table, the meal had arrived, and the time passed by quickly with polite and, at times, enjoyable conversation. Sir Kenneth was a good conversationalist, which was perhaps unsurprising given he was a global leader in an industry where communication was everything. Natalie pushed aside thoughts of Catharine's warning. But it was still a relief when, shortly after finishing dessert, Sir Kenneth announced that he had to leave for an evening business function.

'I'll see you for breakfast,' he said, leaning over for a peck on the cheek. She tried her best not to stiffen as his lips touched her skin. 'Once again, many, many congratulations, Natalie,' he smiled. 'You've got a very bright future ahead of you, and it's great to have you onboard.'

'Thank you.'

Natalie assumed that Tabitha would fill her in on the details for breakfast once Sir Kenneth had left. But she didn't.

'Good night, Natalie. I hope you have a chance to relax upstairs for the rest of the evening and let all of this sink in. I know it must be a lot to deal with, and your head is probably all over the place at the moment. I do understand.'

'Thanks.'

'Now is the time to act with a clear head,' she added. 'Don't make any decisions that you might live to regret.'

Natalie knew what this was about. And now was the

chance to minimise the damage done by anything that Tabitha had overheard. 'You're right, Tabitha. My head is all over the place, but everything's a lot clearer now. I'll be fine.'

Tabitha smiled but seemed to be scrutinising Natalie for signs as to whether she was telling the truth. 'That's great. See you in the morning.'

'Sir Kenneth mentioned breakfast? What time should I...'

'Oh, yes, if you could just wait for a call in the morning. I don't know yet when Sir Kenneth plans to breakfast. It depends really on this evening. It could be a very late night.'

37

'Penny, please do take a seat.'

'Thank you.'

The young girl sitting opposite him didn't look anything like as nervous as Krishna, but like the man who had come before her, she seemed on edge. It could just have been the police thing – Cullen was used to that, people behaving differently when faced with an officer, even if they had done nothing wrong.

'As I explained to Krishna, this isn't an official police interview – more of an informal, initial chat. Are you okay to proceed on that basis?'

Penny nodded.

'If you feel it's getting too much, don't be afraid of letting me know,' Cullen added.

'I'm sure I'll be fine,' she replied.

'How old are you, Penny, if you don't mind me asking?'

'Seventeen.'

'That's amazing,' Cullen said. 'To get through this far in

such a competitive application process at such an early age. Your application must have really stood out.'

She shrugged. 'I guess. I've been quite successful in my career so far.'

My career so far – at seventeen years old! At seventeen, he had been content with sneaking into the local pub and enjoying his rugby at the weekend.

'What is it you do?'

'I've got a baby-naming website, for people in South East Asia, China mainly. But we expanded recently into Japan and next month we're launching in Malaysia.'

The way she spoke about her expanding global business in such a relaxed way was quite remarkable for someone who was still a teenager. 'Sounds interesting.'

Another self-deprecating shrug. 'I enjoy the business development side of things, really. I suppose the baby-naming aspect is secondary to me.' She looked directly at him with keen eyes. 'I'm keen to move onto new things.' And then there was a flash of sadness. 'Which is why I applied for the post with Brand New, I suppose.'

'Did you expect to win?'

'Not really,' she said, without pause for thought. 'There were a lot of really strong people here, who had achieved *a lot*. I knew it was a long shot. And I don't mind, honestly.'

'What about Natalie? Did you think she would win?'

'No,' she answered without hesitation. 'At least, not at first. She didn't really have any experience. To be honest, I wasn't sure how she got shortlisted. Sorry, that sounds rude.'

'It's okay – you're being honest.'

She flushed. 'But actually, as the weekend went on, I saw how good Natalie was. She has a lot of potential. So when she did win, I wasn't surprised at all.'

'Krishna seemed to think that Natalie had been set up to win,' Cullen revealed.

She looked genuinely taken aback by the suggestion. 'Set up to win?'

'Because she had met Sir Kenneth previously.'

'I know about that. She met him at a book signing. He mentioned the opportunity to her, that's all.'

'So you don't think there was anything more to it than that?'

'I spent the whole day on Saturday with Natalie. We were in the same team, so I got to know her quite well. I really don't think she was part of some kind of set-up. Nothing that she knew about, anyway.'

'For what it's worth, I think you're right,' Cullen said. He nearly told her about the family connection, that Natalie was a friend of his daughter, but decided against it. Even if this wasn't an official police investigation, he needed to treat it as such.

'I'm usually a pretty good judge of character,' Penny added. 'And I really liked Natalie. We exchanged numbers, so we could keep in touch.' Her forehead creased up. 'I hope she's okay.'

'So do I.'

'Do you think something bad might have happened to her?'

'I hope not. But that's what I'm trying to find out.'

'Where did she disappear? I mean, did anyone see her after she left this place?'

'There haven't been any sightings, but she sent a text message en route to Paddington station. That's the last confirmed contact with her.'

'She was getting a train back to Bristol, wasn't she? Back

to university. What did she say?'

Cullen decided it could be helpful to reveal that detail. 'Natalie made reference to making a terrible mistake. Do you know what she might be referring to?'

'Terrible mistake?' Penny said, puzzled. 'But she won. When I last saw her, she was happy. At least I thought she was.'

'So there's nothing you can think of that might have happened over the weekend to upset her? Something that might explain why she's disappeared?'

Penny was still thinking. 'Not really.'

'What about Krishna?'

'Krishna?'

'I wondered if you knew anything about what happened between Natalie and Krishna.'

'Sorry, I don't know what you mean. Something happened between them?' She searched his eyes for clarification.

'Krishna admitted that he tried to scare Natalie, to try and frighten her away from the house, out of the recruitment process. He left a note in her room on Friday evening. He said he did it because he was worried that she would win the competition.'

'Right,' she said, taking it in. 'Well, Natalie didn't mention anything to me, and we were together all day Saturday.'

'You don't seem surprised though – that Krishna did that.'

Penny shrugged. 'I knew what it would be like, the weekend. That it would be competitive. And you could feel it during the drinks reception – everyone appraising each other, finding out bits of information, ranking themselves against one another.'

'Is that what you did?'

'Yes, of course.'

'And what about Krishna?'

'A few of the people in the group, they made comments about him, making fun of him, really, about how competitive he was. He wanted to know about everyone, and he kept talking about how great he'd been in business. But he wasn't really any different from the others – it was just that he wasn't as subtle, he wasn't as good at hiding things.'

'What about the rest of the group? You said you got on well with Natalie...'

'Yes, I got on really well with her. Susie, too. The three of us were in the same team on Saturday. We spent the day at EXCEL-ENT.'

'Which is?'

'An entertainment agency. We had to design branding for a new publishing company they are setting up. It was a challenge, part of the recruitment process. The company were scoring us.'

'What about the others? How did you get on with them?'

'Less well. Although to be fair, there wasn't much chance to get to know them. There was Samantha, who, to be honest, I really didn't take to. She seemed like the sort of person who could be two-faced – she said some pretty mean things about Krishna. Then there was Matthew, who seemed okay, but I didn't speak much to him. And Ben, who seemed okay too, but again I didn't really get to know him. The other person was Russell. Natalie got on really well with him, actually, but I have to say that the guy freaked me out.'

'In what way?'

'Well, I know this sounds a bit soft, but to start with it was his business that weirded me out to start with. Do you know what he does?'

'No.' He really didn't know anything about the residents of New House. Not yet, anyway. The list from Tabitha would hopefully help in that regard, and he'd fill in any blanks in discussion with her.

'He arranges funerals,' she said.

'What, he's an undertaker?'

'Well, not really. He organises bespoke funerals for the super-rich. He was telling everyone how he'd arranged for people's ashes to be sent into space, and he'd organised burials in really unusual places. Those things weren't so bad, even though I admit I'm dreadfully squeamish when it comes to dealing with death. I think it's because when I was young my gran died, and it's my earliest memory, being at her funeral, surrounded by sadness. No, what was worse was the story he told about how he arranged for a man to be buried in a container of worms, which... dealt with the body really quickly.' She shivered. 'It was really gross.'

'Not the way I'd like to go,' Cullen admitted. 'But probably good for the planet.'

Penny smiled. 'Yeah, I suppose it is.'

Cullen had held onto something Penny had said a few moments ago. 'You said to start with that it was his business that bothered you about him. What else was it?'

She nodded. 'I mean, I was already a little spooked by his line of business, especially the worms, but then after dinner he started telling us all about the horrible thing that had happened in this house.'

'Oh? What happened?'

She looked a little surprised that Cullen didn't know. 'The mass murder.'

'Mass murder?'

'Sir Thomas Sinclair, he wiped out his family.' She looked

at him, evidently expecting him to have a sudden realisation. 'He killed his wife and children and then himself, in *this* house.'

'I'm not familiar with that story,' Cullen replied.

'Russell told us all about it. It was back in the early eighties. The owner, Thomas Sinclair, he was a successful businessman, a millionaire. But he got into financial difficulties, had a bad gambling problem and was also having an affair, which he feared was about to go public, destroying his reputation. Then one night, he murdered his whole family before shooting himself. It happened right here in this house. The room where we had the drinks reception, that's where they found his body, slumped over a piano.'

'And Russell, he told you about all this?'

'Yes. And he really enjoying telling us, delighting in it.'

'How did he know so much?'

'He'd done his research, I assume. He was the only one of us to know anything about the history of the house, so I guess it made him feel important. But I also believe he was trying to spook us, put us off, just like it seems Krishna did with Natalie. Like I said, there was a lot of competition between us, because the prize was so valuable.'

'I can see why you didn't take to Russell.'

'I know this is going to sound odd, but I felt like Russell had something of the dark about him. Do you understand what I mean?'

Cullen nodded. In his line of work, he had met many people who met that description.

Too many.

'Anyway, I was actually quite relieved when Russell left the house early.'

'He left early?'

'Yes, he left in the middle of the night, in the early hours of Saturday morning.'

'Sounds very strange. Do you know why?'

'No,' she replied. 'But Susie heard him go.'

'Oh?'

'His room was next to hers. She said she heard raised voices coming from his room – Russell and Tabitha. And then she heard the door open and close, and when we came downstairs in the morning for breakfast, they announced that he'd decided to leave the house.'

'They didn't give any more explanation than that?'

'They just said he'd decided it wasn't for him, so he'd decided to leave.'

'In the middle of the night.'

She smiled. 'I know. Sounds very odd, doesn't it?'

'It does.' Cullen pondered on whether this could be in any way related to Natalie's disappearance. On the face of it, probably not, but it was something worth exploring with Tabitha. 'You said that Natalie got on well with Russell.'

'Yes, she seemed to.'

'What makes you say that?'

'They were seated together at dinner, and were laughing and talking a lot. And then on the Saturday morning, when they told us that Russell had left, I saw the look on her face.'

'Which was?'

'Disappointment. She looked *really* disappointed. I think everyone else was just glad that one of the competition had dropped out.'

'Did you speak to her about him?'

'A little. Although there wasn't much time for chitchat, it was pretty full-on on Saturday with the task. I just asked her what she thought about what had happened. I suppose I was fishing, really.'

'And did you catch anything?'

'Sort of. She told me that he'd come to her room that evening. Not for what you might think. She said he'd wanted to show her something in the house.'

'What?'

'I don't know. She was in the middle of telling me when we were interrupted. I meant to catch up with her later about it, because I was quite intrigued, but I forgot.' Penny looked at Cullen, and they both knew that the discussion was coming to a close.

'Is there anything else you think might be useful for me to know?' Cullen asked.

'I can't think of anything. Sorry.'

Cullen smiled sympathetically. 'Don't be. You've been very helpful. Thank you for taking the time and trouble to come along.'

'Don't mention it. As soon as I heard what had happened, I was more than happy to help.'

'Well, thank you.' Cullen was thinking about Russell Cave. 'I don't suppose you have a photo of Russell?'

'Actually, I do. I took a few photos on Friday evening.' She pulled out a handful of Polaroid photographs from her bag. 'We had our phones taken off us, so my favourite camera came in useful - I just love retro things like that. She picked out one photo. 'This one is of the group - Russell is there on the far left, next to Natalie. Would you like to have it?'

'Please.'

She handed it across to him.

'Thanks, that's great.'

They both got to their feet and made their way to the door.

'What do you think has happened to Natalie?' she asked, as they were halfway down the stairs.

'I'm afraid at the moment it's a total mystery. But believe me, I'm doing my best to solve it, and I won't stop until I do.'

Tabitha was waiting for them as they reached the reception area, and she turned as she heard Cullen. Moving away from a chat with the receptionist, she straightened and smiled, now looking at ease once more with the situation. 'Is everything okay?' she said, receiving a nod from each of them.

'Penny has been very helpful,' Cullen said.

'Oh?' Tabitha said. 'That's great.'

If she were waiting for further elaboration, she would be disappointed, as Cullen offered nothing. 'Nice to meet you, Penny.'

Penny shook his hand. 'You too.'

'Yes, thanks Penny,' Tabitha added, also offering a hand.

Cullen watched and waited for Penny to exit, feeling the weight of Tabitha's expectation as she stood unspeaking next to him.

Finally he turned. 'Tabitha, I wonder if you have that list?'

'Oh, yes.' She reached over the reception desk and handed Cullen an A4 sheet of paper, upon which was a table detailing the previous weekend's guests.

Cullen eyed the list. 'Thank you.' This was very interesting. He looked up at Tabitha. 'This is perfect.' Tabitha smiled, looking relaxed, and a bit relieved. Then Cullen said, 'I wonder if you might answer a few questions about one of the applicants in particular?'

'Yes, of course. Which one?'

'Russell Cave.'

Tabitha couldn't hide her reaction and Cullen felt his pulse quicken.

38

Previous Sunday morning

THE CALL CAME JUST after seven thirty in the morning.

'Hi, Natalie. It's Tabitha. Sir Kenneth just called to let me know that he is ready. If you could go up to the third floor, it's the door straight ahead of you.'

'Oh, not the dining room?'

'No, third floor.'

Natalie frowned at the surprise location.

'Will you be there too?'

'Yes,' she replied. 'See you in a few minutes.'

NATALIE CLIMBED up to the third floor, and knocked at the door that was straight in front of the staircase. The door was wider than the other doors in the property, with a different look. It seemed almost like an external door.

'Come in!' she heard Sir Kenneth shout.

She emerged into a surprisingly open-plan room, which put even her plush room to shame with its grand decor. Off to the right was a kitchen full of high-end equipment, while just past it was a lounge area with large windows overlooking Mayfair and beyond. She could only assume there was also a bathroom and bedroom, off the corridor that ran to her left.

She edged nervously around the corner.

'Natalie, lovely to see you again!'

Sir Kenneth was sitting at the table, an impressive breakfast selection spread in front of him. He stood as she approached.

'Please, do take a seat.'

Natalie did so, wondering why Tabitha wasn't here as she'd said she would be. Alarms bells sounded deep inside. She didn't want to be alone with him.

'Do tuck in,' he instructed.

Natalie took a croissant and bit into it, aware that Sir Kenneth was watching her intently.

'How do you like the apartment?' he asked, the moment Natalie had swallowed the first mouthful.

'It's lovely.'

'It's three rooms knocked into one,' he explained. 'I had it done shortly after I purchased the property, as I wanted a place where I could stretch out.' He paused, using his tongue to get something out of his teeth. 'I don't live here permanently, you understand. I have a home in Windsor, that's my permanent base, where I feel most comfortable. And there are a few holiday villas. But this apartment, it's a good hideaway for me in Central London. I use it after events like last night, when it feels like too much trouble to travel back out to

Windsor. It's also perfect if I need to just get my head down and do some work.'

'It's lovely.' Natalie took another bite of her croissant, hoping that Tabitha would appear soon. It was unnerving having this private breakfast in Sir Kenneth's apartment.

'I'm so glad you like it, Natalie. Coffee or tea?'

'Tea, please.'

He poured her a cup.

'Sugar? Or are you sweet enough?' He held eye contact until Natalie looked away.

'Just milk, thank you.'

'Very wise.' He passed across the cup. 'So, Natalie, how does it feel, now that you've had a night to sleep on it?'

'Sorry?'

'How does it feel? To be the victor, the chosen one?'

Natalie shifted at the vaguely messianic reference. 'I'm really pleased,' she nodded. 'Really happy. Thank you. It's such a fantastic opportunity.'

She surprised herself by sounding so convincing, even though this experience was just cementing her decision that next week she would turn down the offer.

'You weren't so sure last night,' he noted.

Natalie felt her face redden.

Had Tabitha said something to him? She must have.

'I was in a bit of a state of shock, I think. It really took me by surprise. I didn't think in a million years that I'd be the last person standing.'

'Well, I did.'

'You did?'

'Yes, of course. The first time I spoke to you, at my book signing, I could just see there was *something* about you.'

He really did remember...

'Something that betrayed your great potential,' he continued. 'In fact, you might say I was really rather taken with you. And that doesn't often happen, believe me. There are lots of people who want to get my attention, and try very hard to do so, but it's quite rare, quite rare indeed, that it happens the other way around.'

He took a sip of his coffee and let out a satisfied sigh, waiting for Natalie's response. He smiled in anticipation, as if he had offered a challenge and was looking forward to seeing how she would react.

'I didn't think you'd remember me,' she said carefully, not liking the direction the conversation was heading. They had only spoken for what could have been sixty seconds at most. And that was on a day when Sir Kenneth must have spoken with hundreds of people – the queue for the book signing had stretched out of the tent. Each of those people would have had a similar conversation with him. She had watched from the queue as he had conversed at some length with dozens of people eager to talk.

And yet he remembered her.

'Of *course* I remember you!'

Unless he was just saying that, to try and impress her with his memory. Maybe somehow during the weekend word had got back to him that she had met him at the book festival – probably via Tabitha. Yes, that was almost certainly it. It was a good trick, designed to be a little ingratiating. To make the other person feel important. Part of the Brand New family.

But surely it was just a trick.

'I remember you with great clarity, Natalie. And my invitation to apply for this great opportunity was one hundred percent genuine. I really wanted you to apply, and I wanted to look out for you if you did. That's why I asked for your full name, do you remember that?'

Natalie nodded. She did remember. He had asked what her name was, for the personal message in the book, but then he had pressed for her surname, too. She'd thought at the time that it was a little strange, but he had said something about looking out for her in the future. She'd brushed it off as him being polite.

'I said I'd remember you, Natalie, and I did. I have a good memory for names of people that matter to me.'

'Thanks,' Natalie replied, still uncomfortable with the attention.

'I can't tell you how happy I was when I saw that you had indeed applied for this opportunity. I was so very happy. I ensured that you got your chance, which I am delighted to say that you took with both hands!'

So the others had been right – their teasing about her being somehow favoured by Sir Kenneth New, having an advantage over them, had been right on the mark. She felt a sudden sense of deflation. She hadn't got there on her own merit, she'd been picked out of the thousands of other applicants because of favouritism.

She'd been handpicked, done a favour.

And now here she was.

In his private apartment.

Alone with him.

39

'Russell Cave is missing from the list,' Cullen said, handing it back to Tabitha.

'Oh,' Tabitha said. She went quiet, staring at the piece of paper. Cullen sensed she was playing for time, working out what she was going to say next. Maybe he was being overly suspicious of her, but he thought not. 'Oh, I see what's happened,' she said at last. 'Milly produced this list based on the check-outs from Sunday.' She looked up at Cullen. 'Russell left us early, so that's why he's missing from this.'

Cullen nodded, hiding the fact that he was far from convinced. 'If you could produce an updated list, that would be great.'

'Of course, I'll get Milly to produce one.'

'Or just jot down Russell's details on that version,' Cullen suggested. 'If it's quicker.'

'No, no, it's okay, we'll update the list, that's no problem whatsoever.' She turned and rang the bell on the reception desk. Milly appeared from the back office, and Tabitha requested the update.

'So,' Tabitha said, turning back to Cullen. She tried to smile, but there was that flash of discomfort again; it was clear and present, no matter how much she was fighting to hide it. 'You wanted to ask me about Russell Cave?'

'I do, if you don't mind.'

She glanced away, and then back at him. 'I can tell you what I know. But he wasn't with us long.'

'So I heard,' Cullen quipped. 'Maybe we should go back upstairs.'

Tabitha agreed, and they returned to the lounge area that had now become a makeshift interview room. The chairs were still in position, and Cullen gestured for her to sit.

'So,' he said, deciding to get down to business. 'Tell me about Russell Cave.'

Tabitha shifted in her seat. 'Well, there's not much to tell, really. Like I said, he wasn't with us for long.'

'Tell me about that.'

'What? Why he left?'

'Yes.'

A pause. 'I... I really don't know, to be honest. He just left, in the middle of the night.'

Cullen thought back to what Penny had said: that Susie had heard raised voices coming from Russell's room, and that one of them was Tabitha's. 'Did you speak to Russell before he left?'

Another pause. Cullen could tell that she was deciding whether to tell the truth, or at least how much of the truth to tell.

'Yes, I did see him,' she admitted at last.

'Where was this?'

'In his room. He dialled reception, in quite an agitated

state. The night porter, Karl, was pretty worried about him, so we went up to the room to see what the matter was.'

'And what was the matter?'

'He'd been drinking. They all had, the residents, well, most of them – at the drinks reception. But he must have brought more alcohol in, because it was hours after everyone had gone to bed and he was pretty drunk. We're very careful that the residents don't drink to excess, as we want them to be at their best for the weekend's activities. And we make that very clear to all residents, both before and when they arrive.'

That could explain the raised voices, Cullen thought – if Tabitha had found that Russell had smuggled in contraband alcohol.

'The ways of working and living are very clear,' she added.

The ways of working and living? It sounded like some kind of cult.

'Are there penalties for those who break the rules?'

'Yes. Anyone who goes against the ways of working and living will be removed from the application process. Sir Kenneth is very clear on that. He needs someone he can trust totally, and following the ways of working and living is the most important indicator that trust has been earned.'

'But you said that you didn't know why Russell left the house. Except he didn't *choose* to leave, you asked him to leave.'

Tabitha was thinking again. 'That's right, yes.'

'So he *was* removed from the house?'

'He was *asked* to leave,' she replied, pushing a strand of hair behind her left ear.

'How did Russell feel about that?'

'He understood the situation, once we explained things to him. I mean, he was upset, and drunk, so it took him a few minutes to get his head around it and see it was the right thing to do.'

'What time was this?'

'Just after two thirty.'

'You threw him out of the house at two thirty in the morning, drunk. It doesn't sound like the most charitable thing to do, if you don't mind me saying. Couldn't you have waited until the morning?'

Tabitha blinked a couple of times. 'Sir Kenneth instructed us to remove him with immediate effect. We were mindful of the time of night, and his state of mind. We ordered him a taxi, made sure he was safe and that he got to suitable accommodation.'

'But you still could have waited.'

'Sir Kenneth thought it would unsettle the remaining residents if Russell waited until the morning before leaving. And that wouldn't have been fair on the others. They shouldn't have to suffer because of one person who couldn't follow the rules.'

'You would also have risked the truth coming out,' Cullen said, 'if Russell had had the chance to talk to the others the next morning.'

'Truth?' Tabitha flushed.

'You told the others what you initially told me: that Russell had decided to leave on his own accord. And they had no reason not to believe the lie.'

She didn't seem to like the insinuation that they had lied. 'As I said, we didn't want to unsettle the other residents. We felt it was better for everyone if they thought that Russell had decided to leave.'

'I can see how it made things easier for you.'

She straightened in the chair, suddenly appearing more

defiant. 'I think it was for the best, how we handled it, but I can see how it might look to others. We were put in a difficult situation, by someone who knew the rules but chose to break them.'

Cullen held her gaze, unspeaking. She filled the gap.

'Is there anything else I can help you with, Detective?'

'That's it for now,' he replied, 'but if you could let me have those contact details for Russell, that would be great.' He got to his feet. 'You do have a phone number for him?'

Tabitha got up from the chair. 'Yes, we will have.'

'You must have had a number when you tried to call him before?'

'Actually I was working from the same list as the one I gave you, so I haven't actually tried to contact him yet. Would you like me to call him from reception?'

'It's okay.' Cullen waved the offer away. 'You just get me the number and I'll take it from there. I'm interested to talk to Russell in particular.'

Again there was something about Tabitha's reaction that excited him.

40

Previous Sunday morning

'You look pensive,' Sir Kenneth noted.

'I'm okay,' Natalie replied. 'It's just all such a lot to take in.'

'I do hope you're okay.'

It was as if he could tell what she was thinking, as if those intense eyes could see through her skin, deep into her being. Or maybe her face was betraying her emotions too clearly.

She forced herself to maintain eye contact. To look away would just bring on more questions from him, raise suspicions as to how she was really feeling.

But if she were feeling uncomfortable, didn't she have every right to say so?

'I'm good, thanks.'

And yet, she felt unable to move from the table, unable to vocalise her feelings. So the only other option would be to play the longer game, make conversation, finish the breakfast, and then she'd be free.

'So, Natalie, tell me a little about yourself.'

'Well, I'm a student at Bristol City University, studying business and marketing...'

He put up a hand. 'No, I mean tell me about *yourself*.' When Natalie looked puzzled, he expanded further. 'Your hopes, your dreams, your inner core that drives you towards your next destination.'

Again, he looked at her with the same intensity that left Natalie feeling exposed right down to her soul. He was trying to read her, and she looked away, as if it might break the spell.

'I'm not sure how to answer that,' she said at last, knowing that it was a response that would surely disappoint her host.

'Just try, Natalie,' he prompted, pressing a finger into the side of his head. 'Look inside yourself and you'll find what drives you, your engine.'

She felt awkward, still not knowing how to answer. 'I want to make a difference,' she said at last.

He smiled sympathetically. 'Well, that's a start. Make a difference to what? Your bank balance?'

'Well, I didn't...'

'World peace?' he stated. If he were teasing, he was playing it straight.

'I... I want to do something that makes a positive difference to people,' she said. 'Makes people's lives better.'

'And you think branding can do that?'

'I'd like to work for a charity, or a development agency,' she explained. 'Help them to connect better with people.'

'Ah,' he said, sitting back, a glow of satisfaction on his face. 'Now that *is* better.' He nodded. 'I like that idea, Natalie. But there's only one problem.'

'Oh?'

'You've just chosen to join me and my company. And we're

not a charity or a development agency, are we? It doesn't seem to tie in with your hopes and dreams.'

Maybe he'd hit the nail right on the head. But she couldn't say that here, to his face.

Fortunately Sir Kenneth filled the space before she had time to think what to say. 'You know, Natalie. We had some amazing talent here at the house this weekend, which is no surprise, given the intense level of competition to get to this point. And I know that many of those people have already achieved great things in business; they're already very successful.'

'Yes,' she agreed.

'But prior success is not what I was looking for. Not that on its own. I wanted someone with that inner passion. That's what I saw in you. And don't worry, you *will* be able to fulfil your inner desires with us at Brand New.'

'That's great,' she said, smiling through her continued discomfort.

'Outsiders may look at us and just see another branding company, albeit one of the most successful ones on the planet. But we're much more than that. We focus on corporate work, yes, and that's how we've built the business over the years. You're very familiar with our work, I'm sure.'

'We studied Brand New in our first year.'

He nodded, as if that is what he had expected. 'Tell me, did your tutors talk about our philanthropic work?'

'Not really, no.'

Again he nodded knowingly. 'I must admit, we haven't talked about it much externally. But we're very active in that sphere. We work on social projects across the world, lending our expertise – very much the kind of thing that you are interested in.'

'Sounds good.'

'I think it's tremendously important to do good, Natalie. For me, business, making money, capitalism – whatever you choose to call it – is a means to an end. My great wealth and the resources of Brand New enable me to take action to make the world a better place. Interested?'

'Yes,' she replied. It was the first time during their discussion that she'd begun to relax, and to also seriously begin to question whether or not she should be walking away from all this. It was still just the word of Catharine. What if she'd simply been trying to cause trouble on her last days in the office?

Sir Kenneth smiled, satisfied that he had piqued Natalie's interest. 'That's fantastic. Because I have special plans for you.'

'Okay...'

'As I said, we've been involved in charitable works now for years. But I want to really ramp it up, make it part of our core purpose. That's why in the next few months we'll be launching the Brand New Foundation. It will enable us to dive deeper and broader into those vital social issues that matter to the people of this planet. That includes gender equality issues, which I'm very passionate about. There's so much that needs to be done to protect and promote the rights of women and girls across the world.'

Natalie nodded, her wariness for this man draining away with each word.

'I've assigned a team of my most trusted colleagues to work on the Foundation, people whom I know well and have complete confidence in. They are the best of the best. The team are working out of our London HQ, liaising closely with me, but we also have small satellite teams based in several of the world's major cities: New York, Delhi, Sydney, Berlin. Natalie, I want *you* to be part of the team.'

'I don't know what to say...'

'Just say "yes"!'

'Yes.' And she meant it. In those few minutes, Sir Kenneth had captured her again, selling his vision so completely that her past concerns evaporated. 'I'd really love that.'

'Fantastic!' he said, clapping his hands together in glee. 'That is the most wonderful news. Truly *wonderful* news! Cheers!' He offered up a toast with the glass of orange juice. She reciprocated, returning his smile. 'You are going to *love* working for us, Natalie, I just know you will. And my team will love you. You'll experience so much.'

'Thank you,' Natalie said. 'It sounds like an amazing opportunity.'

'What are your plans for the rest of the day?' he asked, tearing off some croissant and popping it into his mouth, never taking his attention away from her.

'The rest of the day? I... I'm not sure. I wasn't sure when the selection centre would end, so my advanced fare ticket is for a later train. And it's non-transferable.'

He smiled. 'We were deliberately vague about the timetable. We wanted to see how the weekend played out. What time is your train?'

'Eight thirty-five.'

'From Paddington?'

Natalie looked surprised.

'Well, you *are* studying in Bristol, are you not?'

She nodded.

'Good, good. That means you have got some leisure time available.'

'Well, I did think about contacting one of my friends who lives in London, see if she's free.'

'No need.' Sir Kenneth dismissed the suggestion. 'I'd like you to spend the day as my guest.'

'Well, that's very kind...'

'Please, Natalie, please don't refuse. It would really cause me great pain to know that I could have enjoyed your company for a few more hours, but didn't.'

She struggled for a response. 'I...'

'Have you ever been in a helicopter?'

'No.'

'How would you like to see London from the air? My helicopter is stationed at City Airport. We can take a flight over the capital and around the coast, right over the white cliffs of Dover, skirt over Calais. The sights are amazing. You'll love it. Sound good?'

'It sounds...'

'We can drink champagne in the air, and toast your success.'

'Will there be time?'

He glanced at his watch. 'Of course. It's still early. I can give my people a call now and have them make the preparations.'

Before Natalie could say anything else, Sir Kenneth had leapt up from the table and was half jogging down the corridor. 'My phone's in the bedroom,' he explained. 'Back in a tick.'

Natalie looked around, doubts creeping in about Sir Kenneth and his intentions. She could make a run for the door now, rush down to her room, gather her belongings, and...

'Natalie!' Sir Kenneth called out. 'Can you come here for a moment. I need to ask you something.'

Natalie moved past the living room, hesitating as she reached the bedroom door.

C'mon, she was just being stupid.

She gathered her composure and entered.

Sir Kenneth New was lying face down on the bed, in just his underwear.

41

Cullen exited New House and put a bit of distance between him and the place before pulling out the sheet of paper from his pocket. Tabitha had duly handed him a revised version of the list of the "residents" that contained the phone number for Russell Cave.

He dialled the phone number as he walked.

But the call just rang through to the voice message service. He cut the call, preferring to speak to the guy directly. He would try again in a few minutes. It might be that Russell Cave had nothing to do with Natalie's disappearance. He had, after all, left the property a day before she vanished. But there were enough questions about Russell to place him at the top of the list of people he wanted to speak to.

Krishna, with his strange behaviour, might still be worth talking to again. But in the time since he had spoken to him, Cullen had further cooled on the idea that he had something to do with Natalie vanishing.

He stopped in a quiet back street and scrutinised the

others on the list. There were four remaining, excluding Russell. Samantha, Matthew, Susie and Ben.

He got straight through to Susie, who was back at home up in Edinburgh. She seemed genuinely shocked to hear about Natalie. She confirmed what Penny had said about the raised voices in the middle of the night, prior to Russell's ejection from the premises. And she was certain that the female voice had been Tabitha's. But there was nothing else she could add about the events of the weekend over and above what he had already heard. She promised to get in touch if anything else came to mind.

Matthew also picked up straight away. Cullen wondered just how hard Tabitha had tried to contact these people, given the relative ease with which he was now picking them off. He was at work in the City, but took time away from his desk to tell Cullen what he knew. In truth, it was of little help, but again he promised to get in touch should anything else come to mind. What was becoming clear was that in the short time they had known one another, Natalie had made a good impression with the other residents. It felt less and less likely that one of these people was the explanation for what had happened.

For the first time that day, Cullen's thoughts returned to Natalie's ex-boyfriend, the controlling and manipulative Jack Morton. Maybe he should have pushed the guy further, instead of returning so hastily back to London.

Certainly if something sinister had happened to Natalie, he was still the prime candidate.

He pushed that thought away for the moment, and refocussed on the remaining calls. He got hold of Ben, who was suitably sorry to hear about what had happened, but didn't really offer anything new. But it wasn't possible to reach

Samantha, who didn't pick up. He could follow up with her later, but it wouldn't be a priority, as he strongly suspected she would not be able to add anything over and above what he already knew.

Cullen continued walking, lost in thought, with no particular destination in mind. It was only as he approached a tube station that he remembered about the newspaper article. A man was handing out copies of the London Post to passersby. The newspaper had gone free last year, and was now funded by advertising. It meant the circulation was now sky-high, offering huge publicity for Natalie's disappearance.

If the article had been published.

He strode up to the man and took a copy of the paper, his nerves quickly on edge as he brought up the front page into his line of vision.

And there it was.

RAIL COP HUNTS FOR MISSING GIRL

Accompanying the headline was the headshot of Natalie, smiling right at the camera. The story and image dominated the front page. Simon and Zack had been true to their word.

He read the first few lines.

The London Post can exclusively reveal that rogue rail cop Detective Chief Inspector Paul Cullen, currently suspended while under police investigation for his role in the death of a young man on Monday morning, has defied orders from bosses to launch an unauthorised investigation in the desperate hunt for missing teenager Natalie Long.

The inaccurate and hyperbolic language wasn't a surprise. It was Simon all over. And it *had* got Cullen the coveted front page.

Natalie Long, a Bristol-based student, was reported missing on Monday morning, when she failed to return home from a weekend in London's Mayfair where she was staying at a multi-million-pound mansion owned by Brand New, the international branding company owned by enigmatic billionaire Sir Kenneth New.

The rest of the article was accurate, reflecting well what he had told Zack. He looked again at Natalie's photo that adorned half of the front page. He couldn't have hoped for more. All across London, commuters would be reading the story, scrutinising Natalie's face. Some would be wondering if that girl they had seen on the tube, or passing on Oxford Street, had been her. Fewer still might be certain that they *had* seen her, and would respond to the request for information at the end of the article. The newspaper, at Cullen's request, had asked readers to contact the paper directly with any further information.

Cullen was just wondering how long it would take for Maggie Ferguson to get in touch, when his phone rang. It was Beswick.

'I hope you know what you're doing, Boss,' he said, without preamble.

'I gather you've seen the paper.'

'Just now. The Super is going to go mental when she sees it, you do know that?'

'Of course.'

Beswick exhaled. 'Please, just be careful. I like you too much to see you ruin your career.'

'Understood.'

There was a pause. 'Great effort, though,' said Beswick, softening, 'getting the Post to run a front-page splash. I assume it was your doing?'

'Certainly was.'

'Any developments?'

'Not really. A few irons in the fire, but nothing of note –

nothing I could pass over for a formal investigation. But I'm hoping the publicity today might lead to something.'

'Fingers crossed. Let me know if you need any help.'

'Will do.'

They said their goodbyes.

Cullen fired off a text message to Amy, letting her know about the newspaper story and promising that he was still on the case.

He just hoped it wasn't too late for Natalie.

42

Previous Sunday morning

NATALIE FROZE in horror as Sir Kenneth looked across at her from the bed.

'Natalie, it's my neck,' he said, grimacing with pain and holding onto the offending area. 'I was just turning, and felt something pull.'

She stood there, not knowing what to do.

'Would you like me to call someone? Tabitha, maybe?' she tried, taking a half step backwards.

'No, no, don't worry anyone,' he said. 'I just need someone to mobilise the area for me. I can show you what to do.'

Natalie's mind was buzzing.

'I...'

Sir Kenneth let out a yelp of pain. 'Please, Natalie, it's happened before. I just need a bit of pressure on the area, and it will resolve.'

She felt in an impossible position. If she didn't agree, how would that look?

She took a step forwards.

'Thank you, thank you,' he said, shifting a little on the bed in anticipation as Natalie approached slowly. 'If you can just put your thumb on that point there,' he directed, 'right on the back of my neck. It's a muscle knot. You can squash it, and it will free up the tension.'

Natalie edged up to the bed, so she was standing alongside the prone Sir Kenneth. 'I... I'm not sure what to...'

'It's simple,' he said. 'Just press here.'

'Okay,' she replied, against her basic instincts. She leant over and reached out to his neck, placing her thumb on warm, damp skin. 'Here?'

'Just a little higher.'

'Here?'

'Yes, that's right. Now press. Quite firmly.'

She leant over and pressed down with force.

'Harder,' he said.

She applied more pressure.

'Harder, Natalie.'

Her thumb was actually hurting from the force.

'Yes! That's perfect. Keep it like that. One, two, three, four, five, six, seven, eight, nine, ten! Yes! Thank you!'

Natalie, nervous sweat beading on her back, relaxed a little as she brought her hand away.

'Ouch!' Sir Kenneth shouted, thrusting a hand to the base of his back and arching his back up and down like a landed fish. 'This... sometimes... happens! Referred pain!'

Natalie stood over him, feeling helpless.

'Please, Natalie, my back. You... need to... apply pressure... to the base of... my spine.'

'I… I'm not sure…'

'Please!' he pleaded, his face full of pain. 'If you don't do it now, it will be hell.'

She moved back in. 'Where do I press?'

'Either side of my back, the base. With both hands. Use your thumbs.'

She made contact with skin again. Here it was wetter, and it just felt wrong. Her hands brushed against the fabric of his underwear.

'Press!'

She pushed hard.

'Natalie, it's not hard enough.'

She pushed harder. 'I can't push any harder.'

'You'll have to use your body weight,' he instructed. 'Climb on top of me and use your weight to really push down hard.'

He stared at her as she tried to process the request.

'Climb on top of me, Natalie,' he said slowly.

She found herself shaking her head.

His eyes flared. 'Do it!'

She took a faltering step back, nearly tripping up over the bedroom rug.

'Natalie, please!' he softened. 'Please, just do this one more thing for me.'

Another shake of the head. 'I can't. I've got to go.'

'Natalie!' he screamed, as she retreated into the hallway. 'Come back this instant!'

She almost got to the front door.

'Look here!' he said, catching up with her and wheeling her around by the shoulder. 'What the hell are you doing?'

'I… I've got to go.'

He looked frustrated and angry. 'What's the matter, Natalie? I thought we were getting along well?'

'We were, we are, I just...'

'What?' he snapped.

'I...'

She felt the weight of his intense stare again. 'Oh!' he said, finally. 'I see what this is all about.' In an instant the anger was gone, extinguished. 'You think I was coming onto you?'

'It's not t...'

'You think all this was part of some elaborate set-up, to get you into my bed?'

'No...'

He shook his head sadly. 'Natalie, I thought you knew me better than that.'

'I...'

His face was all disappointment – disappointment with her. 'I think you'd better go, don't you?'

Natalie didn't need asking twice. 'I'm sorry,' she said, exiting.

But as the door closed behind her, a rapid reappraisal of what had just happened left her shaking, and regretting her instinctive apology.

He had moved very quickly for a man who just seconds earlier had been in agony on a bed.

In fact, there had been no sign of pain then at all.

She hurried to her room.

It was time to get out of this place, and fast.

NATALIE PACKED QUICKLY, throwing clothes into her case and rushing to the bathroom to collect her toothbrush and toothpaste. All the time she was on edge, waiting for the knock on the door.

Please, don't let him have followed me...

The room cleared, she grabbed her case and headed for the door, her breathing fast and shallow.

Tabitha was waiting for her on the other side.

'Natalie, is everything okay?' she asked, her face full of concern. But underneath, Natalie could tell that she knew.

'I have to go,' Natalie replied, moving past her towards the staircase.

'Natalie,' Tabitha said, side-stepping into her path. 'I think we need to sit down and talk.'

'I just want to go.'

'I think it would help to talk about things,' she insisted. 'Just so there are no misunderstandings.'

And there was the confirmation. She had already been told about what had happened. She had come here to talk her round, as an envoy, to make the case for Sir Kenneth.

Natalie moved to go around her, but Tabitha moved in step.

'I think you misunderstood Sir Kenneth's intentions. He's really upset about it, and wants to explain. He doesn't want you to get the wrong impression.'

'I didn't,' Natalie replied. 'I know what he did.'

Tabitha shook her head sadly. 'Don't ruin things, Natalie.'

'Ruin things?'

'Don't ruin your big opportunity over a simple misunderstanding.'

'I *know* about him,' Natalie responded.

'Excuse me?'

'I *was warned about him*.'

Tabitha gripped her clipboard tighter. 'I'm afraid, Natalie, that you appear to have been got at by somebody, who has obviously turned your mind against Sir Kenneth.'

'You don't care about me at all, do you?'

Tabitha blinked several times. 'Of course I do.'

'No you don't. You haven't asked me what happened in his apartment just then, what he did.'

'I... Sir Kenneth explained.'

'You aren't interested in my side of the story. You're here to try and persuade me that it was all a simple mistake, or just my imagination.'

'Natalie...'

'I'm going,' she insisted. 'Now get out of my way, Tabitha.'

Tabitha's face hardened into a cruel smile. 'If it's money you're after, then forget it. You'll get nothing from him or the company. It's your word against his, and history has shown that Sir Kenneth's word is worth more than people like you.'

'You know, Tabitha. I've just escaped from one controlling man, someone who treated me like an object. I'm not about to fall into that situation again. I don't want money. All I want is to get out of this messed-up place and never see Sir Kenneth New, or you, again.'

Tabitha opened her mouth, but the shock of Natalie's strong reaction prevented any words coming out.

Natalie took her chance, brushing past her and heading for the stairs. Her heart was thudding in her ears as she reached the reception desk.

Tabitha was in pursuit.

'I want my phone back,' Natalie demanded from the surprised receptionist, who had been tapping away at the computer. 'I'm leaving.'

The receptionist looked across at Tabitha, who had caught up.

'Give it to her,' she stated.

The receptionist nodded, and fetched the mobile from under the desk, handing it to her without question.

Natalie snatched it from her and made for the door and freedom.

43

Amy was in the room, but she wasn't hearing what the lecturer was saying. Her mind was full of worries about her friend. There had been no messages, and each call had rung through. It seemed likely that Natalie's phone had been turned off, or had run out of battery. But that told her nothing about Natalie's welfare.

She still felt sure that Natalie was in great danger.

But she wasn't ready to accept that it was too late.

Amy's vision came back into focus just as the lecturer was summarising the key learning points from the one-hour session on digital marketing. She would have to read up about it later, in case it was in the exam, as she had zoned out after the first couple of slides.

She gathered together her laptop and notebook, slipped out of the seat and headed for the door, trailing behind the other students.

Even though it was still early afternoon, lectures were over for the day. She didn't want to go back to the flat yet; it just felt so weird and empty with Natalie gone. But she also wasn't in the right frame of mind to hit the books in the library. So instead she took a walk, heading for what had been styled as a 'mindfulness garden' around the back of the lecture theatre. The small space, designed to be a refuge of peace and calm amongst the hustle and bustle of the university campus, had a couple of benches around a water feature and was encircled by a low hedge.

Amy took a seat and closed her eyes against the warming afternoon sun. It did feel calming here, with the sound of the water feature and birdsong in the background.

Suddenly she had the feeling that someone was sitting next to her. Her eyes snapped open.

'Hello, Amy.'

It was Jack Morton. He was sitting too close to her on the bench, wearing his trademark skinny jeans and American branded t-shirt. 'I thought it was you when I saw you leaving the building.' He shuffled up some more, smiling at her apparent discomfort. 'Just had a lecture?'

'Yes,' she said tightly. 'I'd better get back.'

She made to stand, but he placed a hand on her shoulder. It was a gentle touch, but aggressive nevertheless, and Amy stiffened in place. She glanced around, but there was no one passing by.

'I'd just like a quick chat,' he said, moving his hand away once he was satisfied that she was going to remain where she was. 'I think we need to clear some things up, Amy. Don't you?'

'I don't know what you mean,' she said. To her annoyance, her voice was shredded with nerves, betraying her inner emotions.

'Oh, I think you do,' he stated. 'I think you know *exactly* what I mean. Would you like me to remind you how you brought the police to my door, into my home, into my *bedroom*.'

Amy didn't know what to say, so she said nothing.

'But it wasn't just any police officer, was it, Amy? It was your father. Tell me, do you always call in Daddy to help you out when things aren't going your way?'

'Leave me alone, Jack.'

'What? Or you'll call Daddy again to come and threaten me?'

'He didn't threaten you.'

'Oh didn't he? I beg to differ on that point. He tried to intimidate me, and he upset my girlfriend.'

Amy found herself shaking her head at that word.

He just smiled. 'And before you ask, our relationship started after Natalie and I broke up.'

'You certainly don't waste any time,' she quipped.

'What's the matter, Amy? Jealous?'

'What?'

'Jealous that I chose Natalie instead of you?'

'You're a real piece of work, Jack.'

'I've seen the way you look at me. Don't think I didn't notice you checking me out, that first time I came around to the house. I saw the spark in your eyes.' He smiled.

Amy fumed silently. Because he was right. He had known. That first time Natalie had brought him back, she *had* been attracted to him, *had* felt that pang of envy as Natalie later retreated upstairs with the good-looking, good-smelling confident older man while she watched the news and ate the rest of the Pringles from the night before.

But that was before she had found out what he was like – his controlling nature, his need for dominance, tightening his grip slowly but deliberately, a boa-constrictor in human form.

'You're really in love with yourself, aren't you?' she managed to say, in spite of her nerves at being alone with this man.

'You don't like me, I understand that,' he replied, avoiding her question. 'And I know that deep down it stems from jealousy, and from the fact that I don't want you. But you've got to understand, I do have standards.'

She just shook her head at that, taken aback by his arrogance and attitude. The guy was poison.

'Anyway,' he continued, 'back to my original point. We need to clarify some things about Natalie. And how you called Daddy down to put the squeeze on me.'

'I just want to find my friend.'

He nodded. 'I know you do. And so do I.' He gauged Amy's disbelieving reaction, half laughing. 'You really think I have something to do with Natalie's disappearance?'

'I don't know.'

'Actually,' he said, putting up his palms in mock surrender, 'you got me. I killed Natalie and buried her in a shallow grave just outside the city boundary. You know that rural road down towards the coast? I hired a van, and transported her body in a rolled-up piece of carpet. It was late at night, no one saw me. The digging was difficult, just to get the grave deep enough...'

'Stop,' Amy pleaded. 'Just stop.'

'What's the matter? You want to know the truth about what happened, don't you?'

'I want to know what really happened to my friend. And if you cared for her at all, you wouldn't be doing this. You'd be helping, not playing games.'

He shook his head. 'It isn't a game, bringing the police to my door, threatening me and my girlfriend.'

'You're so self-centred.'

'And?'

'If I find out you've done anything to Natalie, then I swear you're going to regret it.'

He laughed at that. 'Please, Amy, don't play the strong one, it really doesn't suit you. I know what you're really like. Natalie told me all about you.'

She said nothing, but she knew that her face was betraying her emotions.

'Oh, yes, Natalie told me all about the problems you've had, Amy. How you flunked your exams because of your condition. I mean, you being a headcase with esteem problems, it does explain a lot.'

'Go to hell.'

He smiled tightly. 'Natalie was worried about you. She thought you might not be strong enough to see university through. She told me one time that she wasn't sure you would last the pace.'

She wasn't going to take his bait. 'Why are you here, Jack?'

'Like I said, just to set things straight.'

'You didn't just happen to see me leave the lecture, did you? You were waiting for me.'

This time it was his turn to remain silent.

'You knew my timetable, and you were waiting for me. You were stalking me.'

'Oh, that's a little strong, Amy. I'm not a stalker. And if I were, believe me, I would aim higher.'

Amy ignored the jibe. 'You might not be a stalker, but you are a manipulator, Jack. You're controlling and possessive. You're everything I hate in people.'

To Amy's surprise, this actually did seem to land a blow. Jack pushed his tongue against the inside of his mouth as he looked away. But then he turned, slowly and with menace. Like a wounded predator, caught out by a blow from their prey, his eyes were set on going in for the kill.

Amy summoned up all her strength to face down her aggressor. 'What are you going to do, Jack, rough me up like you roughed up Natalie?'

Suddenly he thrust a hand towards her, grabbing her chin and digging in his nails. Amy flinched but was held in place; their faces remained inches apart. She couldn't look anywhere but deep into his blue-grey eyes. 'Don't *ever* say that again about me. Do you understand?'

At first she was too scared to move.

'Do you *understand?*'

Finally she nodded.

'*Say it!*'

'I... understand.' Her mouth was twisted with the force of his grip, and she could hardly get the words out.

He released her, pushing her face away with disdain. She sat there in shock, looking at the floor, her chin stinging and her jaw aching.

'Hey!' she heard someone call out. 'What the hell are you doing?'

Amy was still looking down, but from the corner of her eye she saw Jack get to his feet. She lifted her head and watched as he hurried off around the pond and dashed out of sight.

'Are you okay?'

She turned to see a well-built guy with messy blond hair crouching to her right. He was wearing a university rugby top.

'I'm okay,' she managed.

'Is he your boyfriend?'

She shook her head.

'But you know him?'

'Yes. He's an acquaintance.'

'Well, it looked really nasty, what he was doing to you. Would you like me to take you somewhere, to report it? The campus security office is just over there.'

'I'm fine.'

'How about the medical centre? Maybe you need to get yourself checked over?'

She realised she was still holding her chin with the pain.

'I'm okay, really. I'll just get off home.'

He didn't look convinced but seemed to realise there was little else he could do. 'As long as you're okay.'

'I am.'

'Look,' he said. 'You can tell me to mind my own business, but any man who can do what I just saw him doing to you – well, I'd be very, very careful of him.'

Amy nodded.

'Trust me, my dad used to beat up my mum when I was young. Men like that, who physically assault women, they're capable of anything, *absolutely* anything.'

Amy watched her good Samaritan leave. He turned one last time to check on her, his face still full of concern and consternation, before he disappeared from view. His words resonated in her head.

They're capable of anything.

Absolutely anything.

She felt a rising panic about the situation she was in. What might happen if Jack came after her again? What if he door-stepped her at the flat?

There would be no one to come to her rescue then.

And then she had another awful thought: his monologue about how he had supposedly killed Natalie and buried her...

Maybe it wasn't what she had instinctively thought – a way for him to wind her up.

Maybe it had been a confession.

PART IV

44

Previous Sunday morning

NATALIE HURRIED ALONG THE PAVEMENT, her breath ragged, as she sought to put as much distance between her and New House as she possibly could. The tube station was only five minutes down the road, but it felt like a long way away. A London bus drifted past on her right, pulling up at the stop just ahead of her. Without thinking, she jogged up to the vehicle and boarded. She didn't even know where it was going, she just had a desperate desire to get away, and it didn't really matter at this moment in time where 'away' was.

'Do you go anywhere near Paddington station?' she asked, as the driver looked on expectantly.

'Hyde Park is the closest we get,' he said. 'You can pick up the Number 60 from there, it'll take you straight to the entrance.'

Natalie nodded with relief, bringing out her debit card to make the contactless payment. She'd walked to Paddington from Hyde Park before. It wasn't far. No more than ten minutes or so.

Downstairs was busy, so she heaved her weekend bag up the stairs to the top deck. As she sat down, the bus moved away. She took a few deep breaths and tried to steady herself. But the relief of escaping that awful place was tempered by the lingering horror of what had happened. She still couldn't really believe it. Sir Kenneth had abused his position, wanting some kind of sexual favour. And the way he had turned on her – the look on his face.

She shuddered at the memory of him, squaring up to her, angry and aggressive.

Then she thought back to what Catharine had said. Or what she had tried to say.

There's something I think you should know, something about Sir Kenneth New...

Had she been trying to warn Natalie that something like that might happen? But how would she have known? Unless he'd done something like that before. She remembered some of the high-profile cases in the news over the past few years, where men in positions of power had got away with such behaviour for years, even though it had been an open secret among sections of their profession. It certainly wasn't far-fetched to believe that the same might have been true with Sir Kenneth New.

Catharine had tried to warn her.

But not Diana Saunders.

And not Tabitha.

Now that this was starting to sink in, she was beginning to think ahead. How would she deal with what had just happened? She already felt conflicted – the urge to run, forget and move on was strong, but so too was the desire for justice. To see justice done, not just for her, but for all the other women that he might have done the same to.

She thought about Jack.

He had got away with it.

He would be free to do the same again, treat other girls with scorn, control them for his own pleasure. She shook her head. She had barely felt able to extract herself from his clutches, never mind turn around and face up to him and what had happened. And that's what reporting him to the authorities would mean – it would mean maintaining that link with him.

So she'd walked away, putting all her energies into the upcoming opportunity at Brand New. It was the thing that had given her the strength to finally end things with Jack. But in reality, she'd been stepping into a new horror. Indeed, it had been planned in advance and in detail by Kenneth New.

She pulled out her mobile and typed a text message to Amy. She desperately wanted to speak to her, but now wasn't the right time, surrounded by strangers on the top deck of this London bus.

She kept the message short, deleting bits several times. She didn't want to worry Amy.

Can't wait to get home. Made a terrible mistake coming here.

NATALIE WAS ALMOST SLEEPING when her phone, perched on her lap, buzzed.

Natalie. So sorry I missed your call yesterday.

It was Russell Cave.

She felt a frisson of excitement as she re-read the message. She typed out a reply.

No worries :)

Before she could type a follow-up message, the call came through.

'Hello?'

'Natalie,' Russell said. 'Lovely to hear from you. I'm so sorry I missed your call yesterday. I tried to call you back, but your phone was off.'

'I was calling from another phone,' she explained. 'They still had my mobile phone behind the reception.'

'Yes, I thought that would be the case. I'm so glad you gave me your mobile number. So, how's things? I assume, given that you've answered your phone, that you're out of the house?'

'I'm on my way back to Paddington,' she said, dodging the question about her well-being. There was no way she could explain things at the moment, so she decided to keep things light. 'Although I got on the wrong bus, so I'm going to have to change at some point – at Hyde Park, I think.'

'Which side?'

'South entrance. Why?'

'I'm not too far away from there now,' he explained. 'I'll come and pick you up. Drop you off at the station.'

'It's okay, you really don't need to...'

'It would be my pleasure,' he interjected. 'And honestly, I'm just a few minutes away. Where are you at the moment?'

Natalie looked out of the window. She knew London well enough to tell they were getting close to Hyde Park. 'Probably about five minutes away.'

'Great, if I'm not there when you arrive, I'll be no more than a few minutes longer!'

~

HE WAS ALREADY STANDING at the bus stop as Natalie alighted.

'Hey,' he smiled, squinting in the bright spring sunshine. He moved towards her for a loose embrace. 'Lovely to see you again, Natalie.'

'You too,' she said, as the bus powered away across the busy junction. She pulled back, feeling rather uncomfortable now with this almost stranger.

'So,' he said in a friendly way. 'How are things?'

She just nodded. 'Okay...'

He frowned. 'Doesn't look like it. What's up?'

'It's a long story.'

'I have time. And so do you, don't you? Isn't your train at eight thirty-five?' He glanced at his smart watch. 'Which means you have quite a few hours to kill.'

'I was hoping I might be able to change my ticket for an earlier service,' she explained.

'You're that desperate to get out of the Big Smoke?' he said.

She shrugged. 'I'm looking forward to getting back to Bristol. It's been a tiring few days.'

'Fair enough. London Paddington it is then. My car's just across the road.'

They crossed and Russell gestured towards the light-blue Porsche parked in the side road.

'Did you think I'd drive a hearse?' he joked, as he popped open the boot.

'I wouldn't have been surprised,' she said, appreciating the lightening of mood after her melancholic bus journey.

She climbed into the passenger seat and belted up, as Russell slipped in beside her. They pulled away and accelerated out towards the row of traffic lights.

'So,' he said, as they waited on red, 'don't keep me in suspense.'

'What?'

He seemed surprised that she didn't immediately know what he was talking about. 'Who won?'

'Oh,' she replied. 'I did.'

'Wow. That's amazing, Natalie! Wow!' He shifted his gaze back to the road as the lights went to green. 'That's just amazing news.' He glanced across. 'I'm so pleased for you.'

'Thanks.'

'We *must* do something to celebrate,' he continued, not seeming to notice how subdued she was at this apparently amazing news. 'Let me show you my place. There's a fantastic deli just around the corner, they do amazing lunches. You won't regret it.'

Natalie was thinking again about those awful minutes in Sir Kenneth's apartment. She shuddered at the image of the billionaire boring into her with his angry eyes.

'Lunch will be on me.'

She nodded, not really listening.

'Fantastic! You won't regret it. It will be another experience to remember.'

45

Cullen had only just pressed send for the text message to Amy and was still standing in front of the tube station when the call came through.

'Detective Chief Inspector? Zack Carter here.'

'Zack.' Cullen took a step away from the station entrance. 'How's things?'

'Good. Very good. Have you seen the front cover?'

'I have. In fact, I'm standing next to a pile of them now.' He watched on as a young guy handed copies to passers-by.

'I hope you're happy with the story?'

Cullen saw a girl with the paper folded in two in her hand, looking intently at the photo of Natalie. 'Very happy.'

'Good, good. I wasn't sure what you'd think of the headline.'

'Goes with the territory,' Cullen reassured him. 'And I know you didn't have control over that.'

'No, I didn't,' Zack said simply.

'So, is there anything I can help you with, Zack?'

'There's something I might be able to help you with,' the young journalist replied.

'Oh?'

'We've had a few calls come in already following the story. Some suspected sightings, which we're passing on to the police as per your wishes, although to be honest they're all a bit vague so far, and I'm not holding out a lot of hope.'

'I know those type of leads well.'

'Yes, well, we've had one more interesting call, just a few minutes ago.'

'Go on.'

'From a lady called Catharine Houghton, works at EXCEL-ENT. She saw the newspaper report and says she wants to speak with you.'

EXCEL-ENT. Cullen had heard that name already today. It was the agency Natalie had visited on Saturday. 'Did she say what about?'

'No, but she was very keen to speak to you in person. I have her number,' Zack added, before Cullen had a chance to reply. 'She said it was okay if I passed it on to you.'

'Thanks, Zack. I'll give her a call now.'

'CATHARINE, IS IT?'

The girl nodded and rose politely from the table.

'Yes, hi,' she smiled, shaking his hand.

'Thank you for coming over to where I was,' Cullen said. 'It's a big help for me.'

'Oh, no problem. Like I said, it's not far from where I live anyway.'

They both ordered coffees.

'So,' Cullen said, while they waited for the drinks to arrive. 'Zack tells me that you work at EXCEL-ENT.'

'Used to,' she corrected. 'I quit at the weekend.'

'Oh?'

'I've been meaning to do it for a long time. I just hadn't plucked up the courage until now. But now I've actually done it, it feels great.'

'Good for you.'

'Thanks.'

'Anything in the pipeline?'

'A charity to improve reading among children.'

'Sounds like a very noble job.'

She smiled sadly. 'I hope so.'

'So, you saw the newspaper story and wanted to talk?'

'Yes,' she said. 'There's something you need to know.'

'I'm all ears.'

'It's about Kenneth New.'

'Go on.'

'There are rumours about him. Strong rumours – about how he treats the women who work for him.'

'Really?'

'One rumour is that he propositioned someone in a hotel room. He invited her back to discuss business and then emerged from the bathroom totally naked, wanting a massage.'

'Sounds like the kind of thing that's been happening in Hollywood.'

She nodded in agreement. 'It's never got into the public eye. Probably because people are scared of taking him on, scared of what he could do to their careers. Plus, he has friends in high places. So in the public eye he remains the generous philanthropist who had donated millions of pounds to local hospitals and charities across London.'

'That's certainly the Kenneth New I've read up on in the past few days. He's very well thought of, by the sounds of it.'

'Exactly.'

'So what do the stories say?'

'That over the past ten years a number of women have alleged that Sir Kenneth propositioned them and pressured them in various ways. I'm sure you know what I mean.'

'How do you know this?'

'It's an open secret in the business. We work closely with his company Brand New, and I've got friends there. But everyone is too scared to say anything publicly. Not only is it risky career-wise, it might also mean financial ruin, as Sir Kenneth is known for going after people with the best lawyers. Rumour has it that some of the accusers were paid off, while others were scared away by threats of litigation.'

Cullen pondered on the hypocrisy. Sir Kenneth's Wikipedia page documented how he was a key voice on equality in the workplace and had come out as a strong advocate of women's rights in the aftermath of the #Me Too movement, where women across the world had come forward with their experiences of harassment.

'You think Natalie's disappearance might have something to do with Sir Kenneth New?'

She shrugged. 'I read that Natalie said in her text message that something had happened over the weekend.'

'And you think that might involve Sir Kenneth?'

Another shrug. 'I don't know. Probably not. But, well, I wanted to warn her about him. I *tried* to warn her, but we were interrupted.'

'You were that concerned?'

'Yes. I was. I know I'd only just met Natalie, but she seemed... she seems like such a nice person, I just wanted to warn her, in case, just warn her to be careful. It was an instinctive thing, you know, to look out for a fellow woman.'

'I understand.'

'So when I saw the headline, I was just so shocked, so upset, I felt responsible. I *had* to speak to someone.'

'You did the right thing. And whatever has happened to Natalie, please, don't blame yourself.'

She thought on that. 'Do you know if he was there, at New House, over the weekend?'

Cullen nodded. 'He was there.'

She looked sick to the stomach. 'Have you questioned him?'

'Not yet. He's on a flight to Australia. But don't worry, I will.'

'That's good. Thank you.'

A thought struck Cullen. 'You worked closely with the group at the weekend? You met them all?'

'Yes, the group who came to EXCEL-ENT, I welcomed them to the building.'

He pulled out the photo that Penny had provided him with – the one that showed Russell at the drinks reception. 'I wondered if you knew anything about this guy.'

He showed her the photo.

'The guy on the left, next to Natalie,' he directed. 'He's the one person I haven't yet been able to get in touch with. I wondered if you'd come into contact with him. His name is Russell Cave.'

She looked confused as she scrutinised the image. Finally,

she looked up. 'Are you sure they said his name is Russell Cave?'

'Yes. Why?'

She looked again at the photograph, her face now settling with certainty. 'Because I know that man, and his name isn't Russell Cave.'

46

Previous Sunday morning

'HERE WE ARE,' Russell said, as they pulled up on the road-side. The road was pretty – tree-lined, with well-kept houses. 'That's my place, Number Thirty-Two. I've lived here for two years,' he added, as Natalie peered out of the window, examining the property. 'Cost me a small fortune, but it's a great little place and the location is amazing.'

'Looks lovely,' she said.

'Are you surprised?' he asked, as he led her up to the front door.

'Surprised?'

'About where I live?'

She looked down at the garden, which was compact but bursting with flowers. 'Maybe.'

'I lived in a dockside apartment for a few years,' he said. 'New build.' He pulled a face. 'I thought it would be paradise, but it was just soulless. I didn't see any of my neighbours, never mind get to speak to them. And the riverside location wasn't what I expected – it was quite industrial. So I learned my lesson.'

'Well, this looks perfect.'

They entered the property and Russell showed Natalie through to the kitchen, which ran down the back of the house, past a small but lovely sitting room. It might sound sexist, but the place looked as if it had benefited from a woman's touch.

'It's not your stereotypical bachelor pad,' Russell said, reading Natalie's mind. 'I like neat and tidy.' He shrugged. 'It's just the way I am.'

'I'm impressed.'

'Coffee?'

Natalie nodded, noticing the impressive bean-to-cup machine.

'Latte, cappuccino?'

'Latte, please.'

'Coming right up.'

Russell busied himself with the preparations as Natalie took a seat on one of the high stools.

'I still can't believe you won,' he said, filling the machine with beans. 'Sorry, that came out wrong.' He stopped to look at her. 'I believed it was possible, but for you to actually have won, well, it's amazing. That's what I can't believe – that you've got this unbelievable opportunity.'

Natalie smiled sadly, unable to play along any longer.

He noticed. 'What's the matter?'

She swallowed her reticence to voice what had happened. 'Sir Kenneth New, he...'

'What is it, Natalie?'

'He assaulted me.'

'What?'

She felt an upwelling from her stomach, and for a moment wondered whether she was going to be physically sick right there in front of Russell. But she held things together. 'He invited me to his apartment, in New House. It was supposed to be for breakfast. But he went off to his bedroom and then called me in, wanting me to touch him...'

'*What!* Touch him where?'

'His back. He said he had a back problem, and he wanted me to massage it for him.'

'But you said he assaulted you?'

'I got out of the room and he came after me. He grabbed me by the wrists, pushed me up against the wall. He said a lot of things. I can't remember all of it, but it was nasty.'

He thought for a moment, staring down, shaking his head. 'That doesn't sound like Sir Kenneth,' he said at last, to her utmost shock.

'I...'

'I mean, I know a lot about him. I've read his book, and books by people he's worked with. He's big on women's rights. The thought of him...'

'It's what happened.' Natalie went to get off the stool. 'Don't you believe me?'

'No, no, of *course* I believe you,' he said, moving over to allay her concerns. 'Of course I do. It's just, maybe you need to look at things a little differently. Maybe from his perspective?'

'What?'

'I mean, what you experienced, it was awful, I can see that. But sometimes, if you think about things from another point of view, things can seem different.'

'I don't understand.'

Russell placed a hand on each of her shoulders. 'Please, Natalie, don't hate me for suggesting this, but maybe it was just a case of misinterpreting intentions.'

She went to shrug him off, but his grip held firm.

'I know that Sir Kenneth does suffer from back problems,' he revealed. 'He talks about it in his autobiography. Ten years ago he fell off a horse while competing in a charity race and damaged the discs in his lower spine. He's had treatment, one of the discs was taken out, but he said in the book that it's an ongoing problem.'

'He was just in his underpants.'

'Have you ever been to an osteopath or chiropractor?' he asked. 'I have. They ask you to remove everything but your underwear.'

'Yes, but...'

'I know it's strange,' he said, 'to just spring it on you like that without warning. It shouldn't happen, I agree. It's not acceptable behaviour.'

'But?'

'But it might just be that he really was in pain at that point, and he trusted you. When you think about it, it's quite a trusting thing to do, to reveal yourself like that, show your weaknesses.'

To her surprise, Russell was actually making sense. Maybe she had overreacted? Maybe she had misinterpreted the events, possibly because of her experiences with Jack. 'I don't know, Russell. The way he came after me.'

'It sounds awful, really awful,' he said. 'But maybe, just maybe, in the heat of the moment, he was angry at being embarrassed. Maybe he lost it for just a moment. You said he grabbed your wrists?'

'Yes. And pushed me up against the wall.'

'How did you get away?'

'He let me go.'

'Without you having to struggle?'

'I... I asked him to let me go.'

Russell smiled sadly. 'He probably realised he had gone too far. The red mist had cleared.'

Natalie closed her eyes.

'I'm not trying to downplay what happened,' Russell continued, 'or to come up with excuses for what he did. But it's worth thinking this through.'

Finally Natalie nodded. 'I need to use the bathroom.'

'It's up the stairs, on the left.'

NATALIE CLIMBED THE STAIRS, thinking through what Russell had said. The scary thing was that it made sense. He'd forced her to think from Sir Kenneth's perspective, and almost immediately the scenario seemed transformed.

But she *had* felt the horror. Could it really just have been an unfortunate misunderstanding?

By the time she had exited the loo, she had shaken off the doubts.

It had been more than an innocent misunderstanding. She was sure of that. All those months of giving Jack the benefit of the doubt when he had used various means to exert power and control, treating her so badly. She recognised what had happened at New House, and it had been sinister.

She paused at the top of the stairs, gazing along the landing to the open bedroom at the end. For some reason she felt compelled to explore. Surely Russell wouldn't mind –

after all, he had been the one to insist on her visiting his place.

She entered the bedroom. As with downstairs, it was perfectly neat and tidy, like a show home. But one item stood out.

The book was on the chest of drawers.

The book about the Sinclair family murders that Russell had been consulting during their evening together at New House.

She picked it up and began to leaf through.

But something was wrong. The text was referring to the English football team during the 1990 Italian World Cup. She flicked through the pages some more, and again, it was just football references.

Then she saw the gap between the cover and the main part of the book. She lifted the outer cover up to reveal the book's true cover.

Italia '90: Travels with England.

The Sinclair cover was merely a facade.

Russell had been lying.

And there on the inside front cover was something else.

47

Previous Sunday morning

NATALIE FELT QUITE sick by the time she returned to the kitchen. Russell smiled as he handed her a coffee.

'Here you go,' he said. 'Hope you like it.'

She took the cup, cradling it in both hands, and steeled herself for the conversation. She wasn't even sure why it was that important that he'd lied about the book, but it *felt* important and she needed to have it out with him. 'The book you had about what happened at New House,' she began.

His face altered, the smile dissolving before her eyes. 'You found it.'

She nodded.

He took a sip of his coffee, his brow furrowed. 'It wasn't meant to be anything serious, just a bit of a game, that's all.'

'A bit of a game,' she echoed.

'Yes.' He shrugged. 'I thought it would add to the

atmosphere of the weekend, the story of the Sinclairs. The book was part of that.'

'So the story about the murders, it wasn't true?'

He shook his head. 'I'm sorry,' he said, when he saw Natalie's reaction. 'It was just a bit of fun.'

'I believed you.'

'Sorry,' he said again, but this time it didn't sound quite as genuine. He took another sip and turned to the sink. 'You've got to remember, Natalie, that the weekend wasn't a real-life situation. People were there to play a game, to take part in a competition. I was just trying to liven things up, that's all. I'm sorry if I've offended you, I really am.'

Natalie watched Russell, not sure how to respond. She had trusted him. And she didn't accept that it wasn't real life. It was.

'Why did you leave the house early?' she asked.

Another shrug. 'I'm not sure, really,' was the surprising reply. 'It was a spur of the moment decision, and it probably had a lot to do with all that whiskey I'd drunk, if I'm honest.'

'So you didn't plan to leave?'

'No, I didn't, honestly. I said goodbye to you, got back to my room, and, I don't know, I just found myself packing up my stuff and heading for the door. I'm sorry I didn't say good-bye. I felt pretty bad about it in the morning. And I thought you probably wouldn't be in touch because of it. So I was glad when you called and left your number.' He tried a smile.

But Natalie wasn't finished with the questions yet – something didn't feel right about this. He'd been lying about the book, and she felt pretty sure he was lying about the circumstances behind his exit from the house. She really didn't want a confrontation, though. After all, she hardly knew him – maybe she knew him even less than she'd thought – and she was in his house. It wouldn't be wise at all to raise tensions. And yet, she wanted to know the truth...

'Susie thought she heard you talking with Tabitha, in your room,' she said, deciding that it was something that she wanted to pursue.

There was just a second or two of hesitation, but it was enough. 'Oh, yes, she came by to see what the matter was because she could hear me banging around. I'm afraid I must have been a bit noisy when I was getting my things together.' He kept his tone as even and light as possible, but there was tension in his voice.

'I don't think you're telling me the truth,' she found herself saying.

He just looked at her.

And then the thought came to her. 'How did you know about the secret room in the attic? About where the secret door was to the staircase? You said it was mentioned in the book you had about the Sinclairs, but it wasn't, because there was no book. So how did you...'

Still he just looked back.

It certainly wasn't the kind of thing you could stumble upon.

Another thought. There was only one explanation she could think of for why Russell would have known about the existence of that room.

'Your name isn't Russell, is it?' she said. 'It's Guy. Guy Clarke.'

'I don't know what you're on about.'

'That's the name in the book. Guy Clarke.'

He gave a half-hearted shake of the head. 'Natalie, you've got this all...'

Natalie brought out her phone. 'If I were to search for Guy Clarke on here, would I find your photo?'

His expression told her yes.

'And would it also tell me who you worked for? You must have a LinkedIn profile.'

This time he nodded. 'Do it,' he conceded. 'Go ahead.'

'I'd rather you told me yourself.'

He drained his coffee and placed the mug on the draining board before turning back to face her, palms spread. 'Fair enough. You're right. My name's Guy Clarke, and I work for Brand New.'

'Let's go through to the sitting room,' he said. 'I can explain everything.'

Natalie followed him through and took a seat opposite him. She watched as he composed himself, and she hoped he wasn't just taking these few minutes to think up some more lies.

'I've worked for Brand New for the past six years. I'm a senior brand manager, focussed on our digital marketing operations.'

Natalie had a lot of questions, but wanted to hear him out.

'I was asked by the company to do a bit of role playing in the weekend's assessment exercise – pretend to be one of the applicants.'

'Why?'

'Sir Kenneth is quite a playful character,' he said. 'It was his idea, to mix things up a bit in the house.'

'Which is where the story of the Sinclair family comes in.'

He nodded. 'Yes. That was Sir Kenneth's idea too. He came up with the story. He's got quite a vivid imagination, which I'm sure won't come as a surprise. He sent along the story and I just had to run with it. It was my idea to come up with the book, with the fake cover. It all added to the authenticity. And we knew that with you guys having no internet access, you wouldn't be able to check the veracity of what we were telling you.'

'Is that why electronic devices were banned?'

'Partly. But it was also because Sir Kenneth wanted to create that feeling of being isolated from the rest of the world. You can't do that with social media notifications pinging around the place.'

'And your job, arranging designer funerals...'

'Also Sir Kenneth's idea, although I wish I could take credit for it.'

'So all along you were working with Tabitha. Her coming to my room, looking for you, it was all an act.'

'Yes.'

'Why focus on me?'

'Because Sir Kenneth instructed me to. He wanted me to test you out, see how you'd react.'

'Test me out?'

He smiled. 'Of course. He wanted to see whether you'd come with me, explore the house, face up to the ghosts of the Sinclair family. He wanted to see how you reacted, how you dealt with the situation.'

'But why?'

Another smile. 'Because you were the winner, Natalie. You always were. He picked you out himself, that day at the book signing. He was waiting and hoping for you to apply. And you did.'

'He told me,' she replied. 'He told me all this. Just before he attacked me.'

Russell shook his head. 'Natalie, as I said, you've got this all wrong. Sir Kenneth really isn't like that.'

Natalie bristled. 'What he did, it wasn't me misunderstanding events. It didn't happen like you said. I know what happened, because it happened to *me*.'

'You're mistaken.'

'I'm not.'

'Natalie, I don't want you to make what could be the biggest mistake of your life. Don't throw away the amazing opportunity that you've been presented with, all because you got the wrong impression. Honestly, it would be a *massive* mistake, believe me.'

'Why should I believe anything you say?'

'I like you, Natalie, I really do. You want the truth?'

'Yes.'

'Okay. I was acting over the weekend, playing a part. But honestly, I really like you. I wasn't faking that. I enjoyed talking with you that evening.'

'While lying to me...'

He nodded. 'Yes, there was that. But later, when we went up to the attic, that moment wasn't fake, I promise. There was something special about that moment under the stars, wasn't there?'

'I was on the rebound,' Natalie replied, more harshly than she had intended. She chose her words more carefully. 'I'm still getting over my relationship with Jack. I just got caught up in the moment. But I did like you. Until I found out what it was all really about.'

'It wasn't fake,' he repeated.

Natalie looked around the room, reappraising the situation that she now found herself in. 'This was all planned too, wasn't it? You calling me, inviting me back to your place. It was all to get me to forget about what happened, to move on, and let Sir Kenneth off without any repercussions. Just like in the house, pretending to be Russell Cave, you're doing your job, serving your employer.'

'I *was* asked to speak to you, yes. But only to see if you were alright. We were – are – worried about you.'

'We?'

'Yes, we. Tabitha, Sir Kenneth, everyone at the company. After you left the house like that, so upset, we were really worried. We're like that in Brand New – we're concerned for one another. We're a family. And we don't want to see one of our family suffering.'

'It was Tabitha who called you, wasn't it?'

'Yes. Tabitha called me. She told me what had happened. She's worried about you, Natalie. Look, I know you're sceptical, I was too when I first started at the company, but in time, in a short time, you'll understand. You'll look back and truly understand what I'm talking about. We really care.'

Natalie couldn't quite believe what she was hearing. He was speaking as if she was still going to accept the job with the company. How on earth could he think that was a possibility, after what had happened?

'I won't be working at Brand New.'

'Don't be too hasty,' he said. 'My advice would be to sleep on it. Things might seem very different in the morning.'

Natalie shook her head. 'You're just not hearing, me, Rus– whoever you are.'

'Guy.'

'Guy, you're not hearing me. Look, I think I'd better go.'

She made to stand, but only got as far as the door before

the room started to twist and turn, as if she were balancing on a floating barrel. She lurched for the doorframe, reaching out desperately for some stability. Suddenly she felt as if she might vomit, and she thrust her other hand to her mouth, to try and catch whatever might emerge.

'Natalie, are you okay?'

The words seemed distant, other-worldly. She tried to say something but no sound came out. She felt the ground rise up to her and the side of her head hit the wooden floor with force. Pain rippled through her temple, as she watched the room undulating like waves, splashing up against her skin. Her power levels were at zero. She felt paralysed, trapped in her own body, and she was scared.

The last thing she could remember was Guy's voice again. His tone was urgent. But she could only pick up isolated words, which echoed through her spinning head.

Natalie... collapsed... big trouble.

48

Previous Monday

NATALIE COULD HEAR VOICES AGAIN, echoing through the fog. She couldn't make out what they were saying, and she certainly couldn't tell if they were directed at her. But then the fog began to lift, and the words began to make sense.

'Natalie, are you okay?'

The voice was soothing. It reminded her of her mother, that time when she had been holed up in bed with the flu.

'Natalie?'

Natalie tried to open her eyes, but it was like lifting a great weight. Her body was rigid, aching; it was a real struggle to move.

What the hell was happening?

'Are you okay, Natalie?'

The voice felt far away again now.

And then there was nothing.

'NATALIE, please, try and wake up. It's been hours now, we're getting worried.'

It was the voice again. This time she realised it was the voice of a female. The voice was familiar too, but she couldn't quite place it.

She willed herself awake. This time, her body obeyed, and her eyes opened. The light was painful, and she brought a shielding hand to her face.

'Natalie!' the voice said excitedly. 'You're awake!'

Her body still aching, she struggled to turn towards the voice.

'It's okay, take it slowly,' someone said. 'You don't want to rush things.'

Natalie flopped back down onto what must have been a pillow as a shard of pain sliced along the side of her head.

She went to speak. 'Where am...'

But the effort was too much.

'I'm getting more worried,' the girl's voice said. 'She should be improving by now.'

'I know,' a man's voice replied.

Then, after a few seconds of lucidity, the conversation swirled away from Natalie. And again she succumbed to the darkness.

NATALIE SAW the outline of the person sitting across the room. They were tapping away on their mobile phone, oblivious to the fact that Natalie had at last opened her eyes.

She was lying in a single bed, on her back, but with her

head propped up with pillows. The covers were up around her chin and tucked in at the side – she could feel the pull of the tension of the sheet, holding her in tightly.

Natalie resisted the temptation to shift into a more comfortable position, as she didn't want to alert the person until she could get some better bearings. She blinked until the room came into better focus.

The girl in the seat.

It was Tabitha.

Almost at the same instant as her realisation, Tabitha looked up.

'Oh,' she said, startled at the sight of the pair of eyes looking back at her. She recovered quickly, smiling. 'Natalie, you're awake! Thank goodness!'

She rushed over to the bed, as Natalie tried to pull off the covers. She was still very weak, but she managed to loosen the sheets and pull herself up into a sitting position.

Her whole body was aching.

'Take it easy,' Tabitha said, placing a hand to Natalie's head. 'You've had a really rough time. Don't rush things.'

Natalie looked around some more. They were in a bedroom, presumably in Guy's house. She thought back to those last lucid moments in the sitting room, before her balance deserted her.

'What happened?' she asked, her voice fragile.

'You collapsed,' Tabitha replied, as she pulled up a chair to the bedside. 'Here,' she said, reaching across to the table, 'have some water. Your throat sounds very dry.'

Natalie sipped at the liquid. It was tepid but nonetheless it felt like heaven for her parched insides.

'I don't understand what happened,' she said. 'One minute I was...'

'You had a temperature,' Tabitha explained. 'And you were sick a few times throughout the night.'

'The night?'

'You've been out for a while.'

'How long?'

Tabitha looked at the time. 'Just over twenty-four hours.'

'What?'

'It's half past one on Monday afternoon,' Tabitha confirmed.

Natalie could hardly believe it. It felt like just a moment ago that she'd been talking with Guy.

'You've not been out all that time,' Tabitha explained. You've been awake at points. But this is the first time that you seem better.'

Natalie winced at the headache again. If this was better, she was glad that she couldn't remember the rest of it. 'My head.'

'It's okay, Natalie,' Tabitha soothed. 'You're bound to take a bit of time to get back to feeling normal.'

'It all happened so suddenly,' Natalie replied. 'I was sitting, talking to Rus– to Guy, and then, when I stood up, I just...'

'Guy was really worried,' Tabitha said. 'He called me straight away and I came right over.'

'I still don't understand what happened. Why I collapsed...'

'You had a temperature,' Tabitha said. 'It was pretty high, touching forty, but it came down pretty quickly.'

'I can't believe I was asleep for over twenty-four hours...'

'We called the health advice number,' Tabitha revealed, 'explained the situation. They asked us a lot of questions, said it sounded like it was just a virus, told us to keep you comfortable and to call them back if you got any worse.'

Natalie yawned, wondering how she could still feel tired after being asleep for more than a day. 'Where's Guy?'

'Popped out to the shops.'

'He told me that he works for Brand New.'

'I know,' Tabitha replied. 'Look, do you really want to talk about this now? Maybe you should get some more rest? I can come back later.'

'I'm fine discussing it now.'

She nodded. 'I'm really sorry, Natalie. Guy told me that you were upset by the situation.'

'I was.'

'I know it might seem like we were playing around with you for our own entertainment, but it really wasn't like that. Honestly, it really wasn't.'

Natalie didn't know what to say.

'I can see how you might feel. But we weren't laughing at you,' Tabitha continued. 'Yes, Guy got carried away, took things too far. He wasn't meant to go as far as he did.'

Was she talking about the incident in the attic?

'Your trip up to the attic room, it wasn't part of the plan. But he'd got himself drunk and started going off-piste. Which is why I told him to leave.'

The raised voices that Susie had overheard. Now it made sense. It had been Tabitha arguing with him.

'I'm so sorry, Natalie. And I'm sorry about what happened with Sir Kenneth, too. It's just been a series of terrible misunderstandings...'

Natalie still wasn't feeling great, but she couldn't let that comment pass. 'You're wrong.'

Tabitha was following the same script as Guy – that what

had happened with Sir Kenneth was a simple misunder-standing.

'Maybe we should come back to this later,' Tabitha said, moving to stand. 'After you've had some more time to rest.'

Natalie reached out and grabbed her sleeve. 'It *wasn't* a misunderstanding.'

'Sir Kenneth isn't like that, Natalie. He's just not that sort of a man.'

'You weren't there.'

Tabitha smiled sympathetically. 'You're bound to be confused, Natalie. You've been really unwell. And after all the excitement of winning. It's been such an emotional roller-coaster for you, it's no wonder you're all over the place.' She patted her arm. 'I'll come back in a bit; you rest up in the meantime.'

Natalie watched the door close.

She wanted to take hold of Tabitha and shake her to her senses, to make her believe. And if she'd had the strength she would have tried to follow.

But less than a minute later she succumbed to sleep again.

49

Previous Tuesday morning

THE NEXT TIME NATALIE WOKE, she felt so much better. The fog had lifted, and the aching in her limbs was gone. When she raised herself up in the bed with ease, she realised that her headache had also cleared.

She swung her legs out of the bed covers. But Tabitha must have heard her shifting around, as she entered before Natalie had a chance to plant a foot on the floor.

'Natalie, how lovely to see you up,' she said, closing the door behind her. 'And you're looking so well!'

Natalie brought her legs down, glad to be upright at long last, as Tabitha pulled the seat back across to the bed next to her.

'How are you feeling?' Tabitha asked.

'A lot better.'

'Good, that's really good, Natalie. I'm so pleased. We were really worried about you!'

Tabitha placed a hand on her leg and held it there for a second or two.

Now Natalie had spoken, she became aware of just how dehydrated she was. 'Is there any water?'

'Yes, yes, of course,' Tabitha said, reaching behind her to the table. The half-full glass had been hidden behind the desk lamp.

Natalie sipped at first but then downed the rest. Her body craved more.

'I'll get you another glass in a minute,' Tabitha said, reading the situation well. 'But first I've got an exciting piece of news.'

'Oh?'

'Yes. I've been in touch with Sir Kenneth, to explain the situation, and he sent you his best wishes from Australia.'

'Right.'

'He's really sorry you've been feeling so unwell. He'll be so pleased to hear that you're on the mend. He wanted me to keep him updated.'

Natalie just nodded. She couldn't think of anything to say. But one thing was certain – she didn't want Sir Kenneth's sympathy. She didn't want anything more to do with him, ever.

'Sir Kenneth also wanted me to let you know how sorry he is for the misunderstanding at the weekend.'

When Natalie didn't say anything, Tabitha continued.

'He's mortified by what happened. He said the last thing he ever wanted to do was to make you feel uncomfortable. He wanted me to let you know that it was a genuine confusion, but he said he takes full responsibility for it.'

Again Natalie offered nothing.

'He's been thinking about it, and he can see how things might have looked from your perspective. As I said, he's beside himself about it. He really likes you, Natalie, and he's looking forward to working with you. He doesn't want you to feel uncomfortable, or think that there was anything untoward about his intentions.'

Natalie shook her head. 'What he did. It wasn't appropriate.'

Tabitha smiled tightly. 'He can see that now. He can see that, for you, it wasn't the appropriate thing to do. And he'll never do it again with you – he gives you his word.'

'It wasn't appropriate *for me*?' Natalie said, acutely aware of the significance of how Tabitha had worded that.

'Yes, Sir Kenneth knows now that it isn't appropriate to do that kind of thing with you. So you've got nothing to be worried about. The last thing he wants is for you to feel worried about being around him.'

'But what about the other times?'

'Pardon me?'

'Catharine tried to warn me,' Natalie revealed.

'Catharine?'

'Diana Saunders' assistant. She tried to warn me about Sir Kenneth. She told me to be careful.'

Tabitha remained impassive. 'I don't understand.'

'We were interrupted, so she never got to finish what she wanted to tell me. But that was it, wasn't it? The thing she was trying to warn me about, it happened to me. And it must have happened to others before me.'

'She's a liar,' Tabitha said finally. 'I hear that Diana fired her.'

'She told me she was planning to resign.'

'That's not what I heard. I do know that Diana had been

considering it for a few weeks, because unfortunately she couldn't trust Catharine.'

'She seemed nice. She said she was going to work for a children's book charity.'

Tabitha smirked. 'Well, I feel sorry for them, because from what I've heard, they might well have trouble with her.'

'In what way?'

'Diana suspected she was stealing from the company.'

'Stealing?'

'Yes. Money had gone missing. On more than one occasion.'

Natalie thought back to her dealings with Catharine. She'd seemed nice. And her reasons for wanting to leave the company seemed extremely plausible, especially when you had first-hand experience of working with Diana.

The sacking story didn't ring true. And neither did the idea that she was a thief. So was Tabitha just trying to smear her, discredit Natalie's source?

That seemed more likely.

And she wasn't going to be put off.

'Has Sir Kenneth ever been accused of anything like this before?'

The hesitation was telling. 'Anything like what?'

Natalie chose her words carefully. 'Has he made people feel uncomfortable?'

'Sir Kenneth is a good man.'

'He has, hasn't he?'

Tabitha shook her head, but it seemed more in frustration than an act of denial. 'What do you want, Natalie?'

'What do you mean?'

'I mean, what do you *want*? What's this all about?'

Natalie frowned at Tabitha's cool tone but decided to fight it with fire. 'It's about your boss, and what he did.'

Tabitha laughed. 'It's money, isn't it?'

'No!'

'Look,' Tabitha said, her face softening. 'I'm sorry I just snapped. Let me speak to Sir Kenneth again.'

'There's no...'

'I'll also get you that fresh glass of water.'

She left the room, closing the door behind her.

Natalie, for the first time in many hours, stood on two feet. She saw the pile of her clothes folded in the corner, and dressed quickly if shakily. Hopefully her shoes would still be by the door, but if not, she could take a pair of Guy's or Tabitha's, or just run in stocking feet. She would do whatever it took to get out of the house, away from this. And then she would decide what to do next.

She hurried for the door and turned the handle.

But it refused to budge.

She'd been locked in.

50

Jack Morton put some distance between him and the garden.

That bloody girl.

He was sweating profusely, his t-shirt sticking to his wet chest and back. His heart was pounding – he could hear the beat in his head.

He shook his head. She had made him do that, prodded him until he'd had no choice but to do what he did.

And it had worked – it had stopped her in her tracks, shut her up. He thought back to the look on her twisted face, the shock and fear in her eyes, the fragility, the desirable femininity laid bare in the face of the danger he posed.

He had almost wanted to kiss her.

He kicked out against the nearby wall, connecting with some force. Running a hand through his hair, he lamented that he'd had to do what he'd done.

Now she would call her daddy, tell him how nasty Jack Morton had attacked her. Cullen would come running, and she would show him the nail marks on her face, and cry like a baby on his broad shoulders.

And then Cullen would come for him. He would find some way of taking vengeance on behalf of his daughter. He would stop at nothing.

'Damn it!' he shouted out loud, crying to the heavens. A couple of first-year girls gave him a wide berth, eyeing him warily. He thought about shouting after them, but decided against it. Instead he retreated further away from the main university buildings. He had lost control in the face of Amy's provocation, and the world was still tilted on its axis. He needed to stabilise things, but until then he had to get away from people who might recognise him. He had a reputation to uphold.

He got back to the flat, which was only a ten-minute walk down the hill. As he approached the door, his phone rang.

It was Sophia, a girl he had met the previous evening at the student event in town. A pretty Spanish first-year language student, friendly and trusting. He'd seen her from across the dance floor, studying her body as she had partied with three less attractive friends. He'd waited until she had peeled away from the group, and had intercepted her as she returned from the bathroom.

They'd struck up a conversation, and she invited him to join them on the dance floor. He hated dancing, but it was often necessary in order to achieve the ultimate goal. Later, he'd suggested going back to his place, but she said she had an early morning class and needed to get home. But after a passionate kiss, they'd swapped numbers and promised to meet up.

He knew that she would phone soon enough.

They always did. Even the ones who played hard to get would phone eventually, intrigued and sometimes strangely anxious by his lack of urgency at calling them first. It was funny how it almost always worked.

And here was Sophia, just as expected.

He stared at the phone, wondering whether to just ignore it. But she would only call again, and now he knew that he didn't want that. He didn't want that at all.

She was still ringing. Desperate. She reminded him of the girl he had met about a year ago, in the Students' Union. As usual, he had peeled her away from her group of friends with relative ease, although convincing her to come back to his place had taken a few drinks and a lot of charm. In the morning, he had woken in horror to find the girl folding his clothes that he had thrown on the floor the previous night. She placed them in a neat pile by the bedside, as if they were some kind of married couple! She had beamed at him like a new bride, as he hid his disgust at her in-your-face act of domesticity.

He'd got her out of the flat as quickly as he could, resisting her overtures to take the day out with her. He had classes to lead, research to get on with; he couldn't just drop everything.

But he could and would drop her.

She didn't take the hint at first. He'd obviously been too good with his excuse, when maybe he should have just swatted her away there and then like the annoying buzz fly she had turned out to be. A few days later she tried to call him, but he just left it to ring. Then again a day later. And again the day after that. She finally got the message after that final call.

He could do the same now, ghost this new girl until she got the hint. They hadn't slept together – there were no emotional ties – so it might only take the one unanswered call. But he was angry. And he wanted to vent on someone.

What did it matter if it was this girl, and not the real target for his annoyance?

He snatched the phone to his ear, full of rage and bitterness at the whole of womankind for the rejection that until now had been simmering but somewhat under control. 'Yes?'

How dare she reject him!

'Oh, hi,' the girl said hesitantly, faced with Jack's abrupt opening word. 'I was... hoping to speak with Jason...'

As he often did, he'd used a false identity. This time he was Jason, a third-year law student. It made it so much easier with one night stands. He had several well-used identities, and had even set up a number of social media accounts for each one.

'I don't know if I've got the right number?' she added.

Her politeness only served to inflame his emotions. His nostrils flared as he thought about Natalie Long, and how she had walked away from him. How dare she! And that friend of hers, she was so pleased about it. Jealous cow.

'Hello?' the girl said. 'Is that you, Jason?'

He was sweating again, his body temperature rising as the blood pumped.

'Hello, is anybody there?'

'I was drunk,' he said at last.

'Sorry?'

'I was drunk,' he repeated. 'That's the only reason I showed any interest in you.'

'Oh...'

'I would never have given you my number if I'd been sober. Delete it from your phone and don't call me again. Do you understand, Little Miss Ugly?'

There was shocked silence on the other end of the line. Then she reacted.

'You can't speak to people like that.'

'I just did.'

'You're a horrible person, do you know that?'

'Maybe I need to go on a course, to address my behaviour. You, on the other hand, I'd recommend cosmetic surgery to fix that face of yours. But it won't be cheap because there's a lot of work to be done.'

'Well, I guess you've got good access to behaviour change courses, haven't you?'

She sounded suddenly assured.

'Excuse me?'

'Maybe you can ask one of your colleagues to fit you in.'

'I...'

'You *are* a postdoc researcher in the psychology department, aren't you?'

He said nothing, suddenly put on the back foot.

'Aren't you, Jack?'

Panic rose up from within. 'I don't know what you're talking about.'

'You're Jack Morton. Don't you want to know who I am?'

He considered cutting the call there and then, but needed to know if this was as bad as he feared. He thought this might happen one day. His luck would run out, he would be exposed for his actions, most likely by a jealous lover: one of those needy girls who wanted revenge and was lucky enough to stumble on the truth about him.

'Who are you?'

'I'm a reporter on *The Spotlight*,' she said. 'I write feature articles.'

He swore under his breath. This was worse than he'd feared.

'I know what you've been doing for the past few years, Jack. How you've been preying on vulnerable young students for your own sexual gratification. How you stalk them out at the Freshers' events. How you use multiple identities, like you did with me last night.'

'It's lies,' was all he could manage.

'You know that's not the case,' came her assured reply.

'This is entrapment.'

'This is protection of our student population. Soon everyone will know what you've been doing.'

'Please, I'll stop.'

'Too late. As soon as we finish this call, I'm contacting the university authorities. I have multiple witnesses who have come forward to back up the claims that we've received.'

He turned on the spot, blood pumping again. He was finished. They would sack him. It was all over. 'Who told you?'

'I can't say that.'

A realisation. 'It was her, wasn't it? Amy?'

'I can't say.'

'She's a liar.'

He had a sudden urge to march back up to the campus and find her. Make her pay.

'I'm going to go now, Jack.'

She cut the call.

'Damn it!' he shouted at the phone. He screamed skyward, stamping his feet hard on the ground like a toddler with a tantrum. 'Argh!'

The panic had turned to rage.

He knew who was really to blame. Natalie. It had all

started with her. The downward spiral. The tailspin from his heady heights of success. And now he was heading for the ground, unprepared for the impact, and it was all her fault.

He had a desperate thought.

His hands shaking with adrenalin, he swiped through his phone until he got to the app he was looking for, buried in the settings of the device.

Find my Friends.

Locate your friends via their mobile phone, no matter where they are. Natalie hadn't known that he had set it up on her device, giving him access to her location. It was meant for parents to keep track of their children. But it was perfect for keeping track of her. He would look at it whenever they were apart, just to make sure he knew what she was up to.

Just in case.

It was also useful to know where she was when he was with other women.

He'd been monitoring her particularly closely for the past two weeks, since she had so cruelly ended their relationship. He'd tracked her to London, her signal following the trainline from Temple Meads to Paddington. He knew she had reached a property in Mayfair on that Friday evening.

But then the signal had gone dead.

At first he wondered whether her battery had died. But when the signal didn't return, he began to think that maybe she had discovered what he had done, and had blocked access.

There had been no signal since that Friday night.

He opened the app, expecting the usual radio silence.

But to his surprise, the blue dot appeared.

It was south of the Thames, in Balham.

He zoomed in and the road names appeared.

Garden Terrace.

The blue dot was over one of the houses. A quick look on Street View confirmed which property.

Number Thirty-Two.

A search of the address brought up a record on Companies House.

A company registered to that address. Director by the name of Guy Clarke.

His blood boiled.

She was with a man.

While his world was falling apart.

Who the hell was he?

This had no doubt started before their break-up. Now it all started to make sense. Maybe there hadn't even been a recruitment event at all. It had just been a ruse to meet up with her lover in the capital.

How dare she!

He grabbed his car keys.

She was going to pay for this.

51

As soon as Cullen left Catharine, armed with the new knowledge about the person who had been pretending to be Russell Cave, he called Tabitha.

A minute later, he set off for the address that Tabitha, after a bit of persuasion and pressure, had provided him with.

He was closing in on the truth.

He could feel it.

But there wasn't much time.

52

Tuesday afternoon, present day

GUY MADE himself his fifth espresso of the day. He was buzzing. He heard the banging and shouting from upstairs.

Natalie had realised the door was locked.

Tabitha had left for work half an hour ago, stipulating that he wasn't to engage with Natalie while she was out. But the noise from above was beginning to grate, and even though he knew the neighbours were out, and the bedroom window was locked and only looked out onto the back garden, there was a chance that someone might hear her.

His worrying was interrupted by a ping from a mobile phone. It came from the living room, and he realised it was Natalie's phone. He'd taken it from her after her collapse and turned it off.

On several occasions over the past few days they'd turned it back on again, using Natalie's thumbprint while she lay immobile and unaware in bed, just for a few minutes at a time, anxious to know who might be looking for her, and what they were saying. And early Monday morning he and Tabitha had decided to reply to the numerous text messages that had been sent by a girl called Amy.

He'd sent just one text, pretending to be Natalie, saying that she was taking time out to be with friends.

This morning he had again turned the phone on.

But had forgotten to turn it off.

It was another message from Amy. He was careful not to click on the message, so she wouldn't know someone had read it.

He turned the phone off, placing it back on the fireplace. Then he headed for the stairs, but as he reached the bottom, Natalie shouted out again.

'Let me out of here!'

He climbed the stairs without replying. But halfway up the staircase, his phone, which had been left in the kitchen, began ringing.

'Damn.'

He rushed back through into the kitchen. It was Tabitha calling through.

'Guy, the police will be coming around.'

Guy placed a hand to his head. 'The police, what do you mean?'

'Paul Cullen, the detective, he called me just now, asking questions. I gave him our address.'

'You did *what*?'

'I had to. He was going to search for your address on the police system – he would have realised that the name was false.'

Guy circled in panic. 'What the hell are we going to do?'

'Get out of the house. With Natalie.'

'I can't. How can I do that?'

'I don't know.'

'She's shouting. I can't take her anywhere.'

'What about the drugs. Have you got any more left?'

'Yes, but you know what happened last time. We thought we'd killed...'

'Just do it. Give her less.'

'How, though?'

'The same as last time. In a drink. Take her up a drink. She'll be thirsty.'

'I don't know...'

'Guy, just *do* it!'

'Okay, okay,' he said, looking around the kitchen for a cup. 'I'll do it, I'll do it. But where should we go?'

'I don't know.'

'And how do I get her from the house to the car without people seeing?'

'I don't know, just do something.'

He was really panicking now. A cup he'd grabbed slipped out of his hands and smashed on the tiled floor. 'Damn it!'

'Guy, you've got to calm down!' Tabitha said. 'We can sort this out. We can make it right.'

'We can't. We can't,' he replied, crunching over the smashed crockery.

A loud bang came from upstairs.

'Will you *shut up*!' he screamed towards the ceiling.

'You're losing it,' Tabitha said. 'Pull yourself together.'

Guy cut the call in spite. 'It's all your fault, you evil witch!'

No sooner had the words left his lips that the doorbell rang out.

Guy stiffened.

It rang again.

He looked up towards the ceiling. Natalie had gone quiet.

Then a hard knock on the front door.

Cullen had already arrived.

'I can do this,' he said. 'I can do this.' He would talk to the officer at the doorstep, then he would leave, and things would be okay. He moved into the hallway, seeing the human shape on the other side of the glass-panelled door. 'I can do this.'

He was just a few feet away from the door. 'Hello, officer,' he whispered in rehearsal. 'How can I help you?'

He was sweating profusely.

'Hello, officer, how can I help you?' he tried again, his breathed words ragged with nerves.

The figure was waiting.

He put on a smile and opened the door.

'Hello, officer, how can I...'

The blow thundered straight into his face, knocking him off his feet, and sending his head crashing into the edge of the radiator.

53

Natalie banged and banged on the door, shouting for Tabitha and Guy. She figured if she kept it up long enough, then they would have to respond. But her throat was hurting.

'Let me out, please!'

'Will you *shut up*!' she heard Guy scream from below.

Natalie sat back down on the bed. Maybe it wasn't such a good idea, antagonising them like this. It certainly wasn't doing her throat any favours. She moved over to the window and looked out over the back garden. There was no house overlooking theirs. No chance to raise the alarm via that route.

They had thought carefully about where to put her.

She continued watching the garden as a blackbird hopped across the lawn. A plane crossed the sky. Life was going on outside, while she was a prisoner.

She watched for a few more minutes before being startled by the noise behind her. The lock had been slid back, and the door opened.

It was Jack.

'Your lover is dead,' he stated with icy coolness. 'And it's all your fault.'

54

Natalie felt a sickening swell in her stomach as she took in the sight of Jack standing in front of her.

How had he found her?

She noticed his hands were stained with blood, and there was a smear of crimson across his left cheek.

She stepped back against the wall, keeping her eyes on her ex-boyfriend, who was standing stock-still, blocking the doorway.

'Didn't you hear me?' he said, smiling in a weird, vacant way. 'Your lover is dead. It was the radiator. Cracked his head wide open.'

'You've killed him?'

'And it's all your fault.'

'Guy isn't my lover, Jack.'

That weird smile again. Deranged. 'Don't lie to me, Natalie.' He took a small step towards her.

'I met him at the recruitment event. He works for the company.'

'Don't lie to me!' he exploded, taking another step

forward, jabbing an accusing finger at her, his face blood-red. 'Don't you dare lie to me!'

'It's the truth.' She tried to keep her voice calm and measured, her eyes desperately seeking out some reason within him, to calm the rage.

He shook his head dismissively, lost in the swirling mass of anger within.

Natalie had played through many times what she wanted to say the next time she saw Jack Morton. She had fantasied about telling him how escaping from his clutches had been the best thing she had ever done. She wanted to tell him how small men like him really were. But here and now, cornered by this man as he claimed to have killed another, she was just desperate to get out. So all those things she wanted to say could wait for another time, another place. 'I wanted to thank you.'

That confused him. '*Thank* me?'

'For rescuing me.'

'*Rescuing* you? You're lying.'

'They were holding me hostage here. In this room.'

'What?' He looked around.

'That's why the door was locked.'

If she could just bring him down from his murderous high, even get him on side, she might have a chance of getting out of here...

'I don't understand.'

'I think they drugged me, locked me up.'

She was getting through to him.

'But... why?'

'I'll explain when we get out of here. But we need to get out now, before the others come back.'

Once outside the house, she would run at her first opportunity.
Run and not look back. Run for her life.

'The others?'

'The other men who took me. They'll be back very soon.'

There was a flash of fear on his face.

'Jack, we need to go now.'

He nodded. 'Don't worry, I'll protect you. I won't let you go again.'

55

She didn't plan it, but as they emerged from the room, with Jack leading the way, Natalie saw her chance and reacted on pure instinct.

She pushed him down the stairs with all her might.

Caught off-balance, Jack twisted to his left, corkscrewing down the carpeted stairs. Natalie watched from the top as he landed with a thud at the bottom, legs and arms in a tangled mass.

But he was moving.

He recovered with shocking speed, eyes burning, the anger again raging.

Natalie stood frozen at the top of the stairs. She'd made a terrible error of judgement. The escape route was blocked again, and there would be no way now of placating Jack. She forced herself to break away from his stare and headed across the landing to one of the front rooms.

Maybe she could barricade herself in and then try to climb out of a window.

But she could hear Jack running back up the stairs.

She entered the main bedroom, but only got the door three-quarters closed before Jack appeared on the other side.

'You're a liar, Natalie,' he spat, straining against her weight as she battled to shut the door.

She was losing the fight; despite her best efforts, Jack was gaining traction, and he knew it, his anger spurring him on to increase the force.

The breaking point was reached and Jack almost fell into the room, as Natalie scooted around the double bed, evading his grasp.

But there was nowhere left to run.

He chased her down, pushing her against the wardrobe. She had flashbacks of Sir Kenneth. There was the same look on Jack's face.

Hatred.

Natalie tried to resist, but Jack grabbed her collar and slammed her into the back of the wardrobe.

Then she brought her knee up hard and fast, connecting with his groin.

He folded in agony.

She pushed him down and scrambled across the bed and back out onto the landing. But as she reached the stairs he caught up with her, shoving her back into the room in which she had been held captive.

'Jack, no!' she shouted, as he grabbed her around the neck.

Teeth bared like a rabid dog, he applied pressure with both thumbs, choking off her airway.

Paul Cullen approached Number Thirty-Two Garden Terrace. He went to press the doorbell but noticed that the door wasn't quite shut. He pushed gently and stepped into the hallway. The first thing he noticed were the blood marks on the carpet. There was also a streak on the radiator to the left of the door.

The marks looked fresh.

He waited, thinking through his next move. There was no use in calling for backup. He was in here now, and it was only him.

He listened for any signs of movement.

Nothing. But then.

'Jack, no!'

Without a second thought, Cullen ran for the stairs.

Natalie felt the pressure in her head rising and rising, as if it were a balloon being over-inflated. Jack's eyes bored into her as she tried to free herself from his deathly grip.

'P-l-e-a-s-e...'

But there was no mercy there.

And then, suddenly, his head snapped right, towards the open door, and he released his grip. He took a step behind the door as another man appeared at the top of the stairs, making concerned eye contact with Natalie.

'Natalie?' he mouthed.

She tried to warn him, but she was too weak, merely able to raise a single hand.

As the man stepped into the room, Jack emerged from behind the door, shouting and swinging a wild punch at the man's head.

58

Despite the element of surprise, Jack's punch did not land. Cullen batted the blow away as if he were swatting a bothersome fly, before putting a hard shoulder into the man's body just below the ribs. They both crashed back against the wall.

Jack tried to struggle, but he was no match for the power and weight of Cullen, who sat astride him.

'It's all your fault!' Jack spat in Natalie's direction.

Cullen pressed down just that little bit harder, on Natalie's behalf, before turning Jack Morton onto his front. He yanked the man's hands around his back and applied the handcuffs. There was no struggle left in him. And no more accusations.

Cullen looked back up at Natalie, who still feeling her throat. 'Are you okay?'

She nodded.

'Good. Amy will be delighted to hear it.'

He turned his attention back to his captive. 'Jack Morton, you're under arrest...'

59

Cullen called through for backup as he remained astride Jack Morton, who was still quiet, with his cheek planted firmly in the carpet. Natalie was sitting on the bed, regaining her strength.

After a few minutes they made their way downstairs.

And there waiting for them in the living room was Tabitha.

Tears in her eyes.

And a knife in her hand.

'He's *dead*!' she shouted, her shaking hand clenched tightly around the knife. Her face was crumpled with extreme grief. 'He's dead,' she repeated, her voice now soft and broken.

Cullen looked on, feeling constrained as he was still holding onto a handcuffed Jack Morton. 'Tabitha, please, put the knife down.'

She shook her head lamentedly. 'It's too late. Everything is ruined.'

Natalie stepped forwards, beyond Cullen, towards Tabitha. 'It's okay, Tabitha.'

Another shake of the head before she looked up with drowning eyes. 'It's all his fault. It's all *his* fault.'

At first Natalie thought she was referring to Jack, but she wasn't.

'I *told* them to be careful,' she continued. 'They *knew* what my uncle was like. They *knew* he'd done it before.'

'You're Kenneth New's niece?'

She nodded.

'We *tried* to protect you, Natalie. We tried to put in safeguards. He *wasn't* even meant to be there. He was meant to already be in Australia. That was the plan. But the old fool just couldn't help himself. He never can.'

Natalie took a small step forward, with more than half an eye on the knife. 'Tabitha…'

'Even after it happened, we tried to protect him, to limit the damage. We were loyal to the company and to him. We must be idiots.'

Natalie edged closer. 'It will be okay.'

'And now my fiancé is *dead*!' Tabitha shouted. 'Guy is dead…'

Without warning, she launched the knife with force. It spun at speed through the air, lodging straight in Jack Morton's head.

He was dead before he hit the floor.

61

'Come in!'

Paul Cullen took a deep breath and entered. Maggie Ferguson stood behind her desk, her back to him, gazing out of the window.

'Ma'am.'

She stood there for a moment longer without replying, while Cullen hovered by one of the chairs. He noticed that this afternoon's paper displaying his story was on her desk.

He didn't regret what he had done. Not for one moment. It was the act that had cracked the case. So it was all worth it.

Whatever came next, he was ready for it.

Finally she turned around. 'Paul. Thank you for coming in at such short notice, and so late in the day. Please, do take a seat.'

Cullen did as requested, and Maggie Ferguson took the seat opposite. 'I had quite a surprise this afternoon,' she said, 'when I was shown the front page of the London Daily Post.'

'Yes.'

She picked up the paper and held it up facing Cullen.

'I'm sure I don't need to explain to you that when you agreed to take a break, you were supposed to actually take a break.'

'I know. I'm sorry.'

She raised an eyebrow. 'Are you?'

Cullen played the answer around in his head, but decided to just tell it the way it was. 'To be honest, not really.'

She surprised him by cracking a wicked smile, accompanied by a half-laugh. 'No, of course you're not. You came to your daughter's aid and saved the day. I get it.'

'A dad has to do what a dad has to do,' he said simply.

'Indeed,' she mused. 'You could have been more careful though.'

'I was. Until I had to be less careful.'

She nodded her understanding. And then, ominously, her face hardened. 'What if I were to tell you that your stunt this week has cost you your job?'

He opened his mouth to speak, but the wind had been taken out of him. As much as he had steeled himself for the consequences, he now realised that he hadn't truly thought he would face the ultimate punishment. He'd thought he was bullet-proof, but the truth was it depended on who was firing the shots. So he just sat there, mouth ajar, feeling as if he were in freefall.

'I'm really sorry, Paul, but you crossed the line. Now, if you'll please excuse me, I've got a call to take.'

Cullen stood, still in shocked disbelief. 'Yes, ma'am.'

He walked to the door like a man condemned, gripping and twisting the brass handle as a swell of sickness washed over him.

Was this really it?

Was this really the end of the career that he loved so much?

But still, he couldn't find a place for regret.

He would do the same again. And again.

'The inquiry has concluded its investigation,' Maggie Ferguson announced from over his shoulder.

Cullen turned.

'You've been cleared, Paul. Totally exonerated. Which of course I had every confidence that you would be.'

'How so quickly?'

'We received some information earlier today from your friends at the London Daily Post.'

Cullen thought back to what the young journalist Zack had said, how he had promised that there was news that would really help his case. 'What information?'

'Monday morning, when you spotted the guy outside Euston, he'd exited a shop.'

'Yes, a pastry shop. The one just outside the train station.'

'He'd just made a drop,' she revealed.

'Drugs? But there was no...'

'Evidence of anything in his possession? That's true. But that was only because he'd managed to dump it when you appeared on the scene.'

Cullen stepped back towards her, rapt at the news. 'But how...'

'When you moved to apprehend the suspect, can you remember what he was doing?'

'Eating, from a paper bag.'

'Which he dropped when he heard you shout.'

Cullen nodded, beginning to understand where this was going. 'The bag, it didn't contain food.'

'Precisely.'

'He dropped the evidence and took off,' Cullen thought out loud. 'I didn't give it a second thought. I was focussed on catching him.'

'And why would you? It was a paper food bag, he'd just come out of a pastry shop.'

'So what was in it?'

'Money. Just over five thousand pounds in fifty-pound notes.'

'How did you retrieve it?'

'Your friends at the Daily Post passed on information from the girlfriend. In their interview with her, she'd got very upset and angry about what had happened, as you can understand. But it wasn't you she was angry with.'

'No?'

'She told your friend Zack that the shop had stolen their money.'

'She named the shop?'

'Yes. She admitted he was planning a drugs drop, in exchange for cash.'

'And she knew that he didn't have either the drugs or money on his possession at the time of the road traffic collision, because she was right there,' Cullen said.

'Yes.'

'So she decided to come clean.'

'They've got a two-year-old daughter, and she's worried about how they'll survive without his income. From what your journalist friend said, she wanted to punish those who had stolen from her.'

'Do we know the shop took the money?'

'We looked through the CCTV again. This time we focussed more on the area where he'd dropped the bag.

About twenty seconds after the bag hit the floor, an individual from the shop picked the bag up and took it back inside.'

'Bingo.'

She nodded. 'Officers visited the shop just over an hour ago. They found what we presume to be the bag of money, and a significant quantity of drugs – more than could have been part of that particular deal, I'm sure. Seems like they had quite an operation going on there. One of the workers also matched the person in the camera footage.'

'Good work.'

'Thanks to the Daily Post,' she accepted. 'Do pass on my thanks to your contact.'

'I will.'

'So as I said, the independent police investigation is over. You're in the clear, Paul.'

'Thanks, ma'am. It's been good working with...' He suddenly felt choked up, and couldn't get the rest of the words out.

He turned again towards the door.

'Paul,' she said, as he reached the threshold.

'Yes?'

'You know me well enough not to try something like this again, don't you?'

'But I thought...'

Her eyes narrowed. 'I like you, Paul, a lot. I wouldn't have given you the DCI post if I didn't have the utmost respect for you. I also trust you. Or at least I thought I did.'

She let the statement hang there like a noose for Cullen to step into headfirst.

'You can trust me.'

Her smile was tight. 'Trust is hard won, but easily lost.'

'I know,' he said sadly.

She mused on something. 'Don't let me down again, Paul.'

'I won't.'

'Take the rest of the week off,' she said. 'And I mean off. I don't want to see or hear of you until first thing Monday morning. Do whatever you like, as long as it doesn't have anything to do with policing.'

'I'm okay...'

'No arguments,' she said. 'Call it a washout period.'

'Okay,' he conceded.

She nodded at that. 'Dismissed.'

Cullen nodded back and left, reflecting on his narrow escape as he descended the staircase to the offices of his team. It was gone six thirty and the place was quiet. Margaret, the cleaner, was emptying the bins and they exchanged a hello.

Cullen surveyed the open-plan office, with the side rooms leading off it. This was his patch. This was where he wanted to be. He'd worked hard to get here, and the thought of losing it all had stung.

He would be more careful. Next time Maggie Ferguson wouldn't be as charitable; of that he was certain.

'Boss.' A voice came from behind him.

Cullen turned. 'Tony! Didn't realise you were still here. You do know what time it is? Brenda will be wondering where you've got to.'

'I saw you arrive, thought I'd wait around until you came out from your meeting. I figured you might welcome a chat afterwards.'

Cullen placed a hand on his shoulder. 'You're a good friend.'

'Just tell me she hasn't sacked you.'

'Nearly,' he smiled. 'But not quite.'

'Well, thank God for that. We need you here.'

'Nice of you to say so. Fancy a quick pint?'

Beswick grinned. 'Now you're talking.'

EPILOGUE

London Daily Post

BRAND NEW TROUBLE FOR SIR KENNETH

MAVERICK BILLIONAIRE SIR Kenneth New is facing mounting calls to resign from the company that he created as more women from across the world come forward with details of alleged assaults. What started with the revelations from Bristol-based university student Natalie Long has very quickly snowballed, with now over twenty current and former employees of Brand New breaking cover to accuse Sir Kenneth of inappropriate behaviour. It is reported that Sir Kenneth has flown back early from a business trip in Sydney to meet with his Board of Directors who called a crisis meeting following the scandal, which has resulted in a sharp drop in the company's share price on the London Stock Exchange. One unnamed member of the board is quoted as saying: 'Sir Kenneth is finished. And I'm sure he knows it. For too long people have turned a blind eye to the rumours, but no longer. Time is running out for people like him.'

PAUL CULLEN WILL RETURN IN 2020

Pre-order FALLEN ANGEL, the gripping second novel in the Detective Paul Cullen Mystery Series, which will be published in 2020.

Click here to visit the Kindle Store on your device and find out more.

To be alerted when FALLEN ANGEL is released, add your email address here: https://www.subscribepage.com/paulcullenmysteries

ACKNOWLEDGMENTS

First of all, thank you to my family for all the support you give me - I couldn't do this without you! Thank you to all who have bought and read Long Gone - I hope you enjoyed it and will continue to follow the adventures of Detective Paul Cullen. Special thanks to those readers who read and commented on a draft of the novel, providing me with extremely useful feedback during those final stages of production: Eileen Mintonye, Marje Hirst, Christal Worth, John Campbell, Elizabeth Bowen, Tricia Northall, Patricia Cheshire, Nina Izard, Bev Colthorpe, Kelly Ryan, Sharon Nunnerley, Renee Crosbie, Kimberly Daigle, Tracey Moss, Jac Eden, Julie Murrell, Claire Frith, Tracey Silvestri, John-paul Coe, Vicky Larios, Elsi Gabrielsen, Michelle Nelder, David Gildea, Heather Anderson, Michelle Gonzalez, Alexa Toth, Jennifer Moore, Jennifer Clark, Alex Turner, John Lowrey, Rachael Sweeting, Rebecca Casbeard, Angela Casbeard, Stella Ash, Patty Younts, Quindella Ewing, Pat Field, Jennifer Olow, Kristal Ginn, Anca Andronic, Zahira Soto, Dawn Watson, Sylvia Stottlemyer, and Gayle Valentine. Also a big thank you to the following who were among the hundreds of people who pre-ordered the novel: Patricia Cheshire, Angela Casbeard, Andrew Gibbons, Anne Waters, Ruth Bufton, Lisa Furfie, Dorothy Lancaster, Dale DePrima, Wes and Lynn Whittemore, Julie Putt, Mimi Zwerling, Trevor Flowerdew, Kristal Ginn, Yvonne Pearson, Charlotte Stone, Vicky Larios, Eileen Mintonye, Nicki Payne, Tracey Moss, Sarah Wood, Jim Eisele, Laja DeCuir, Margaret Still, Bev Colthorpe, Patricia Cheshire, Kimberley Vials, Bonnie Fowler, Louise Taylor, Tricia Northall, Jessica Pickering, Stuart Tonge, Marsha Laprade, Rochelle Eames, Nikki "Fluffy Fluffster", John Campbell, Helinka, Jo, Monique Shorts, Linda Freier, Zena Swansbury, Lynda Ross, Sara Starling, Dorothy Lancaster, Starla, Lynn Walker, Montse Ipas, Craig Adamson, Bev Boyle, Alyssa Biediger, Denise Hanby, Pauline Barnes, Vicky Larios, MJ Ilsley, Anita Friel, Gloria Acque, Steph Clayson, Ashleigh Campbell, Liz Wells, Cathy Evans, Jann Spriggs, brconrad, Gillian Ross, Susan O'Connor, John Doublecarol, Sarah Stephens (and Duke!), Sharuqh Bhuiyan, Diane Winter, Rose Thompson, Molly Burian, Michelle Cummins, rrostrowski, Juanita Nokeley, Laura David, Nichole Gearhardt, Michele Selway, Kristy Younger, Kathy Fisher, Karen Bickford, Duane Taylor, Rae Gunter, Rhonda Cook, Megan Kensinger, Jerry Gentry, Gayle Valentine, Anca Andronic, Patricia Bristow, Yvonne Pearson, Michelle Janssen, Pamela Murray, Carlene Lee, Kay Peet, Linda Shelley, Meredith Lucarelli, Gladys Anderson, Jayne Harris, Marcy Dell, Debbie Hunt, Bernie Desmul, Nicola Falkingham, and Ekta Garg. Finally, a big thanks to everyone in the publishing industry who have helped me on my journey over the past few years - it's been a dream and you have all played your part in helping it to come true! To find out more about my writing you can visit my website at: www.paulpilkington.com

Best wishes, Paul

August 2019

ABOUT THE AUTHOR

Known for his fast-paced, emotive thrillers and mysteries packed with suspense, twists, turns and cliffhangers, Paul Pilkington is a British writer from the north-west of England. He is the author of the Emma Holden suspense mystery trilogy, the first of which, The One You Love, was number one in the Bookseller Fiction Heatseekers Chart. The second in the series, The One You Fear, was named as one of the Best Kindle Books of 2013. The final instalment, The One You Trust, has helped the series to achieve over 4,000 five-star reviews on Amazon. He is also the author of standalone mystery thrillers Someone to Save You and For Your Own Protection. Long Gone is the first novel in Paul's new mystery series featuring Detective Chief Inspector Paul Cullen. The second novel in the Paul Cullen series will be published in 2020.

facebook.com/paulpilkingtonauthor
twitter.com/paulpilkauthor
amazon.com/author/paulpilkington

,

Printed in Great Britain
by Amazon